Time After Time

Book 1 - Catch Me

Fair Warning Dear Reader

Dear readers, this book contains references to assault, suicidal thoughts, detailed sex scenes with multiple partners and A LOT of swearing.

Eden

A red haze of rage slides over my vision as I block, counter, and hit with the Bo I'm fighting with. My Bo-Jitsu sparring partner fades and is replaced by the attackers who taunted, laughed, and beat me after they killed my partner. I'm so consumed by the rage and memories that I have no awareness of the damage I'm doing to my opponent until a brutal shove sends me back across the ring and my trainer, Diesel barks harshly at me.

"That's enough, Eden!"

The red haze clears and I look down at the poor guy I have just annihilated on the mat of the fighting ring. I take in the arm he's clutching to his stomach in pain and the blood streaming from his nose and mouth. I can already see the swelling around one of his eyes. I wince at the damage I did to him and take a step towards him with a contrite expression but the way he flitches back and the look in his eyes tells me he already thinks I'm a psycho and no amount of apologizing will make any difference. Diesel steps between us blocking my view of the guy with a hard look on his face before sighing and shaking his head.

"You're done. Go hit the bag for twenty but after that, we need to talk." He tells me sternly.

I open my mouth to try and defend myself but the look on his face tells me I've finally pushed him too far after multiple warnings so I just give him a small nod and lean to one side to see the guy still on the mat nursing his arm.

"Sorry, man. It got away from me."

I tell him with as much contrition as I can manage in my tone. The guy's face turns into a glare of hate so with my shoulders slumped I turn away and climb out of the ring, heading towards the punching bags.

As I wrap my hands up to go to work on the bag my mind tracks through all the options I have to convince Diesel not to drop me as a client and ban me from the gym for my latest infraction of the rules but comes up empty. It's been ten months since the attack that killed my EMT partner and left me ravaged with PTSD. The easy way the gang members who attacked us had taken my partner out and beaten me had driven me to learn how to defend myself in all ways.

When first I came to Diesel and asked for help, I hadn't even known how to make a proper fist for a punch. With his teaching and encouragement, I had single-mindedly dedicated most of my waking hours since the attack to training and now could confidently go up against any sized man who wished me harm. I learned how to fight hand to hand, with a knife, a bo fighting staff and I was a dead shot with a handgun.

I beat all of my frustrations into the leather punching bag as I worry about the red haze that takes me over when I'm sparring with an opponent. On the one hand, it helps get the job done but on the other, I'm going to end up killing someone who doesn't deserve it if I can't get myself under control. By the time my trainer comes over to deal with me, I have a fine sheen of sweat coating my body from the savage work I'm doing and he has to call my name twice to break through the fighting zone I'm in. With a final roundhouse kick to the bag, I turn to him knowing that this is it, I'm out.

I stand silently as he steps forward and uses his huge hands to bring the bag to a stop from its wide-swinging before pinning me with a frustrated look.

"Eden, you could have seriously hurt or killed that guy." When I just nod miserably, he huffs out a breath and rubs a hand over his shaved and tatted head. "Look, you know you're my favorite student and I'm so proud of how far you've come but you have no control. You're dangerous and I can't risk you hurting someone here under my watch." When I still only nod, his face fills with sympathy. "You need to see someone, a counselor or therapist. You need to work through everything that happened to you and find a way to get yourself under control. I'm sorry, Eden, until you do, I can't let you train here anymore. I could lose my license if you seriously hurt someone."

I swallow down the lump in my throat and blink back the burning of tears that threaten before nodding again. "I get it. I understand where you're coming from. I'll clean out my locker." I can't handle the pity I see shining in his eyes so I look down as I work at unwrapping my hands. "I just want to make sure you know how much I appreciate everything you've done for me. You took a fucked up hot mess and made me strong enough to be a functioning fucked up mess. Thank you, Diesel."

A groan from him has me glancing up to see the look of exasperation on his face. "Come on, kid, do us both a favor and get some therapy and then get your ass back here so we can get back to work."

My lips twitch with a smile at hearing him call me kid considering he is all of two years older than my twenty-nine, fast approaching thirty but I just nod and slide past him with a small wave. I hit the locker room and when I open the metal door of my locker just stand clutching it with a white-knuckled grip. Fuck, what am I going to do now? With a shaky breath, I swipe all the contents of my locker into my gym bag before throwing an oversized hoodie over my sweaty tank and black workout capris. As a rule, I don't shower at the gym but wait until I get home because I still don't feel safe enough to be so vulnerable in a public place. I rearrange my bag so that my handgun is resting on the top within easy reach before zipping it closed. The switchblade I carry everywhere with me is in my front hoodie pocket ready to be flicked out if needed. Am I paranoid? Fuck yes. I've learned the hard way that they really are out to get you so I'm good with being prepared for whatever.

I keep my head down as I thread my way out of the gym, not wanting anyone to see the devastation I feel at losing the last thing in my life that gives me any peace. As I step out into the overcast Seattle evening the glass door behind me closes in a whisper that feels like a slam. With my head still down I turn away to walk down the busy street in search of a taxi, too drained to consider walking the few miles home. I only make it ten steps when a hand lands lightly on my shoulder. The terror that floods me is automatic and a rushing noise fills my head so that I don't hear my name being called. The reaction is automatic as I spin with my fist raised only to check it at the last second before I make contact with the surprised face in front of me that I recognize.

"Jesus, Eden! I'm sorry. I called your name twice!" Kevin sputters as he throws his hands up in defense and takes a step back from my threatening stance.

I feel heat rush to my cheeks in embarrassment at almost clocking a former co-worker. Swallowing down the shame I feel at the crazy reaction, I send him a tight smile.

"Kevin, sorry about that. I was lost in thought. How are you? It's been a while."

He nods cautiously as he studies my face. "Good, good. It has been a while. We miss you down at the station. How are you? We thought you'd be back at work by now."

My eyes dart away from him at the sympathy that I see in his eyes. It was him and his partner's rig that had responded to the call in the aftermath of the attack. He saw first-hand what the gang had done to my partner and me. Kevin had worked on my injuries to stabilize me as the ambulance had careened through the night to get me to the hospital. He knew exactly what I had suffered through and seeing him tonight has vivid images of the attack flashing through my mind. I have to clear my throat twice before I'm able to answer him as I ruthlessly shove the panic rising in my chest back down.

"I'm fine, thanks. Super busy with life. I'm not sure when I'll be back on shift."

He nods slowly. "Soon, I hope. We could really use you. You were one of the best EMTs we had, even as a rookie." When I just reply with another tight smile, he sighs. "Eden, have you talked to anyone? About what happened? You know the station covers counseling sessions after a traumatic event. It's helped a lot of our guys to work through the aftermath of things from on the job."

I grit my teeth against the sharp retort I want to spew. It's like the gods decided today was intervention day. This is the second person in the last hour to tell me to get some therapy. Instead of telling him to shove his therapy up his ass, I fake a smile.

"Yeah, I have a private service I use. It really helps. Anyway, it was great to see you." I lie. "Tell everyone at the station I miss them too. I'll try and stop by soon to catch up."

He knows I'm lying, I can see it in his eyes but he does me a solid by just lifting a hand in a wave goodbye with a sad smile on his face as I turn away. I pick up the pace as I flee down the block no longer searching for a taxi. I need to move, to pound at the pavement to try and get my emotions under control. The three-mile walk home is just what I need to keep it together. I try to blank my thoughts as I go wanting the mindless zone of pushing my body but the wreckage of my life is a relentless deluge in my mind.

The attack I lived through was just the latest hell that has consumed my life over the last three years. I might be coming up to thirty but my soul feels as tired as an eighty-year-old's from the pain it's lived through. Three years ago, I lost my parents and little sitter to a horrific car accident that had sent me into a tailspin of grief. My soon-to-be ex-husband had taken that time to show his true colors. I had no defenses against his vicious emotional abuse as I tried to make my way through the waves of grief that swamped me from losing almost my entire family in one go. He had gleefully taken control of my weakness by isolating me even further from the world and spending my inheritance on whatever he wanted. It finally took my great aunt Adera's intervention to pull me from the marriage and depression I was lost to. She was my last blood relative and even though I didn't know her well, I let her yank me from the carnage of my world like a life raft.

I walked away from my marriage with nothing but the clothes on my back, a greatly reduced inheritance, and a glimmer of hope that I could get back who I once dreamed to be. I worked so hard to create a home in the tiny apartment I found to live in and took the EMT courses I needed to have a job where I could help others. I was just edging into happy and finally feeling like my sassy self again with a year on the job and my divorce from Troy on the books when the attack happened. When I woke in the hospital three days later, it was to an estate lawyer informing me of Adera's death and that she had left everything to me.

Physically and mentally broken and now completely alone in the world I could barely function for a month. I hid in my tiny apartment afraid of every noise in the night. The mail stacked up and all calls went unanswered until a knock on my door finally pulled me out of it enough to turn the corner. Adera's lawyer wouldn't take no for an answer until I caved and let him in. He handed me the keys to what I later found out was an old Victorian home packed to the eaves with a hoarders paradise and bank and investment accounts with balances that had more zeros than I'd ever seen in my life. The shock of it all had me trying once again to get my life back on track. The PTSD I suffered from decided otherwise.

My long walk home ends in front of the Victorian monstrosity of a house that I equally love and hate but choose to live in. When I close the door behind me and flip the three heavy locks, I just lean against it and take a slow scan of the rooms I can see from there. It had taken me long, work-filled months to clear and sort the piles of belongings Adera had crammed into the house but the main and second floor was finally clear. All that remained was the third-floor turret and then I had to decide if I wanted to gut and reno the place or sell it.

None of that matters at the moment as I feel tears burning behind my eyes. The one thing, the one anchor I clung to against the trauma I lived with had just been taken from me. Not being able to work out and train with Diesel was tripping me back towards the hole I had worked so hard to crawl out of these last few months.

Swiping at my eyes in anger, I fish out the gun and my cell phone before I drop my gym bag and shove away from the door. I need a shower and something to eat before I can let myself think about what comes next. I make a quick stop in my room to plug in my phone before I strip my sweat-soaked workout clothes and leave them on the floor as I wait for the ancient pipes to heat up, refusing to look at myself in the mirror above the sink. I don't think I can handle the lost devastated look in my shadow-filled green eyes. With steam finally beginning to build from the showerhead, I ruthlessly yank the bands that hold my waist-length hair in its tightly braided bun and step under the flow of near scalding water.

I stand with my eyes closed as the water beats down on me trying to hold back the flood of pain but the water's warm embrace weakens me until a sob escapes and throws open the door. It's not just all the awful events that have happened to me over the last few years, it's the crushing loneliness that brings me to my knees in the claw-footed tub. The pain is a physical ache in my chest that I clutch at while gasping sobs spill from my mouth. I'm so tired of being alone. I just want someone to lean on. Someone I can love and be loved by in return. Without the gym and Diesel to look forward to, I can't think of a single reason to get out of bed in the morning. I don't want to do this anymore.

The water begins to cool before I finally beat back my emotions and push to my feet to get on with shampooing and conditioning my hair and washing my body. The flow is borderline icy before I close the taps and step out, completely drained and feeling hallow. By the time I've dried myself and combed out my hair, I'm ready to skip the meal and climb into bed to end this day. I force myself to turn away from the bed, afraid I won't ever get out of it again if I crawl in and dress instead. I slide on soft black leggings and a black tank top over a matching set of black lace underwear and bra. I ignore the fact that black seems to be the only color I wear anymore as I reach into the closet to pull out my favorite piece of comfort clothing. The robe cost me more than I've spent on any item of clothing, including my favorite tall black leather boots with the red soles but as soon as I touched it in the store I was helpless not to buy it. Thick, plush, and soft as silk, the black fabric swings out at the waist to reach down to my ankles making it perfect to curl my legs up into on the couch. The wide double-breasted collar just looks cool as shit as it tapers down to a fitted waist and the wide hood makes me think of medieval maidens wandering in a forest. I like that there are two ties, one inside and the belt outside to keep the robe securely closed. Shrugging it on feels like a warm hug and it's just what I need right now.

I snag my phone back from the charger and my favorite brand of cherry lip balm and drop them into one of the deep pockets of the robe before picking up my gun and head to the kitchen. After warming up leftover Thai takeout from the night before, I eat standing over the sink, looking out at the overgrown backyard, and try to decide what to do with the rest of the night. I could curl up and binge something on Netflix or try and read one of the paranormal romances I have stacked up on my e-reader but I know I'm not in the right headspace to engage in any storyline so instead I drop the empty carton of takeout in the trash and head up to the third-floor turret to get to work cleaning it out. Mindless work is what I need right now.

I stop at the front door first to double-check the locks and slide my feet into a pair of soft, black TOMS canvas slip-ons. The floorboards on the third level are in rough shape and the last thing I need is wood splinters in my toes. I feel safe enough inside this house that I'm not compelled to carry my switchblade or gun with me everywhere so I leave the gun on a small landing table to free my hands up to carry a stack of folded boxes and a roll of packing tape up to the top level. My body feels fresh and clean from the shower but I know I'll need another one after sorting through the dusty mess on the final floor to be cleared.

At the top of the stairs, I dump the packing supplies and pull open the double doors to the turret before waving my hand inside to find the light switch. When I finally locate it, the lights come on with a pop of noise as two burn out leaving the large circular room half in shadows. Great, I'll just add that to the shit sandwich my day has become.

I sigh at the stacks of junk in front of me. Aunt Adera was so kind to me when I desperately needed it but I didn't know her very well. She was that weird aunt that flit into our lives randomly between long absents as she traveled the world. Cleaning out a lifetime's worth of belongings has been eye-opening. The woman was obsessed with history. I've sorted through stacks of old - like hundreds of years old - newspapers, research books, thick historical tomes, and documents all wedged in between the most beautiful antique furniture. There was so much crammed into the house that I had to rent two storage units, one for the papers and books and one for the furniture. Once I finish clearing out the turret, I plan on having a few different assessors go through the storage units to see what should be donated to historical societies and museums and to evaluate the antique furniture for auction. Before that can be done though, I need to clean out this final room.

I pause just inside the doorway and imagine the stacks toppling over me, trapping me under the piles of history until I smother. Shaking my head at the dreary image, I slide sideways between stacks and work my way deeper into the room to see just how bad it is before I start sorting. I suck in my stomach as I squeeze through another passage and find a pleasant surprise on the other side. I judge I'm halfway through the room when it opens up into a cleared space. Turning to look back I can see the boxes and stacks of books and papers creates a sort of wall that hid the second half of the room. Shaking my head at Adera's eccentricities I turn back and take in the space.

The first thing I notice is a beautiful cushioned window seat with bright throw pillows dulled by dust. Beside it sits a small table with a china teacup on a matching saucer. I can just imagine my aunt sitting there while reading one of her history books. Turning away from the view I spot a dressing table with old pots of dried makeup and a hairbrush scattered across it. On one side of the table there's a clothing rack filled with what can only be described as period piece costumes and on the other, the most gorgeous full-length mirror leaning against the wall. I feel goosebumps flash across my skin as I take in its stunning beauty. What looks like ancient runes twine around the frame, made up of crystals in every imaginable color. If I didn't know better, I'd swear they were real diamonds, rubies, emeralds, and sapphires but that would make the mirror worth millions of dollars.

I'm so in awe of the mirror that I can't take my eyes off of it and I find myself stepping in front of it. My eyes shift from the sparkly frame to my reflection and I frown as I take in the wild red curls streaked with gold that hang to my waist and the tired, lonely eyes that have faint purple smudges underneath them. The only thing I'm happy about in my reflection is the kick-ass bathrobe I'm wearing and I have a moment to think how sad that is before I see my hair start to lift in a sudden breeze. I try and turn my head away to search for an open window I must have overlooked but find that I'm frozen in place. I can't move a single part of my body. I see the fear bloom in my eyes as a rushing roar fills my ears and a silent scream chokes in my throat when a light so bright and white fills the mirror and I feel myself thrust forward where my body spins and tumbles out of control. The last thing that goes through my mind as darkness takes hold is…fuck my life!

Sebastian

We ride through the gates of the King's gardens and leave Versailles in the direction the informant had pointed us. The wolves, Finn and Cade gallop ahead on their mounts, still young enough to be eager for the hunt. Luca and I keep a steady measured gait as we follow behind. In the millennia and a half that I have been alive, time has made me understand that there's no point rushing anywhere. It's always the same year after year, decade after decade. There will always be royal intrigue, crises, and wars to fight. Nothing ever changes. If not for my brothers in arms I would find a vault to lock myself away in and sleep away the centuries. As for Luca, it's been over a hundred years since I saw him eager for anything. He's only twenty some odd years older than the wolves but the way his human life was ended has left him scarred and hallow even after almost two hundred years. I often wonder if he hates me for turning him into an immortal. I scoff to myself, hate is the wrong emotion for the man riding beside me. It's much too strong for someone who shows no emotion at all.

"I'm somewhat surprised Pierre didn't know who is behind this latest threat to the King. Do you think he was holding back on us?" Luca asks. All traces of his Spanish accent lost long ago.

I lift one shoulder indifferently. "Does it matter? There will be another next week or next month and so on until the man dies and then his successor will continue in the same manner."

"True. However, it seems to me that these assassination attempts are gaining in frequency. Would it not be more efficient for us to take out the root of the threat instead of constantly chasing after the men hired to do the deed?"

I send him a knowing look. "Come now, Luca, you can't lock yourself away in your studio forever. It's healthy for you to get out and feel your blood pumping from a good fight. Besides, at the rate you're going there will not be enough space left anywhere in France to house your creations."

He turns his head and sends me a bland look with one of his dark eyebrows raised. "That would make sense if health mattered to us or our blood pumped." He turns back to the trail we are following and nods ahead towards the top of a rise where our companions have come to a stop. "It would seem that the wolves have found our prey. Let us join them and be done with this matter."

Moments later we rein in our mounts beside Finn and Cade's. The cousins are the polar opposite to Luca and me in both looks and dispositions. Where we are both dark-haired and stoic, rarely showing emotion, the cousins are both blond with their temperaments mimicking the playfulness of the wolves they shift into.

I look past them and shake my head at what I see, bored already.

"The eejits aren't even trying to hide! An hour from the castle and they make their camp out in the open for anyone to stumble upon. Bloody hell, they probably won't even put up a fight!" Cade complains, disappointed he won't get a challenge.

I sigh in agreement but before I have a chance to nudge my horse forward down the slope to get on with it, a bright flash of white fills the air between us and the assassin's camp followed by a loud crack of thunder. All four of us are blinking away spots from our eyes when a shout goes up from the camp. Finn is the first to recover.

"What the bloody hell is that?" He asks in surprise.

I narrow my gaze at what's appeared but it's Luca that responds in his bland way. "That is a woman and I believe she is vomiting. Based on the reaction of the men in that camp, I would say they weren't expecting her."

I feel a small surge of interest. "If whoever mastermind this latest plot has engaged in witchcraft, things have just become more interesting."

All four of us loose our weapons. Luca and I our swords, Finn and Cade their bows.

Finn hums in the back of his throat. "Aye, witchcraft it might be but those men mean to attack the lass so she must not be on their side." He turns to me with a grin. "Should we not intercede? Witch or no, the lass is outnumbered six to one."

I watch the witch shove to her feet and face the six men running her way with swords drawn and tilt my head to the side in consideration. "No. Let us see how this plays out. It's been decades since I saw a witch in action. We will have to deal with her if she successfully defends so best for us to know how strong she is."

I hear a whine come from both the wolves but ignore them as I wait to see how the witch will respond to the attack. It surprises me when she casts off her cloak leaving her body clothed in form-fitting pants and a shirt that leaves her arms bare. Her stance changes and I see the form of a fighter in how she holds herself. We all make a surprised noise when her first move is a strange spin that results in her foot lashing out to connect with the lead assassin's face. A drop and a roll have her coming to her feet with the downed man's sword in her hands and we all watch in slight awe at the dance of her spinning, blocking, and hitting out at her opponents without ever using magic that we can see. When she's down to the last two, she fights them with a berserker's rage that shows in the savage jerky stabs and swipes, all the finesse of her earlier movements gone.

With the spell broken, I nudge my mount to head down the slope with the others following me. Closer now I can see the heaving of the woman's chest and when she spins to block, the blankness in her eyes. Whoever she's fighting, it's not the two men in front of her. A vicious thrust from her has the second last man going down as blood gushes from the wound in his throat, his head only left attached by skin. The final man's eyes are filled with terror as he chooses to throw his sword down, whirling to run away from the banshee instead of facing her in single combat.

"Finn," I command and he lets loose an arrow that drives deep into the fleeing man's back.

The witch stands with her back to us for a few moments and we can all hear her gasping breaths before she turns slowly on one foot to face us. Awareness slowly comes to her eyes as I study her. Even with blood and gore covering her arms, she's the most beautiful woman I have ever seen. I feel my cock twitch when I take in the strange clothing that molds itself to every curve of her figure. The partial shirt she wears allows her heaving breasts to display without shame. It's been hundreds of years since I've last laid with a woman or had any interest in one but this witch has my fingers itching to touch. All the shades of red are represented in her waist-length hair. It ripples in soft waves and curls as the sun turns it into a living fire. Her cat-like green eyes dart from each one of us in confusion before she glances over her shoulder to the man Finn had dispatched and then back to us.

She zeros in on me and with a trembling voice asks, "What the fuck just happened?"

Eden

When the red haze clears I see a man running away from me. He only makes it a few feet before an arrow flies past my head and impales deeply into his back. His arms throw wide at the impact before he faceplants into the ground. I stand in place with my chest heaving and look at the slaughter I've just committed. There are five other bodies littering the ground and each one is covered in blood. I did this. Diesel's words echo in my brain. I've not just hurt people, I've killed them. I'm now a murderer. This can't be real. I must be dreaming or I've finally cracked up completely. One minute I'm in my aunt's house on the third floor and the next I'm in an empty field puking my guts out with a pack of men attacking me with swords. None of this can possibly be real. If there was anything left in my stomach, I would be puking again at the carnage at my feet.

My eyes scan over the bodies again and land on the one who was running away from me. I know I sure as hell didn't shoot him in the back with an arrow so I turn slowly to see who is behind me that had taken the shot. My eyes go wide at the four men on horses who are staring back at me. My brain has no problem ranking their extreme hotness as I look to each one in confusion. Seriously? Horses? What the hell is going on here?

I finally zero in on the one that just screams leader and ask, "What the fuck just happened?"

I hate having to look up at this guy. He has the sculpted features and smoldering good looks of a Greek god that tells me he's either going to be a total playboy or arrogant as fuck. Yup, it's the second. He does that one eyebrow lift thing that just screams "You must be an idiot."

"It appears you've just done our job for us. Who sent you?" He asks in a cold arrogant tone.

"Huh? No one sent me. I…I think we need to call the police." I stammer out starting to lose it.

When they just keep looking at me like I'm speaking a foreign language, I try again.

"I just killed five people! Can one of you please call 911?"

The second dark-haired man leans forward in his saddle. He has the face of a sweet angel and sad grey eyes with brown curls tied back at the nape of his neck.

"911? Is that a code for your master?"

I feel my body start to shake as I make a noise of confusion and frustration. Who are these guys and why do they not seemed to be bothered by what I've just done? I need answers, like where the hell I am and why did the guys I killed come at me the way they did? I finally turn to the last two, blond and smoking hot as well but at least I see some kindness in their eyes along with a hint of amusement.

"Where am I? I think I'm lost." I plead for an answer.

A grin tugs at the lips of the one holding a bow with an arrow ready to be pulled.

"We're about an hour from the palace, lass. Do you often get lost in your travels?" He asks me in a teasing tone with a panty-dampening Scottish accent that confuses me even more.

"Palace? What palace?" I ask incredulously.

"Versailles. Were you expecting a different one?"

The cute blond guy beside bow and arrow guy says with a laugh but nothing about this is funny to me. I gape at him in shock.

"France? Fucking France? How the hell did I end up here?" I practically wail.

I go to scrub my face to clear my head and that's when I realize I'm still holding a sword. My whole body starts to shake harder when I take in the blood practically dripping off my arms. I throw down the sword and crash to my knees, staring at the evidence of my crime. I hear an exasperated sigh come from leader guy before he starts barking commands.

"Finn, Luca, go search the bodies for any sign of who sent them. Cade, assist the witch. We will be taking her with us. The King's men will throw her into the lower levels for the inquisitors before burning her. I want some answers before that happens."

The words, witch and burn register in the back of my mind but I'm going into shock staring at the gore dripping from my arms. A pair of muscular thighs encased in tight, fawn-colored riding pants tucked into tall boots appear in front of me causing me to blink up at one of the blonds. He cocks his head to the side and scans my face with a furrowed brow like he's trying to figure me out before shrugging one of his broad shoulders. Blond guy, wait, leader guy called him Cade, so Cade pours water on a white linen handkerchief, who even uses those anymore, and proceeds to wipe my arms down as best as he can. My voice shakes when I try and speak.

"I…I th-think we really need to call the police. I…need to turn myself in."

He looks at me with his twinkling, blue-green eyes as he finishes wiping blood from my face.

"Are you meaning the magistrate? The King's watch? That would go very badly for you, lass. They will torture you for answers and then burn you at the stake. It's best if you come with us and answer Sebastian's questions. We will be much more forgiving of your nature than the King."

My mouth drops open in disbelief and confusion. Last I heard France doesn't torture or burn women at the stake and it's been like centuries since it had a King. My heart starts rapidly pounding in my chest again at the creeping suspicion of just how fucked I am so I whisper,

"What year is it?"

Cade's eyes narrow at the question but he goes ahead and wrecks my world with his answer.

"1667."

I'm left sputtering in disbelief but am interrupted by the other blond hottie. "Here you go, lass." He says as he holds out my bathrobe. "As much as I enjoy the look of you in those breeches, it's best if you cover up with your cloak." He tells me as his cobalt blue eyes track down my body in admiration.

"Cloak? Uh, right, my cloak." I play along and snatch the robe from his hands and quickly slide it on. If these guys aren't punking me and I'm really in 1667 then I need to get with the program right fucking quick. There's like a hundred and one ways I could end up dead in this era, from drinking the water to the previously threatened burning at the stake. Down the rabbit hole or mental breakdown, I still feel like there should some kind of consequence for me killing five men beyond my own crushing guilt so I ask, "You shot the last one with an arrow, right?"

"Aye, although you did the bulk of the work for us."

"Why? Why did you kill him? Who are, were these men?" I ask him with a catch in my throat.

"Och aye, lass, dinnae fash yourself about it. They were assassins sent to murder our King. They were bound to die today. By your hand or ours."

I swallow some of the guilt choking me. It makes what I did somewhat better but it doesn't change the fact that I'm now and forever will be a killer. I have a lot of questions but before I can ask any of them, sad eyes, Luca, strides past us calling out, "Riders coming!"

Leader guy, uh, Sebastian, merely nods from on top of his horse. "Finn, the witch can ride with you." That earns a glare from me at being called a witch again but he doesn't react to my death glare in the slightest, just nudges his horse to get it moving.

With one last probing look at me, Luca turns away and vaults into his saddle following after mister cold and frosty. The other guy, Cade, sits atop his horse waiting for us. I feel a hand press against the small of my back and glance toward Finn.

"Come, lass. Best we be gone before the watch arrives else you will have trouble this day."

I take one last glance back at the dead bodies before swallowing hard and follow him to his horse. I don't really have a choice. If what they say is true about what will happen if the King's men take me, I have to go with these guys and hope I will be safe with them until I can figure out what the hell is going on.

He motions me to climb into the saddle first and even though it's been years since I've last ridden I still remember well enough to get up and straddled on its back. A snort of laughter has me looking down at Finn's amused face with a look of confusion. He shakes his head before vaulting up behind me. The way he wraps his arm around my waist and pulls my butt snugly against his crotch has me letting out a small gasp. It's been forever since a man had his arms around me. As he gets the horse moving in the direction the others went, I feel his hot breath against my ear.

"Most ladies choose to ride side saddle but like your breeches, I much prefer this position."

I can't help but roll my eyes as I settle back against him cautiously. It seems men are players no matter what century they're in. If I've truly traveled into the past, I'm going to have to tread very carefully and make some allies to survive here. Before my life turned to ashes a few years ago, I had an A-plus flirting game so I channel the old me and reply with,

"Well, I'm not a lady and I prefer ALL the positions."

The choked noise that comes from behind me tells me I've hit the mark dead-on. Huh, good to know that twenty-first century flirting works in this one just as well.

The shock of what's happened as well as the adrenaline starts to wear off and at some point in the ride, I must have fallen asleep. You would think that the crazy I was living would have me on high alert but apparently time travel, mass killing and being held by a pair of strong, warm arms really tuckers a girl out. I had bombarded Finn with question after question but only received grunts in reply to most of them. The only question he actually answered outright was who his King was. I was as relieved as I could be, considering, when he told me that Louis the fourteenth was the current monarch. Digging deep into my high school history, I realized that there were still a hundred or so odd years before the royalty of this country would lose their heads so that meant no revolution to live through for me. Not getting any other answers, the boredom of riding through forests and fields as well as the warm hard body cradling mine pushed me into sleep.

The rumble of his chest against my back and his low biting tone wakes me but I keep my eyes closed to see if I can learn anything.

"Bloody hell, you need to take her, man! My cock can't take much more. I've been as hard as a rock since I settled behind her." A snort of half amusement half disgust comes from one of the other men.

"I swear, you and your cousin are more dog than wolf! You need to learn to control yourselves." Sebastian bites out causing Finn to scoff behind me.

"Ha! I'd wager you'd not fare much better even with your famous bloody control, Bas. The lass smells like the most fragrant perfumed meadow with a loaded dessert table in the middle of it. That and her tight arse cupping my cock for the last hour has done me in."

I'm laughing inside at his description of how I smell. It's just gardenia scented shampoo and vanilla body lotion when reality hits me. I can't suppress the groan as my eyes pop wide open at the thought of NO INDOOR PLUMBING! Fuck no, just NO.

"Look now, you've woken the lass with your bellyaching." Cade laughs.

Sebastian must not find the delay funny as he nudges his horse next to ours and with one powerful hand, wraps around my waist and drags me across to sit sideways in front of him on his horse. Clamping this other arm around me, he kicks his horse into a fast gallop that has me clutching onto him. Sitting sideways gives me next to no control of my balance and I'm afraid I'll fly off at any moment.

Being sideways makes it easy for me to turn my head and study his face once I realize he's not going to let me fall. I'm met with a hard glare that I ignore as I take in his chiseled jawline, cinnamon-colored eyes flecked with gold and stupidly long lashes. When my eyes drop to his mouth I find myself wiggling slightly. Even if he is mister frostbite, those lips are…well, let's just say any sane woman would want them on her, full stop.

"Sit still, witch. I'm not a young pup you can sway with your charms." He growls at me through gritted teeth. I roll my eyes and face forward again but have to suppress the laugh that bubbles up when I hear him take a deep sniff of my hair. I should be terrified at the situation I'm in but something tells me these men won't hurt me. It's irrational not to be afraid after all I've been through in the past but that's what my gut says and I'm tired of being afraid all the time so I'm going with my gut on this one.

Wide awake now, I try and sort through how I ended up in the here and now. I was in the turret getting ready to pack Adera's junk when I found the cleared area. That's when I saw…the mirror! As soon as I stepped in front of it, I was locked in place. I remember the wind and then the white light and roar, then tumbling before hitting the ground and puking my guts out. The pieces start clicking into place. The hidden area, the rack of period costumes, and the fucking drop-dead gorgeous crystal…no, jewel-framed mirror? Bibbidi-bobbidi-boo, bitches. I got my ass magik'd! It's the only explanation that makes any kind of sense.

So now I'm figuring that all those long absences when Adera was 'traveling' the world were actually her traveling time. Fuck me, that blows my mind. OK, that's how I got here but how the hell do I get back and how do I survive this time period until I do? Seriously, I'm wearing a bathrobe! I have no money or jewelry to hock. All I have is, I pat discreetly at the deep pockets of my robe to make sure, my iPhone 20Pro is in it, and yeah, it the latest and greatest model but I'm pretty sure Siri, Alexa, and Cortana combined isn't going to be able to get me out of this mess. I still my fingers as they itch to reach for the final item I've brought through with me. Although I will have yummy kissable lips, I don't think my cherry lip balm is going to be my salvation either.

After what seems like forever, the snow-man turns the horse to gallop down a wide lane that has a double row of over groomed hedges leading to what would be called a mansion in my time frame and you can tack on Estate with capital letters judging by the manicured grounds and too many fountains for me to count. I side-eye the guy behind me and check the boxes. Leadership role, check. Square jaw and all the hot fixins' to go with it, check. Arrogant and up on a high horse, check, check. There's no doubt in my mind. I'm riding with the Lord of the fucking manor.

Sebastian

Servants spill from the house as I slide from the back of the horse and I toss the reins to the nearest one before reaching up and grasping the witch around her small waist to lift her down. I keep my expression completely blank as I use my strength to keep a foot of space between us when I would very much like to feel her chest crushed against mine. I would eat broken glass before I let her or Finn know that she affected me in a similar way to what Finn had complained about. This witch must have strong powers to affect me like this when no other has. No matter the spell she casts, I won't be distracted by my cock. I mastered it long ago.

I leave the witch and the others to follow behind as I stride through the door tossing my cloak and gloves to a servant to deal with and head to the library expecting the others to follow along. I pour myself a crystal glass of brandy, both for the enjoyment of the liquor and to help shake off the effects of the witch's spell. By the time I've downed the glass, I can hear the others enter the room behind me. I turn slowly and spear the woman with a piercing glare that has broken many a man before her. I try to not react when she rolls her eyes and turns away from me. I watch with narrowed eyes as she scans the room and see her eyes trail up the bookshelves that rise to the high ceiling. My sharp hearing catches her whispered words, "I'm dead. This has to be heaven." Her tiny squeal of excitement has my eyebrows raising in surprise as she rushes across the room and latches onto a wooden ladder on rollers and rails that is used to access the higher shelves.

What the devil is wrong with this witch? I send a look to my companions and am not surprised to see the wolves grinning at the witch's antics but it's Luca that has me confounded. There is the smallest of smiles gracing his pouty lips that has not been there in the last two hundred years since his almost death and me siring him. Furious that his reaction could only be the result of her witchcraft, I stomp across the room and haul the menace back to the center of the room dropping her arm like I've been burned.

"Time for some answers, witch! Who sent you?"

Instead of cowering at my thundering tone as most would, she squares up to me with a face filled with anger. A hand comes up and one pretty finger jabs in my direction. "Listen, Iceman, you might be

Lord of the manor or whatever but that doesn't mean you can act like an asshole! Stop calling me a witch! No one sent me. Seriously, it's a case of wrong place, wrong time."

In my one thousand, four hundred and twenty-six years in this mortal realm, I have never been left speechless but this, this demon witch with her jabbing finger and words…did she actually just call me an…asshole?…has finally stunned me speechless. Finn and Cade are howling with laughter at my flabbergasted expression no doubt and Luca is leaning against a bookshelf with an avid expression of interest that I've never seen on his face before. He is clearly hexed by the witch.

Fury fills me at her defiant expression so I can't help myself when I rush the few feet between us and drag her against my chest in a crushing hold. I'm about to show her exactly who she's dealing with and anticipate the terror I will see in her pretty, wide green eyes when I feel something hard and rigid against my thigh. I push her away from me enough to be able to run my hands down her body. Her curves are enticing enough without being covered by the most sinfully soft material that her cloak is made of. Smooth like silk and satin but thick like the softest fur, it's the type of material that only the wealthiest would own.

My hands complete the slow journey down the witch's body sending a slight shiver through her until they reach the two hard objects I had felt. I see the widening of her eyes in panic when I slip my hands into the pockets sewn into the cloak and grasp a hard rectangle and small cylinder from each. I smirk in triumph when her hands come up and latch onto both my wrists. A tiny shake of her head and the one whispered word of, "Don't," tell me I've found her secrets. The witch is strong, surprisingly so for a woman but not strong enough to stop me from pulling the items out and exposing them to the room.

We both look down at what I'm holding, her with a small sigh and me in confusion. I have no idea what either of the items are. The cylinder is red with white writing on it and made from no material that I have ever seen before. I turn my eyes to the rectangle and lift it higher to examine it more closely. The front surface is black and shiny smooth. It looks like obsidian but if it is, the craftsmanship to make a slab of it so perfectly smooth like this is beyond anything I've seen in my long lifetime. The black stone is edged along the sides and back with a material that sparkles in all the colors of opal or pearl, changing when it is looked at from different angles. Whatever the object is, it's priceless in value. How this woman came to be in possession of it is another secret I vow to solve. The lightness of weight surprises me as a piece of obsidian this large should be heavier. I can't help but rub my thumb over its smoothness and the action has the object flaring with light causing me to jerk it away from my face. That's all the witch needs to snatch it from my hand and hide it behind her back. The light from the object is all the evidence I need to prove her a user of the dark arts.

"Not a witch you say and yet here is the proof of your lies!" I accuse in a cold tone.

I expect her to deny my words, beg or plead but once again this woman does what I least expect.

She groans out a frustrated screech, tilts her head back and looks to the ceiling before calling out, "Seriously? Tried for witchcraft and burnt at the stake for a fucking iPhone? Seriously?"

The other three men in the room have moved closer and loosely encircle her. It's Cade that asks, "Are you calling to the one you worship, lass? Or the one you serve?"

She shakes her head and whispers, "Jesus," under her breath but then says it again louder. "Jesus! That is who I worship and serve, in my own way if I have to pick one. I…am…not…a…witch!" She spits out before whipping the magical object out and holding it up for all of us to see. "THIS is not magic. It's…it's technology. Where I'm from, almost everyone, rich or poor, owns some version of one and none of them are witches!" She sighs and lowers it down and uses her thumb to brighten it again before holding it out, offering it to any of us to take. When none of us do, her shoulders slump. "It won't hurt you. It's not dangerous…unless you have an Amazon Prime membership and an addiction to online shopping." As we all take a step back, she laughs. "Joke, I was making a sarcastic joke! Honestly, it's just a device that is common where I come from."

Luca steps closer to her and leans his upper body to get a better look at what is displayed on the front of the object. He frowns and asks, "Where are you from, then? It must be a wealthy land if all people have such a marvel."

She snorts out a laugh and uses her free hand to swipe away a thick hank of her red curls and push them behind her back.

"You wouldn't believe me if I told you."

When he just lifts his eyebrows in dispute, sadness crosses her face and she gives a tiny shake of her head. "No one could believe me. I hardly believe it myself."

Luca lifts a hand and cups the witch's face causing me and the wolves to rear back in shock. Luca refuses to touch others unless it's during a fight or by accident. Should anyone touch him, he will flinch from it or lash out. Seeing this out-of-character behavior from him is just one more instance that proves to me that the woman has cast a spell on him.

"You would be surprised at what we would believe. Try us." He tells her in a soothing tone.

I see her face softening and the longing and loneliness I can read in her expression have me doubting my belief for a moment. She chews on her bottom lip in indecision and something about that sends a bolt of heat down to my cock. Such attraction for a woman this quickly doesn't happen to me and my mind is again swayed back to her being a witch that has spelled us. We don't even know the hellion's name, for Hell's sake.

Her eyes dart around the room to look at each one of us before she takes a deep breath and then blows it out, causing my eyes to dip down to her breasts. I force them away and focus on her face to see the lie that I know is coming.

"My name is Eden Kelly and I'm from the future. The year I come from is 2028. If math is hard for you all, that's three hundred and sixty-one years in the future, to be exact."

The room is dead silent for a moment after her ridiculous lie of a statement until I let out a roar of anger, done with this foolishness. She swings her face my way, still filled with defiance so I show her a truth that will force her to reveal every secret she has. I let the change come over me and feel my canines lengthening to fangs as my eyes blaze the red of the depths of hell. I step towards her with a snarl so my teeth are on full display and wait for the screaming to begin. The witch's eyes widen but not with the terror I expect, instead, they almost seem to be filled with wonder. Her mouth drops open in surprise but quickly snaps into a grin of...delight? Nothing in her reaction is how it is supposed to be so I find that I'm the one who is shocked instead of her when she takes a few steps towards me instead of fleeing for her life. She lifts a hand as if she's going to touch my face but quickly shakes her head and drops it to her side, still with that infuriating grin.

"Holy shit! You're a vampire! Boy, did Twilight ever get it wrong. Not a single sparkle to be seen!"

And then the witch laughs…She laughs!

Eden

Holy cracker jackers! A vampire? A real live…er…dead vampire is standing in front of me right now. As if time travel wasn't enough to scramble my fragile brain the universe is going to throw this at me too? Not that it isn't freaking amazing but now I'm wondering what other crazy is headed my way. I'm grinning like an idiot at vampire guy and try not to giggle when he loses the fangs and red glowy eyes, leaving a small pout on his sexy lips. I guess he was expecting a different reaction from me but as a huge fan of Buffy, True Blood, and The Originals not to mention the hundreds of kindle vampire ebooks I've read, well, I could be scared but I'm more intrigued than anything else. I can't help the sassy wink I toss at him before I spin away to take a closer look at the other three shocked men in the room. My eyes lock onto Luca and I slowly start to nod my head while lifting my hand to point at him.

"Vampire." It's more of a statement than a question and my heart does a little flutter when he nods back just as slowly that I'm right. I grace him with another big smile and switch my focus to the blonds, Finn and Cade. Here I pause while squinting my eyes in consideration but then shake my head.

"Not vampire but..."

Both of them lean forward like they're eager to hear what I'm going to guess. They just don't give off the vamp vibe that fits the other two men now that they've revealed themselves. I track back to all the things I've heard since I landed in this time and focus on the words dog, pup, and...wolf! My eyes go wide and I practically choke out, "Wolves! Oh my god, are you guys wolf shifters?"

The huge grins that plaster across both of their faces tells me that I've nailed my guess and I just stand there in total shock.

"How did you know that, lass? Are there many shifters where...uh...when you come from?" Cade asks in excitement.

I let out a shocked laugh. "In real life, no clue. But in books, TV shows, and movies, yes. So many."

Cade elbows Finn in the side. "Do you hear that, cousin? We're famous in the future! There are many books written about us and the other two things she said that I don't understand. Many, she said!"

Cade opens his mouth to ask me something but a thought crosses my mind like a lightning bolt so I cut him off and spin to look at the others and blurt out, "Time travel, vampires and wolf shifters, for all that's holy, please, please say there are dragons too?"

Luca barks out a laugh causing the other three men to stare at him like he has two heads but only for a second before Sebastian finally loses his patience and roars,

"Enough! Enough of your incessant chatter and lies! I'm done dealing with this nonsense." He points to Finn and Cade. "Take her to one of the guest rooms and lock her in. I will get the truth from her tomorrow." He turns his glare on Luca. "And you! I don't know what spell the witch has cast over you but I don't like it. You will come with me to the palace to inform the King of what transpired today." When Luca frowns, Sebastian throws up a hand. "No arguments. The further away from her the more the spell will weaken."

With that proclamation, he steps up to me and pries the iPhone from my hand and stomps past me, leaving the room.

I glare at the empty door he's disappeared through for a moment before switching my gaze to

Luca. The expression on my face changes to a look of hope as I ask a one-word question.

"Dragons?"

He smiles softly at me but shakes his head before leaving the room as well. As the two wolves escort me to a guest bedroom I mutter under my breath.

"Dammit, why couldn't there be dragons too?"

They leave me in a pretty room with a four-poster bed that is so high there's a small wooden staircase placed beside it to climb up onto it. They promise me food will be brought later and then shut the door.

When I hear the sound of the lock I sigh and feel the energy drain from me as I look around the room slash prison. There's a low divan placed under one of the tall windows and on top of the dresser is a large bowl with a jug of water set inside of it but what catches my eye the most is a wood-framed, full-length mirror in one corner.

I freeze in place and wonder if the mirror is my ticket out of here and back home. Surprisingly, I don't race over to it and that makes me think about why. I'm in an unbelievable situation that any sane person would want out of but the honest truth is that I've felt more alive in the last few hours than I have in years. I mean, killing those men certainty wasn't a highlight and I'm going to have to face the fallout from that soon I'm sure but everything else has been a roller-coaster of adventure. Looking at the mirror on the other side of the room, I can't help but wonder why I would want to go back. A few hours ago I was alone and heartbroken from losing my last friend and place of refuge. There isn't anyone back there that will even care that I'm gone.

Shaking my head at the pity party I'm having in my mind, I do the responsible thing and slowly walk across the room until I'm standing in front of the mirror. When nothing happens after a few minutes, I let out a breath of relief and take a closer look at my reflection. A shudder wracks my body when I spot the streaks and splatters of blood that have dried on my chest and face. When I see a few clumps of my hair that has dried stiff with the gore my stomach heaves. Spinning away from my reflection, I shrug off my bathrobe and go to work with the cold water from the jug until my skin is rubbed raw and the blood is removed from my hair. The lack of a hot steamy shower has me looking over at the mirror again and considering clicking my heels together to see if that would work. Knowing it won't, I use the last of the water to scrub at my tank top and a few blood spots I find on my leggings, glad that they are both black and will hide the stains well enough.

I shrug my bathrobe back on and tie it securely before eyeing the bed. It's been a crazy day and back in my timeframe it would be close to midnight. Judging by the light shining through the tall windows of the room it looks like mid-afternoon. A wave of exhaustion swamps me and I huff a laugh at thinking that time travel jet leg is a thing but before I can climb up onto the bed, there's a sharp knock on the door. Whirling to face the door, I brace for what comes next but when it doesn't open I clear my throat and call out, "Come in."

The lock snicks and the door opens to a pretty, young blond woman with tightly braided hair circling her head like a crown. She carries a tray with food in and sets it on top of the dresser beside the bowl filled with bloody water. A squawk of French comes out of her in a rush as she waves towards the empty jug and blood-tinted water that fills the bowl but I can only shrug having no idea what she's said. A male voice answers her in French causing me to flinch and I see Cade leaning against the doorframe. Whatever he says to her has the woman scowling at me before removing both from the room with her cute little French nose stuck in the air.

I eye Cade warily but when he makes no move to enter the room or leave I take my time looking him over. The man is like serious eye candy with his dark gold hair, sea-blue eyes, and square jaw. His hair must be at least shoulder length and judging by the lone ringlet that has escaped from the leather tie securing it behind his head, thick with curls. He's wearing a billowy, cream-colored dress shirt with the top three wooden buttons open, letting me glimpse a smooth, tanned chest. My eyes drop down to the tight fawn-colored breaches that hug muscular thighs and do nothing to hide an impressive bulge. Feeling heat rising up to my face I turn away and walk over to the tray to take a look at what food is being offered and to compose myself. A partial baguette of bread, cheese, and grapes all look good but the small plate of what looks like dried fish is a hard pass so I pick it up off the tray and hand it over to Cade to take away. With my body cleaned, food waiting to be eaten, and a bed to sleep in all my current needs are being met except for one final thing.

I chew on my bottom lip in slight embarrassment but fuck it, it is what it is.

"Where does a person, uh, relieve themselves? Is there a separate room?"

He looks confused for a moment but then laughs when he gets it and strides past me towards the bed. Leaning over he pulls out a pot from under it with two handles on it and holds it out to me. "Aye, here's the chamber pot for your needs. Leave it under the bed and Bridgette will empty it for you when she comes back for the tray."

My nose wrinkles with a major eww vibe causing his eyebrows to shoot up in amusement. "If you were a man, I'd tell you to piss outside but it's a mite harder for a lass, innit?"

I glare at his amusement and groan out between clenched teeth, "Barbarians! Where I'm from, we have a separate room with a seated bowl attached to a pipe that goes into the wall and flushes the…waste away." I close my eyes and dream for a second about standing under a hot shower before opening them and telling him, "We also have water that's heated in pipes that you can stand under and have hot water shower down on you to get clean. Sadly you won't get to experience that for another two hundred and fifty-ish years."

Cade studies me with his gorgeous blue-green eyes and then shakes his head wistfully. "What a marvel that would be, then. So far I'm liking what you say the future holds." He looks down at the plate of fish and then shrugs. "Eat and rest, lass for you will have to reckon with Sebastian on the morrow. As much as you don't seem afeared of him, you'll need your strength to face him once again." As he goes to walk past me he tilts his head towards my hair and takes a deep sniff and then with a cheeky grin and a wink leaves the room, locking the door behind him.

Eden

My dreams are filled with violence when the men that I killed in this time merge with the gang that attacked me and killed my partner, Sam in my own time. I spend the night thrashing as I fight them off in my nightmares. I swear at some point I hear soothing voices with Scottish accents trying to calm me but I'm trapped in my nightmares. When I finally wake up, I feel more tired than when I climbed up into the bed the day before and the blankets are twisted around me like knots. As soon as I open my eyes I know I'm not alone without even looking. I lay still and let my pounding heart slow as the dreams start to fade away. I make no move to wipe away the tears that are drying on my face and just wait for whoever is in my room to speak. It doesn't take long.

"We know you're awake, lass. There's no reason to pretend you're not. 'Tis the first time you've settled in hours."

I'm so tired I don't even bother sitting up just turn my head on the pillow to look towards the blonds who are sitting in a pair of chairs beside the bed that hadn't been there when I went to sleep the night before. I swallow the dryness in my throat before asking,

"Am I to be interrogated before breakfast? Is it normal for you to invade a woman's bedroom while she's sleeping?"

Finn is slumped in one of the chairs watching me with tired eyes while he taps my iPhone against his chin. Cade is in a matching chair but leaned forward with his elbows on his knees. It's him that answers me.

"Och, nay it's not bloody normal but we didn't have much choice in the matter with you screaming into the wee hours of the night, now did we? You had the servants so flummoxed that they were wanting to call out a priest to do an exorcism." He leans back and rubs at the sexy stubble on his jaw that's grown since I last saw him. "You have some savage night terrors, lass. Who is Sam? Is he your man, then? You called for him over and over again in desperation."

My body freezes hearing that and I can't stand the sympathy I see in both of their eyes so I turn my head away to look up at the canopy over the bed. "No, he's not my man. He is, was my partner, uh, co-worker where I used to work. He, he died." I blink back the new tears that burn in my eyes. "I'm sorry. I…it was a bad night. I'm sorry I woke you and the servants."

"Aye, well, we'll just have to have a kip later today. Don't worry yourself, lass."

"It's Eden, not lass. My name, I mean. It's Eden."

"To be sure, it's a lovely name. One from the bible, isn't it? Will you tell us who you were fighting in your dreams, Eden?"

That is the last thing I want to talk about so I switch topics to one slightly less terrifying.

"I thought Sebastian was going to beat the truth from me this morning. Is he running late?"

Finn snorts a laugh. "Fat chance of himself ever being late for anything! No, he tore out of here at dawn for a long ride. Your screams seemed to bother him a mite. Be assured he won't be harming you, Eden but he will want some answers to his many questions, as do we."

I let out a deep sigh and close my eyes. "I told you the truth last night but here's the cliff notes version. I was born in 1998, I will be thirty years old in a few months and the year I was living in when I traveled here was 2028. I live in a city called Seattle that is in the state of Washington in the country of the United States of America which is on the continent of North America. In this time you would call it the colonies, I believe. I think France has settlements in the northeast, what we call Canada now. I have no idea how I managed to travel through time three hundred and sixty-one years. No one sent me and I have no interest in your business or your King. I was in my aunt's house cleaning out a bunch of old junk when I came across a beautiful, jewel-encrusted mirror and the next thing I know, I'm puking my guts out in a field in France. If I had more answers, I would gladly tell you." I turn my head back to look at them and hope they can see the truth in my eyes.

Finn taps my phone on his chin one more time before dropping his hand to hold it in his lap. "It's a wild tale for sure and it sounds like a fine adventure but you have to agree it's a tad unbelievable."

I narrow my eyes at him in annoyance. "So says the wolf shifter that chums around with a pair of vampires." The guys share a look before Cade nods.

"Fair point, lass, I mean, Eden. It would just be easier to swallow if you could give us some sort of proof."

I press my lips together to stop myself from screeching in frustration but then realize I might have some proof that would convince them.

"Siri, open photo gallery," I call out and then lift a hand to point down at Finn's lap and try not to laugh when Siri answers me and freaks the guys right out.

"OK. Opening photo gallery to the last picture saved."

They both jump to their feet and Finn tosses the phone away from himself but thankfully it lands on the bed. Cade is glowering at me and stabbing an angry finger my way.

"Magic! You are a witch!"

I roll my eyes and finally sit up so I can pick up my phone and hold it back out to him. "NOT MAGIC! I told you last night, it's technology. It's a computer that can do basic functions. Here, take it back and look at the pictures of where I'm from. That should be all the proof you need." When he snatches his hand back and eyes the phone like it's going to attack him, I play on the man's ego. "Are you two big bad wolves seriously afraid of a little box? Come on, it's not going to hurt you! Take it and look at the pictures. All you have to do is swipe the screen to go to the next image."

Cade turns to Finn and nudges him forward. "Go ahead, Finn."

"I'm not bloody touching it! You take it!" He scoffs and takes another step back.

With a huff of annoyance, I untangle from the blanket ropes around my legs and slide over to the side of the bed so my legs dangle off and hold the phone up screen out so they can see it. "You big babies! Here, I will hold it so you don't have to touch the scary box." I tell them in a teasing tone. "The last picture I took was a city view from the second-floor windows of my aunt's house. Lean in and take a look."

After a couple of seconds they gather enough courage to lean closer and study the screen. I try not to smirk as their eyes get large and they take in the downtown view and the space needle.

After a few minutes of ogling the picture, Cade asks, "This is where you live?" At my nod he continues, "Is there more…pictures as you call them?"

"Hundreds," I tell him and swipe to the next. We spent the next few minutes with me swiping and them oohing and ahhing over each picture. I answer questions until a look of fury takes over Finn's face and he yanks the phone from my hand to bring it closer to his face. I haven't been looking at the pictures but holding the phone up in their direction to see so I have no idea what picture I have that could possibly cause such a reaction. When Cade leans in to see what has Finn so angry, his amused expression flips to one so fierce I find myself scooting back away from them on the bed and shaking slightly when I see his blue eyes begin to glow gold.

"Who the hell did this to you?" He rages as he swipes the phone from Finn and spins it my way to show me.

I choke back the bile that fills my throat at the picture that a nurse had taken for me in the hospital a day after I had woken up. I couldn't get out of bed to see the damage in a mirror so after I begged and begged she had taken it so I could see how bad it was. I hadn't looked at it again after that and had forgotten it was even on my phone. My eyes are glued to the image of my broken face and body.

The bruising and swelling had been at their worst by then and the jagged, sewn-up wound that ran up the side of my forehead and into my hairline looked like Dr. Frankenstein had stitched me up. Thankfully, it had healed into a thin scar that wasn't all that noticeable after a religious twice daily application of bio-oil serum. My hand lifts unconsciously up to it and my fingers trace the scar before I lunge towards the phone and try and yank it from Cade but he pulls it back.

"Answer me, lass! Who did this to you?" He demands again.

I glare defiantly back at him. "As you can see, I'm perfectly fine. It happened a while ago but I've healed and I'm fine now."

He chuffs in disagreement before looking down at the picture again but his voice is soft when he says, "This explains your night terrors, then. I'm sorry, this happened to you." His eyes flash back up to mine. "Do you not have a man in this city to protect you?" When I don't answer but keep glaring he nods in understanding and says, "Sam. Your partner, you said. He died to protect you, then. A good death, that."

Bitter anger sends me off the bed until he's forced to take a step back.

"Either move on to the next picture or give me my phone back. I won't discuss this with you again," I spit through a clenched jaw.

Finn tries to break the tension by running a hand down my arm. "Och, lass, you slept in your cloak? As soft and fine as it is, you shouldn't have to sleep in it. I'll be sure to have Bridgette fetch you some clothing and a nightdress to wear."

Ready to leave the topic of my injuries, I jump on the chance to ask a question I've been wondering about.

"You speak French to the staff but you spoke English to me from the start. Why? And if none of you are French why do you live here?"

His lips quirk into a smile. "Aye, most hereabouts are Frenchies and we speak the language well enough. Why not live here? It's been a good home to us for many decades. You spoke to us first in English, remember? You asked what the fuck just happened so that's how we replied. Which reminds me, I've wondered what that word…fuck…means as I've not heard it in such a phrase."

I feel the blood rush to my cheeks, the curse of a redhead, and consider the words to best explain the many, many meanings of that swear word. When I chew on my bottom lip, I see Finn's eyes lock onto it and heat up making what I'm about to say even more cringy. It's only fair to explain the different meanings to them as I tend to overuse that word.

"Uh, so fuck is considered a swear or curse word in my time. It's used to intensify a statement. It gets used in a lot of ways - in anger and excitement. Um, here's a few examples, shut the fuck up. This is fucking ridiculous. Go fuck yourself. I'm going to kill that fucker. I'm totally fucked and many others." Heat blooms even more in my face as I tell them the literal meaning. "Fuck is also a vulgar way to say sex." I have to clear my throat to get out the next bit. "Like you would say, I want to fuck her or um, we fucked like rabbits last night."

Cade lifts his gaze from my phone at this and Finn steps closer with a spreading grin on his face. He reaches over and gives a tug on one of my sleep-tangled curls. "Well now - I believe I've just found my new favorite term." He says in a husky, sexy murmur filled with promise.

I feel my core clench at the look in his eyes and I swear the temperature in the room doubles as Cade takes a step towards us but before anything else happens the door crashes open and Sebastian storms into the room. A bark of laughter shoots out of my mouth when Finn rightly uses the new-to-him word and groans out, "Fucking hell!"

Sebastian

The witch's nightmares drive me from the house before the sun has crested the horizon. I don't trust or believe anything she says but the sounds of anguish, desperation, and fear that come from her room have every fiber of my being wanting to go to her rescue. My arms ache to gather her close and promise her she will always be safe with me. It's complete rubbish. I'm not the hero and humans, especially female humans haven't held my interest in centuries. The hex I know she's placed on me and judging by Luca's uncharacteristic behavior last night, him as well is hard to resist but no mere witch will best me. The wolves are taken with her as well but they rut with any willing female so I send them into her room to comfort her knowing she will do the least amount of damage to them with her charm spells.

My horse is lathered from the hard ride we took to help clear my mind and I'm ready to face her once again to get to the truth of her presence. It's too much of a coincidence her appearing in the same place as the assassins sent to kill the King. I need to find out who her master is before he makes another attempt on the current monarch's life.

Determined to have the answers I need, I vault from the saddle and throw the reins to a groom before striding into the manor. When I reach the bedchamber she's locked in, I'm relieved for a moment to not hear sounds of distress coming through the door but I do hear male voices so I throw open the door to make sure she's not weaving her magic against my mates.

She's standing beside the bed with the wolves close by and when she spins my way and laughs I feel my jaw clench and my hands form into fists. She is still defiant and unafraid and I glare as I slowly look her up and down. She's wearing the same strange clothing as the day before but I see that she's cleaned the blood from her skin. The sun shining through the window lights up her hair and I grind my teeth against reacting to the beauty of all the shades of gold and red blending in a wild curly mane. The witch is tousled like she just spent a night of pleasure with a lover. The thought has me glaring at the wolves but they both look at her like they want to throw her onto the bed and have their way with her so I know they haven't yet. I want my answers and her to be gone before that happens. Looking back at her, I open my mouth to make my demand but she throws both hands up palms facing me before I speak. I wait for the blast of magical power to hit me but all I get is her laughing words.

"Wait! Before you break out the thumbscrews and torture rack, can I get a minute to wake up? I need to, uh, some privacy please, and also, have toothbrushes been invented yet? If not, how about a cup of coffee? Do you guys know what coffee is?"

Cade jumps in before I have a chance to remind her that she is our prisoner and that she doesn't get to make demands.

"Bas and Luca drink that foul brew, yes. You'll be wanting to have a morning wash, then. We will leave you and I'll have a servant bring you hot water to freshen up with." He meets my annoyed gaze and nods toward the door with a firm look. "I'm sure Sebastian's questions can wait. We can discuss everything he wants to know while we break our fast in the morning room. You can meet us there, Eden. Once you are ready, a servant will guide you to us."

The sweet smile of gratitude the witch sends him has my thumb wanting to rub against her lips so instead, I turn and leave the room with a scowl. Finn must have information to share with me if he's accommodating her in such a way. I lead the way to the morning room where a buffet of breakfast dishes has been assembled and take my seat at the head of the table as Luca joins us, waiting for the attendant to pour me a cup of the thick Turkish coffee I have imported.

Where Luca and I do not need to eat or drink to thrive, the wolves have ravenous appetites and over the hundred-plus years they have been with us, we have developed a routine to dine together whenever possible. It also helps keep the servants from speculating too much about our nature.

"Well, what have you learned about the witch, then?" I ask the wolves over my cup as I savor the thick, rich brew.

Cade laughs. "You aren't going to like it, Bas. You have your mind set on her being a threat but she's not."

"Surely you both haven't succumbed to her charms so quickly?" I scoff. "I will admit that she's exceptionally beautiful but that hardly means that she's an innocent."

Finn holds up the witch's magic device. "No, not innocent but not the threat you want her to be. We've learned that she's no maid but a woman of twenty-nine. She showed us how to use this device and from what we can tell, there's no danger from it. There are pictures as she calls them, like the paintings on the walls here that show the future she lives in. Bas, if the lass was a witch with magical powers, wouldn't she have tried to use them to leave by now or tried to do us harm?"

I shrug one shoulder. "There is a game afoot. I'm sure of it. She wants to be here for some plot or plan we have yet to determine."

"Show them, cousin," Cade instructs with an angry expression I have rarely seen on his good-natured face. "Show them the damage done to her as well. No witch with powers would allow that to happen. No matter what fighting skills they have."

My interest is piqued by his words but I'm still wary of the device that flares to life with a swipe of Finn's thumb. He brings it over and takes the chair beside me with Luca on the other side leaning over to see. He shows us the pictures of a great city with buildings that defy gravity soaring into the sky. All the buildings glow with light that cannot possibly come from torches or oil lamps alone. In other images, people smile dressed in strange costumes and clothing and still others with horseless carriages filling perfectly straight streets. I have traveled extensively throughout my existence and have never seen such wonders.

I see Finn's fingers clench and turn white from the pressure of holding the device before he swipes to the next image. It takes me a moment to process what I'm seeing but the red hair tells me it's the beaten bloody witch. Luca makes a choked noise at the sight and I slam my fist against the table in rage. I've seen many a damaged woman in all my years and I'm well aware of how despicable men can be to women but seeing the abuse of the witch in such a vivid image makes my blood boil to the point I can't stand the thought of any more harm coming to the woman who I've only known for less than a day. I quickly swipe the offending image away and study each new image as they appear as Finn defends the witch.

"Don't you think Eden would have used magic to stop such injuries to herself if she had any? Or at least used it to heal herself? She's not a witch, Bas, and these pictures make a good case for her telling the truth about where or rather when, she's from."

I consider his words as I flip through image after image that shows a world I can hardly believe until the next swipe is something different. Sound comes blaring out of the device as the image starts to move, causing me to flinch back. A group of people gather around the witch and another woman that looks like a younger version of her. There's a large cake with script written on it and tiny blazing candles stuck into it. The crowd around them sings out a song about a happy birthday as the two women beam at each other with so much love I can feel it where my heart use to feel such things. When the song ends, the younger woman blows the candles out to cheers and throws her arms around the witch gushing, "I love you, Eden! You are the best sister a girl could ever have!"

"Shut it off!"

The four of us look up in surprise to see the witch standing in the doorway with a look of heartbreaking devastation on her too pale face that quickly shifts to fury. She runs towards us and I'm so surprised by her actions that I let her yank the device from my hand. She glances down at the moving image and just freezes as the fury melts away to be replaced with an expression of deep grief and loss. A quick swipe silences the noise coming from the moving image and then she clutches it against her chest and squeezes her eye closed whispering,

"Hope. I miss you so much, Hope."

I see the single tear trickle down her perfect cheek and feel my stomach clench at the pain radiating off her. I know this isn't a simple loss from being separated from a loved one. This is the agony of death. The woman, Hope, was the witch's sister and I know without a doubt that she is dead. The four of us stay silent as we wait for her next reaction and we are all relieved when she opens her eyes and swipes at her tear before making her next demand in a curt tone.

"Coffee! You said there's coffee?"

Cade is quick to guide her to a chair and pours her a cup of the Turkish brew. He stands back as she takes her first sip but starts when she chokes out a cough with her eyes going wide in surprise.

"What is it, lass, uh, Eden? What can I get for you?" he asks in concern as he pats her back gently.

"Good lord! That's like the strongest espresso I've ever tasted!" She blinks a few times, considers her cup, and then gently sets it back on its saucer. "Would it be possible to get some hot water, cream and sugar?"

Completely smitten with the witch, Cade calls out to one of the attendants standing against the wall in French to get her what she wants before settling into the chair beside her. He starts piling food on the plate in front of her, urging her to eat but her green eyes are glaring my way.

"So are we done with invading my privacy because I've had about all I can take with the trip down memory lane today?" She spits in my direction.

The woman bounces from emotion to emotion so fast it makes my head ache. Most females that I've encountered would be crumbling, weeping messes from the situation she's in - not to mention the painful memories we've forced on her this day. The fact that she's sitting there glaring at me instead makes me want to either admire her strength or chalk it all up to an act on her part. Only time will give me the answer. I pick up the device she's set down beside her plate and tap it softly so as to not bring it back to life.

"I've seen the images and they do point to you being from a more advanced place than here but magic would be the simpler explanation. That, I have witnessed with my own eyes. Traveling back in time, well, it's hard to believe. The timing of your appearance is suspect as well. A mere human would also not have reacted the way you did when you found out our...abilities. A witch on the other hand would accept it in a similar way or would have already known of our existence. There isn't a way for you to prove either, witch."

She groans and rubs between her eyes. I can see the depth of her weariness and feel a pang that I've had a part in it but I need answers before I can decide where to go from here. Her hand drops from her eyes to reveal the frustration in them.

"Stop calling me witch! My name is Eden. E-D-E-N, Eden." She spells it out like I'm a simpleton or a child before glancing around at the servants stationed against the walls of the room. "You, yourself said they burn witches at the stake here so I can only assume you are trying to get me killed by calling me that over and over again. If you want me dead so badly then just go ahead and do it already. Honestly, I could use the rest and peace at this point."

Eden

The look on Mc Icy's face at me telling him to go ahead and kill me already would be almost comical if I wasn't so tired and sad. Hearing Hope's voice out of the blue like that has knocked me for a loop and I feel the darkness closing in again after fighting so long to get back into the twilight I've been living in. Even after almost two years, the grief is still so raw and deep that it takes my breath away. Sebastian holds his reply when a servant, I'm going to have to learn some names if I'm here for a while, brings a tray with the items I asked for. I'm desperate for a cup of coffee that is palatable to a mere human so I go to work filling the new cup with half of the thick coffee and half with hot water to cut the strength and then add the coarse sugar and thick cream until it looks and tastes closer to the brew I'm used to. I ignore the curious looks from the four men but stop the servant from taking away the first cup of energizer strength coffee that is now only half-filled and go about fixing it in the same way. I'm positive I will need at least two cups to get through the rest of this breakfast.

I hum as I savor the coffee just how I like it and finally wave my hand towards Sebastian that he can continue causing his curious expression to settle back into his customary glare.

Cade leans over the table and sniffs at the freshly doctored coffee in the second cup before asking, "Does it taste better that way?"

When I smile a satisfied smile and nod his eyes linger on my lips before picking the cup up.

"May I?" he says.

I nod again and my smile grows when his reaction is surprised pleasure.

"Well, now, that's a mite better, isn't it? I quite fancy coffee this way."

He hands the cup across the table to Finn to try and his cousin has the same reaction before they both turn scowls towards Luca and Sebastian like the two men had been hiding it from them.

Seeing Sebastian close to losing his patience, I get us back on track. "Anyways, I truly don't know how I got here or how to get home. Like I told Cade and Finn earlier, I have no interest in a plot against your King or any of your business for that matter. I'm no threat to you all. At best, I'm a nuisance. I would leave here and never darken your door again if I had any idea on where to go or any money to get me there. So it's up to you to decide what to do with me. I guess what I'm saying is, I'm at your mercy, my Lord. Do with me as you please."

I meant that last part sarcastically but the heat and red tinge in his eyes tell me he's taken it literally and I try hard not to squirm in my seat when all the ideas of how he can use me come to mind with the way he's looking at me.

Luca speaks for the first time since I came into the room, interrupting the sexual stare-down going on.

"For now, I think it's best for all if you stay with us while we see if we can come up with some answers to your dilemma. Sending you out into a foreign country and time would be akin to sending a sheep out to deal with a wolf pack." He slides his chair back from the table and gets to his feet. "You will need supplies that a house filled with men does not have on hand. Bas, we will need to go to court and have some gowns and other garments either made or purchased for her. She will be our guest and we cannot have her wearing the same clothing day in and day out. Who knows how long she will be with us until we find a way for her to return to her home.

Do you wish to accompany me? We can speak to Pierre and see if there has been any reaction to the latest failed plot while we are there."

Sebastian doesn't reply but stands from the table instead never taking his eyes off of me. He comes around and stops next to my chair and surprises me when he holds my phone out to me. "I apologize for us invading your privacy and stirring up painful memories."

He glares at Cade and Finn. "See that she doesn't leave the estate. She might not be a threat to us but others are. Until we can learn more of her situation, she must remain unseen."

When he and Luca leave the room it's like all the air is sucked out with them and I slump in my seat clutching my phone to my chest. I'm relieved that the whole witch business is passed for now but I still have no idea how I'm going to get home or why I'm here in the first place. With no answers in sight, I shake off the dark thoughts and dive into the food growing cold on my plate happy that there's no dried fish in sight. After we finish eating the guys take me to the library where I happily spend a few hours combing through the shelves. I climb the ladder and have fun rolling it back and forth along the stacks. There are thousands of books to run my fingers over as I search the shelves for anything I might recognize. In the end, I laugh at myself when I realize that even the books I would call classics haven't been written yet.

Finally choosing a small book of poetry, I curl up onto a cushioned window seat with my robe tucked around my legs and open the book to get lost in the beauty of poetry for a few hours. Right away I know that's not going to happen with the extreme amount of thees and thous filling the poems. Sighing, I close the book and just rest it in my lap and stare out at the gorgeous gardens and fountains that I can see outside the window.

From what I've seen of it, France is a beautiful country. I guess if I had to get stuck in a foreign country it's not a bad location. Not real happy about the timeframe but I try and make myself feel better by thinking about how it could have been so much worse. I could have landed in the middle of one of the world wars or even worse, 2020. There's just so much I don't know about this timeframe and how the whole time travel deal works. Aunt Adera showed up in our lives now and again so clearly there's a way to get back but I have no idea how. She must have known how to control it but without a user's manual I might end up stuck here. If that's the case then I'm going to have to find a way to make a life here for myself. I can't just assume that the four men who have taken me on will want to support me until I die. The warm sun beaming onto me through the window has me drifting off to sleep as I try and think of a way to make a living and a life in this time.

I wake with my head pressed against the window and can tell that I've slept away many hours of the day as the sun is no longer in sight. It seems like I've done a lot of sleeping since I landed here, especially considering how little I would sleep at home. Anxiety and nightmares have turned me into an insomniac since the attack but for some reason, I have no problem dozing off during the day here. I stretch my legs out and arch my back to try and loosen the stiffness from sleeping in one curled-up position for so long before swinging my legs over the side of the window seat and push to my feet. I only make it a few feet before I flinch in surprise when I spot Luca leaning against a bookshelf watching me from the shadows.

"Um, hi? I guess I fell asleep there for a bit." I say tentatively. He's been kind to me so far but no matter how sexy he is with his sad watchful eyes and sweet good looks, I don't lose sight of the fact that he's a vampire and I'm probably at the top of his food pyramid. So far I haven't felt any fear by being around these supernatural men, probably because of the shock and wonder of their existence but I don't kid myself that they aren't incredibly dangerous figures. Life isn't like a romance novel and if they choose to turn on me for whatever reason, I'm a goner. He pushes away from the shelf and steps towards me out of the shadow.

"You looked so peaceful. I was just enjoying the sight. Have you been in here all day?"

I look down at the book in my hands trying to remember where I got it so I can put it back as I nod. He takes it from my hands and reads the title with a wry, half-smile.

"Rather pretentious poetry, I found. I will be sure to recommend better for you to read." He sets the book on one of the small tables that dot the room. "A servant will shelve it when they next come in to dust. Would you care for a stroll in the gardens before retiring to dress for supper?"

Hell yes, I would! I'm used to being much more physically active at home so a walk sounds fantastic. When he sees the happy expression on my face, he holds out his arm in the direction to go with a slight bow in the most old-fashioned but charming way.

We leave directly from the library through a pair of French doors that lead out to a pretty little courtyard surrounded by flowerbeds and tall hedges. I'm so in love with the little private area that I can easily picture a table and chairs set to sit and enjoy a good book and afternoon coffee break. Luca guides me out of the courtyard and onto the pathways that wind through the gardens and around fountains. I can stop taking deep breaths of the fresh air without a hint of pollution. It's almost like the air has more oxygen in it. As we stroll, I catch sight of many statues hidden away in corners and bends on the path. Each one is more stunning than the last but all of them feature faces filled with agony and loss. I stop looking at them too closely as I find myself recognizing the pain and it stirs my own.

Luca seems content to walk with me in silence but after a while I can't help but start asking him questions.

"So, vampire, huh? Was that a personal choice or just something you stumbled into?" I ask jokingly.

He looks down at me with a hint of a smile on his pouty lips and I try to ignore the flush of heat that travels through me. The man, er, Vampire is so good looking with the sun picking out reddish highlights in his dark curls. It's the kind of hair that you want to dig your fingers into to pull his mouth closer. Swallowing the thought, I look away quickly as he answers.

"It was a choice, in a way. I chose not to die, I suppose. A choice I've questioned every moment of the past few hundred years."

I feel a pang in my chest at his words. How many times in the last few years have I had similar questions? There have been many times I've felt it would have been easier if I had just died with my family or later with my partner, Sam.

"Sometimes, the pain is not worth the price of the next breath," I say in a low voice.

We share a look of understanding and I feel something shift inside of me. An empty space that doesn't feel quite so empty now. A cloud slides in front of the sun darkening his face and I see a brief glimpse of the depths of his pain and sadness before he quickly turns his head away. Wanting to lighten the vibe, I ask my next question.

"The sun, it doesn't cause you harm? In the stories told in my time, a vampire's greatest weakness is the sun. Legend has it they burn to ash in it."

As the cloud moves away and the sun beams down once again he turns his hand this way and that in the brightness.

"There is a kernel of truth to that. The weakest of my kind, ones whose blood has been diluted from the originals suffer and weaken from sunlight but it would take prolonged exposure to actually kill them. The one who sired me was sired himself by an original so I suffer no infliction from the sun."

I sneak a peek up at his face but he doesn't seem to be bothered with my question so I forge ahead.

"Do you mind if I ask how old you are?"

I feel the sadness come off him in a wave and regret asking right away but he answers me anyway. "I was born in the year 1434 and was reborn to this curse in 1461. I am two hundred and thirty-three years old." He steers me around the corner in the path and back towards the house without ever touching me. "Come, you will require time to bathe and dress for the evening meal. The servants will have delivered everything you should require to be more comfortable to your room by now. I was able to procure four gowns that will only need minor adjustments. The others will be delivered by the end of the week. I hope you will be pleased with the choices I have selected for you."

I reach out to pull him to a stop but when he flinches from my touch I snatch my hand back and look up at him with hesitation. "Thank you so much for your thoughtfulness but I have no money or means to earn any to pay you back for the cost of so many gowns. One would have been more than enough."

He waves my words and concern away and I see amusement dancing in his eyes. "There is no need. We are wealthy beyond what we could spend in many lifetimes. As our guest, it is my honor to see you without want. I look forward to seeing you dressed in the finest silks and satins the court's merchants had available."

I can only smile my gratitude and follow him into the huge house where thankfully, he leads me back to my room. I'm going to have to see about drawing a map of this place or I'm going to end up lost every time I go anywhere without a guide. He leaves me at the door with another small bow and I just lean against the frame and watch him walk away. My eyes drop to his tight breeches and I let out a dreamy sigh at the way the fabric clings to a superior ass. When he turns a corner I shake my head at my thirsty girl antics. It's been well over two years since I've been

with a man and temptation is thick with the four hot
as sin men I'm now sharing my time with.

Eden

Turning from the empty hall I push open the door to my room and freeze at the changes since I was last in it. The bed and dresser are piled high with boxes and cloth bags of all sizes that account for way more than the four gowns Luca said he purchased for me. A dressing table with an attached mirror and small stool now sits in one corner and the top is covered with an assortment of glass bottles of all different sizes, shapes, and colors. There are also slim flat boxes stacked on one corner of the table. I don't know what to say or where to start until I spot the large tub filled with steaming water on the other side of the bed. It's not the shower I've been longing for but after almost two days without a proper wash and in the same clothing, I'm thrilled to finally be able to get fully clean. I've just tossed off my bathrobe and am about to whip off the rest of my clothes when the door to my room opens causing me to spin around with a squeak.

My heart slows down when an older woman with steel-grey hair pulled back into a loose bun and Bridgette come into the room carrying jugs of more steaming water. The older lady gives me a kind smile as she dips her head but Bridgette sails past me with a look on her face like she smells something bad and they set the jugs beside the tub. I roll my eyes at the seventeenth-century mean girl and focus on the woman to introduce myself.

"Bonjour, Je m'appelle Eden and that's all I got in French," I say with a laugh.

Bridgette sniffs disdainfully and launches into rapid-fire French but the woman throws a hand up to stop her and points to the door with a stern finger sending the maid out with a pout and a nasty side-eye towards me. The woman steps to me and takes one of my hands in both of her own.

"Bonjour, Mademoiselle Eden. I am Claudette and I'm here to help you bathe and dress. His Grace has informed us that you do not speak French. While not without an accent, I am fairly fluent so please do not hesitate to ask for anything you might need. Oui?" She tells me in charmingly accented English. A real smile widens across my face.

"Thank you and thank you for preparing the bath for me! It is very welcome." I turn and look at the steaming tub but don't see any soap or towels so I ask her and she takes me through what is in all the bottles on the dressing table and shows me the stack of what I would consider sheets to dry off with. When she tries to help me undress, I shake my head.

"Thank you but I will manage alone. But would you help me after with the gown? I'm not sure I can manage it on my own."

"Mais oui, bien sur. I will set the privacy screen for you and begin unpacking the gowns and accouterments if that is acceptable?"

I glance around at all the things Luca has bought for me and nod eagerly before insisting on helping her open up and move a wooden folding panel to screen the tub. As soon as it's in place I strip naked and take the opportunity to wash out my bra, underwear, tank top, and leggings draping them over the screen to dry. Sliding down into the tub of hot water is a dream and I sit and relax for a few moments enjoying the heat of the water as I listen to Claudette hum a tune as she works in the other half of the room. I don't give myself too long as I know the water will cool quickly. The soap is in a crumbly cake that smells lovely but doesn't lather at all. It's more like a scrub than soap.

With no shampoo in sight, I'm forced to make do with the same soap to wash my hair. I use the jug of warm water to rinse my hair as best I can before standing and pouring the second jug over my body to rinse away the bathwater. Ringing out my long hair I know it's going to be a mess of frizzy curls when it dries without conditioner or hair products to tame it. The best I can do is rub some of the fragrant oil over my hands and use it like a hair serum. I dry off as best I can with one of the sheets provided and squeeze out as much dampness from my hair before wrapping a new, dry sheet toga style around my body. I'm contemplating just cutting a good foot and a half from my hair length to make it more manageable in this time frame when I come around the screen and see what Claudette has accomplished.

My mouth falls open in awe as I see the bed filled with the new gowns, all laid out and piles of other fabric garments that I have no idea how to wear. My fingers can't help but reach out to touch the gorgeous gowns. There's a deep emerald-colored one that has black embroidered ivy and small flowers along the neckline. The pattern trails down to wrap around under the chest like a wide belt and then continues down both sides of the full skirt until it travels across the hem in another thick band. If I didn't know it was already mine I would steal it from whoever owns it. There are three other dresses of different colors but I can't keep my eyes off of the emerald one.

"C'est beau, n'est-ce pas?" Claudette says beside me with a sigh of admiration.

"It's freaking incredibly beau! But where would I even wear such a dress?"

Claudette chuckles. "You will don it for supper this evening, but of course."

I turn big eyes her way and ask nervous, "Is there a party? Are we having a ball?" I'm not sure I'm ready to see other people yet. She smiles and shakes her head.

"Non, it is only le famille. There are no other guests joining you."

"Hun, don't you think this gown is a little fancy for just having supper in?"

Claudette laughs like I've just told the funniest joke so I let her steer me as she's the native in the room and she gets down to it like a drill sergeant. She whips the sheet from my body without a blink of an eye and starts by holding out what I would call bloomers to take the place of underwear. Next up is a torturous contraption that's part satin, part boning, and a whole lot of ribbon. As she goes to wrap it around my waist her eyes land on the four tattoos I have. They make a half-circle under my left breast and heart. Four moons in different phases. Three of them mark the phase of the moon when each of my parents and sister were born and the last is the phase of the moon the night they died.

The tips of her fingers brush over them and she whispers, "La lune" before she snatches her hand back and wraps the corset around me. After that it's pain and punishment as she presses her knee into my back to heave on the ribbons to tighten the damn thing. I'm about to cry uncle and tell her to take it off when she finally ties it off and guides me over to the dressing table stool and pushes me down to sit on it. Holy fucking posture. There's no choice but to sit perfectly straight in this sucker or suffer a popped rib. I'm thinking this is a lot of effort just to go to dinner but I have to admire the way the thing has cinched in my waist and thrusted my boobs up higher than God ever intended.

I thought getting into the corset was bad but the sweet, kind French woman turns into a master dominatrix as she literally attacks my hair. By the time she's done, I'm a full sub and I'm wishing I knew the safe word. Knowing my luck it would be some weird French word I can't even pronounce. I won't need to cut any of my hair off because I'm pretty sure she's pulled at least half of it out. It might not have been so bad if I could have at least seen how she styled it but every time I try and turn my head to look in the mirror she yanks it back with a stern, "Non!"

By the time she's done my hair and goes to work on my face with what looks like tiny paintbrushes, I'm sore and tired and ready to say screw supper and just go to bed. The only thing that keeps me in place is that I'm a little bit terrified of the woman. After she's done with the brushes on my eyes and lips she picks up what looks like a piece of coal, flicks a few drops of water on it, swishes her finger around on the top, and holds it up to my eyes instructing me to blink against it. A grin tugs at my lips when I figure out that it's medieval mascara. After a few more dabs and smudges to my face she stands back and looks me over with a critical eye and then nods brusquely.

"Now for the jew-*els* and the gown."

I nod meekly, afraid of what I'm going to see in the mirror. I can already imagine the clown's face she's painted on me but I'm in it now so I let her fasten a necklace around my neck and position jeweled combs into my hair without a word. Beckoning me to stand, again with my back to the mirror, she holds open the dress for me to step into. It slides onto me silky soft but once on my shoulders I'm surprised at the weight of it. I have to give mad props to Renaissance ladies. The sheer amount of work that goes into dressing for and then wearing these costumes just to have supper brings new meaning to the term high maintenance but then again, I'm pretty sure these chicks have never experienced the joy of a Brazilian wax job so I'm holding that in the win column for twenty-first-century girls.

Once Claudette has finished buttoning up a thousand tiny buttons on my back she comes around in front of me and scans me from head to toe before holding up a stern finger for me to wait. At this point I'm basically her bitch so I stay still even though I'm dying to turn and look at myself in the mirror. She kneels in front of me and slips matching slippers with tiny square heels on my feet before standing and doing the twirl motion with her finger. I swallow back the nerves that tell me I'm going to look like a fool and slowly turn to face the full-length mirror behind me.

I gasp at the woman that is revealed. I barely recognize myself staring back. My hair is half piled up on top of my head with glossy black ivy dotted with tiny green gem combs anchored to look like a crown. The rest tumbles down my back in fat glossy ringlets. My worry about the makeup was a waste of time because it's just as flawless as if a MAC counter artist had done it. My eyes move down to the necklace that matches the combs in my hair. It's so delicate the way the black metal looks like ivy circling my neck with the dark green gems looking like leaves. My fingers trail over it and down across the swell of my breasts that have been replaced with a Victoria's Secret model's rack. All that's missing is the angel wings and I could walk that catwalk. The gown fits tightly across my chest and waist before flaring out in what looks like miles of skirt.

As I stare at my reflection I feel tears burn in my eyes. The last time I was this done up was for my ill-fated wedding day but even that pales in comparison. I have barely worn makeup or done anything to my hair in the last few years and what I'm looking at right now is the woman I could have, should have been if so much tragedy hadn't hit me. I'm starting to get more and more emotional but when Claudette cranes her head over my shoulder and sees the sheen of tears in my eyes, she yanks me around.

"Non! You will *ru*-in the eyes!" She glowers at me for a moment before her face softens and she gently cups my cheek. "Not soft, strong. A great beauty. N'est-ce pas?"

I swallow the tears back and throw my arms around the woman who was a stranger to me a few short hours ago, missing my mother so bad it's like a dagger in my heart. She hugs me back with a tinkling laugh and then gently escorts me to the door and waves me out.

I walk down the hallway with the fancy shoes only pinching my toes a little and the gown making a satisfying whoosh with every step. When I reach the top of the grand staircase I can't help but pause as I see all four of the men waiting at the bottom in the entryway. I haven't seen them dressed so formally yet and it's a feast for my eyes.

I think it should be a law that all men have to wear those tight muscle-clinging breeches that show a woman exactly what they are packing. Beautiful waistcoats and tailored jackets complete the picture of elegant drool worthiness. As one, they all turn and look up at me. Four sets of admiring eyes blaze a trail over every inch of me bringing a flush to my cheeks. They watch as I step down each stair but Sebastian turns away when I'm halfway down, his expression turning to one of boredom. I can't help but stare at his wide shoulders covered in of course, black and wonder if he's ever going to cut me some slack. And then I wonder why I care.

Eden

Cade, Finn, and Luca greet me at the bottom of the stairs with Cade elbowing Finn out of the way to offer me his arm.

"You look a right picture, my lady. Such beauty should be at Court. You would outshine all the simpering ladies there."

"Yeah, no thanks! This is about as formal as I can handle." I laugh and turn to Luca. "I can't thank you enough for the dress and everything else you filled my room with. It was very kind of you."

He gives me another of his little bows with a small, soft smile. "It was my pleasure. More so now that I see how your beauty shines in it. The color is a perfect complement for your lovely hair color." He turns and gestures to the right. "Shall we?"

Finn steps in front of him and offers his arm on my other side causing me to…giggle? Ok, enough, I don't giggle but I go with it anyways, feeling like a princess, so both the blonds escort me past a glaring Sebastian to a new room that must be the formal dining room. There's a long, like twenty feet long, elegantly set table waiting for us with attendants hovering at the ready. It's a beautiful table setting but when I see Sebastian go to one end, Luca the other and the blonds escort me to a chair right in the middle with two other chairs across from me I pause before sitting, glancing to either end. Sebastian notices my hesitation and shoots me an annoyed look.

"Is there a problem, witch?"

I grit my teeth at him calling me that once again glancing around quickly at all the servants in the room who must have heard him before giving him a pointed look.

"Not at all, *vampire*."

I feel a small, petty flush of satisfaction at the way he flinches at me using that term before he also looks around the room at the servants with a scowl. I turn and look to Luca, Finn, and Cade.

"Are we meant to yell at each other for conversation?"

At their confused expressions, I sigh. "It's just that we will be so far apart, speaking to each other will be difficult unless we yell." I turn back to Sebastian. "Or is that the point?"

He looks down his nose at me in disdain but before he can say his cutting reply Luca gets to his feet and calls out.

"You are absolutely right."

He waves a few attendants to the table and speaks to them in French.

I smile sweetly at him and back away from my chair so that the servants can rearrange the table. I can practically feel the death glare burning into my skin from Sebastian but don't look his way again until we are all seated. Cade claims the chair beside me with Luca and Finn across from us and of course the Iceman himself at the head of the table. The waves of anger, resentment or whatever grumpy bug crawled up his ass wash over me throwing my anxiety through the roof so I seize the wine glass in front of me that has just been filled and down half of it. Within minutes I feel the warmth and mellowness fill me. This right here is the reason I don't let myself drink. I always knew if I went down the alcohol numbing road to manage my pain I would drown in it. Now I'm a total lightweight with no tolerance.

The first course of soup comes and goes with me barely touching it at the tension smothering the table from Sebastian's bad attitude. With a glass and a half of wine in me, I'm starting to not give two shits about the buzz kill sitting next to me so when Finn breaks the silence I send him a dazzling smile.

"Eden, you mentioned your age as twenty-nine which I find hard to believe. You look like a much younger maid."

"That's so sweet of you to say! I imagine where I come from, life isn't as physically hard as it is here."

His blue-green eyes dip down to my lips as a small smile tugs at his own.

"Well, surely a woman as beautiful as you must be wed. Will your husband not be frantic with worry at your disappearance?"

A laugh spills out of me at the idea of my ex, Troy, being worried about me. He would be delighted if I never came back. With the divorce not quite finalized, it would give him access to all my inheritance without a fight.

"Again, things are very different where I come from. Many women choose not to marry at all or wait until they are older so they can focus on their careers first. I was married but my husband and I are finalizing our divorce. It's been two years since we were together."

Sebastian scoffs. "And what does the church have to say about that?" He asks in the most judgmental tone possible causing me to fight back a snarl.

"Not one damn thing. The church no longer has a say in private matters for the majority of the general population in my country. They no longer have the power they do in this era. Church and State are completely separate." I turn back to Finn and the others. "Women in my time are extremely independent. We work at whatever job we choose and make our own money. We have complete control over our own lives." The wine is making me bold and the shock on their faces causes me to laugh again. "Brace yourselves, boys, we can also be soldiers in the military, choose not to have children and have sex with whoever we choose, married or not." I have the biggest grin on my face at the shocked silence that causes so I hold my glass up and nod at the attendant. "More wine, please?"

Sebastian looks like he just sucked on a whole lemon his face is so sour but Luca leans forwards with a considering expression. "What of France? Do you know what happens here in the future?"

"Oh, of course! France is still a country but it's not like it is now. After the Sun King dies...wait, should I be telling you guys this? Is it going to mess up history?"

Sebastian seems to be over his sulk with the change of subject and he waves my concerns away.

"We don't involve ourselves in matters of state and politics often. Small intrigues such as the one we were dealing with help pass the time but there is always someone somewhere plotting to kill a King. I'm interested to hear what you have to say on the course of your history as entertainment but I don't believe for a moment you are actually from the future. So please, entertain us with your exaggerated tales."

I glare daggers at the infuriating man but just give him a sharp nod and turn back to the others.

"Your King lives until his seventies. After that, there's two more Kings but the second one and his wife along with a bunch of other nobles have their heads cut off in the guillotine when the peasants revolt. History calls that the French revolution. There's no more true Kings after that in France. There's a small little man that goes to war with most of Europe at the beginning of the eighteen hundreds and crowns himself Emperor but even that doesn't last." I let them absorb that as I take a few bites of the next course, a beef pie of some kind, and ask for a glass of water to try and slow down on the wine. I struggle to remember anything else about France's history but come up blank so I switch to other parts of the world.

"North America gets pretty busy in about a hundred years from now. They go to war with England twice to be their own country and eventually win. Then work on building more States for another bunch of decades before they have another war but this time it's a Civil war to stop slavery. Slavery is abolished and then they get even busier building and expanding. I'm sure there are other things going on in the world but I'm just hitting the highlights for you guys. The eighteen hundreds are an explosion of industry. Um, steam engines, telegraphs, and electricity start to really change the world. The nineteen hundreds is probably the biggest century to change how the world lives. Two major world wars happen that drive technology forward at a never-before-seen pace. By nineteen sixty-nine we send men in a rocket into space to land on the moon. The day I got sucked through the mirror to here, there was a space ship already a year into its journey to Mars to set up the groundwork for a colony."

I leave it there for now and take another sip of wine and wait for reactions. Sebastian and Luca both lean back in their chairs, thinking hard on what I've said but Finn and Cade have grins on their faces and the first thing Finn asks almost has me spitting out my wine.

"Let's go back to what you said about women. You really choose whoever you want to have sex with? Outside of wedlock?"

When I nod my head slowly that it's true his eyes heat up and then drop down to my elevated tits. He's so damn cute and I've had enough to drink that I'm not even mad.

"Eyes up here, wolf boy. Just because I'm free to choose doesn't mean I'm a sure thing for you. It is MY choice, not yours."

The hungry look in his eyes has me wanting to wiggle in my seat as I feel my pussy clench with its own need. It has been so long since I was with a man or even wanted to be that I had begun to think my sex drive was dead. As if he knows exactly what I'm thinking, Finn flashes me a devilish smile from across the table that almost seals the deal when two dimples flash my way.

"Och, of course, what fun would it be if the lass wasn't just as willing?"

I'm saved from answering him by Cade beside me when he rests a hand on my arm. "Do you work, then? You said women make their own money in your time."

"Oh, yes, I mean, I did. I was an, uh, a healer I guess you would call it here. I would treat and stabilize people who were hurt until we could get them to the hospital and doctors."

His eyebrows shoot up. "A noble calling, to help others. Do you not do that anymore?"

I look down at my plate not wanting to explain why I'm not an EMT anymore and just say. "I'm taking a break from it right now." Cade must sense that I don't want to talk about it because he doesn't follow up. We both lean back as a servant removes our plates and another sets bowls of candied fruit in front of us.

"So no husband and no work as you call it. Tell me, witch, what do you do to fill your days then?" Sebastian asks. I sigh. At least he said witch at a lower volume than he normally does.

"I inherited a very large property when my aunt passed away. I've been working on clearing it out.

That's where I found the mirror that brought me here. When I'm not working on the house I spend the rest of my time training to fight."

His eyes dip down my body in consideration. "Hmm, we did witness your fighting skills. It was quite surprising. I've never seen a woman as skilled as you in battle. Tell me, is the time you claim to be from very dangerous that you need those skills?"

I stare down at the small bowl in front of me and toy with a sugary berry for a moment trying to think of a way to explain without going too deep into my issues.

Sighing in defeat I tell him, "Sometimes, yes. There are criminals just like I'm sure there are here that will take advantage when they think they can get away with it. My partner and I were attacked by a gang. He died and I barely survived. After that, I chose to do everything possible to never be a victim again. So I trained and learned to fight."

I lift my eyes enough to see his face but the anger in his eyes has me looking quickly back down. I have no idea what I've said that pissed him off again.

Luca speaks from across from me. "You should join us in the morning, then. We usually spend a few hours sparring and working on our battle skills. I would be interested in learning some of the tactics we saw you use in the fight yesterday."

A wide smile fills my face but my reply is cut short when Sebastian groans and shoves to his feet. "I'm retiring to the library. I find myself in need of stronger spirits." With a sharp nod to the rest of us, he leaves the table and then the room.

I guess that means supper is over. I look down at the gorgeous gown I've barely gotten to wear in disappointment that I'll be taking it off so soon. The other three get to their feet so I stand as well ready to ask to be escorted back to my room when Cade takes my hand and lifts it to his mouth. My knuckles feel singed from the heat of his lips as he places a gentle kiss on them.

With a teasing twinkle in his eyes he asks, "Tell me, Eden, would you be interested in playing a card game with us in the library?"

A smile of satisfaction tugs my lips up as I nod my head eagerly. Not only do I get to keep wearing this killer dress for a while longer but I'm positive my presence in the library will annoy the fuck out of Sebastian. Win, win!

Sebastian

I pour what will be the first of many drinks this evening and settle into my favorite chair with a thick book, glad to have some distance from the alluring witch. The picture she paints of the future is mind boggling and must be pure fantasy. I've seen a lot of changes in the world in my fourteen hundred plus years but the idea of the church giving up power to control rulers and women being allowed, encouraged even, to choose how they live their lives is utterly unbelievable.

I myself was once fiercely devoted to Christianity. I converted hundreds to the faith and still stayed true even after I was tied to a tree and shot full of arrows. The fact that I recovered and lived only cemented my fervor for the faith. It took being beaten by the Emperor's guards and then thrown in a sewer to die to finally rock my faith.

When it was an ancient creature that intervened and saved me from death instead of the so-called Lord and Savior my faith was completely gutted. The bloodlust and depravity that overtook me in the first few years after the change had me knowing without a doubt that no God was gazing down on me. The savagery my maker and I committed together before I came to my senses and managed to escape her clutches stripped any belief and faith that remained. If there was truly a God, he would never allow such as myself to roam his earth.

As I sip at my drink, I scoff at the notion that the church would lose so much power that women would be allowed to make such free choices as the witch had spoken about. I could almost see one day women being allowed to earn their own money and own property, possibly even being allowed to soldier but the rest? Choosing not to marry, divorce, and engage in premarital sexual intercourse without consequences? Ha! Even if the church did lose some of its power, mortal men would never allow such change that would threaten the power they wielded. No, the witch's stories of time travel and the future show that she is mentally unbalanced, delusional even. I will watch her closely over the next few days, watch for the moment she shows her true purpose for being here and then deal with her accordingly.

My jaw tenses when I hear her sweet laugh come through the door followed closely by my brothers escorting her. When she spots me and sends a smile my way that is more teeth-baring challenge than smile I have to force myself to stay seated and not react. Her beauty is only exaggerated by the emerald green dress that displays her assets so temptingly. I have to force my fingers to unclench from around the glass in my hand less I shatter the crystal and wear the brandy it contains.

"Bas."

Delusional or not, the physical need to touch and possess the witch and her beauty is like a fire burning under my skin.

"Sebastian?"

I want to thread my fingers into her wild red mane and yank her head back so that I could devour those defiant lips before moving down to her...

"Your Grace, Duc du Gaul!"

The exclamation breaks through my heated thoughts, causing me to snap my eyes from the witch to Finn - who has clearly been calling my name multiple times judging by the amused, knowing, grin plastered across his face. If that isn't bad enough the other three are all staring at me with raised eyebrows.

"What?" I practically snarl in Finn's direction.

"Och well, I was gonna ask if you wanted ta play cards with us but I think I changed my mind. You don't seem to be in a playing mood!"

I wave his words away in dismissal and force myself to stop thinking about playing with the witch. Picking up my book, I attempt to read but find myself rereading the same line over and over again as my eyes keep wandering to the foursome playing cards around a low table between two couches. As Cade explains the rules of the game, the witch is forced to lean forwards over the table causing her breasts to practically fall out of her gown. I watch the wolves lean forward as well with their eyes glued to her chest and almost snort in disbelief when I see Luca's dip down to the smooth, lovely orbs on display. My gaze tracks back to the witch's face expecting to see a satisfied, coy expression that her charms are working but instead I see the heat of a blush staining her cheeks. A frown crosses my face as I watch her casually lean back and cup her chin so that her forearm covers a good portion of her cleavage. Every time I think I have a handle on this witch she does the opposite of what I think she will.

They finish explaining the game but the wolves bicker over who gets to be her partner in the game so Luca intervenes and takes the spot for himself. Once the cards are dealt, she leans over to pick them up but stops halfway.

"Hold on a second, guys. I need a little bit of space here to be comfortable."

She pushes the low table closer to Luca and Finn, who are sitting on the couch across from her, and reaches down, gathers up the fabric of her skirt and removes her shoes, setting them to the side. Then she slides down off the couch until she's sitting right on the rug-covered floor, rearranges her dress, and pulls the table back toward her, and picks up the cards she was dealt. A small smirk tugs at my lips. She's solved the breasts spilling out issue but now they rest even with the table, almost more on display. Clever girl takes care of that when she rests her elbows on the table, crosses her arms, and holds up her hand of cards in front of her face completely blocking the tantalizing view from the men surrounding her. I hold back a chuckle when I spot the pout on both the wolves' faces at her block.

The game starts slowly as they give the witch time to catch on to the rules but once she and Luca win three hands in a row, the wolves step up their play. I've completely given up on the pretense of reading my book and set it aside as I drain and pour another drink. Now that she's fully committed to the game, the table talk cheating comes out in full force by the two pups.

"Cade, did you see the poor job the groundskeeper did on the flower beds? He left his tools laying out and I almost stepped on a *spade!*" Finn says in a bland voice. I see the witch shoot him a suspicious look but she continues playing and loses the hand with a frown.

"Why that's terrible, cousin. If you had been hurt I surely would have beaten the man with a *club.*"

The witch gasps in outrage and glares with mock menace at the two with a shake of her head. The next hand is dealt out and before the pups have a chance to cheat, Luca leans towards her.

"May I say again how lovely you look tonight? The emeralds perfectly match your eyes."

My forehead furrows at the compliment and I stiffen when I see her blush prettily again but he isn't finished. Luca stares into her eyes like she's the only woman in the world and I see her eyes turn soft and dreamy as he continues to speak.

"I believe next time I would like to see you draped in...*diamonds.*"

The table goes dead silent for a few beats as the witch blinks in surprise before throwing her head back and letting out a loud, genuine belly laugh while the wolves roar in outrage that he has honed in on their cheating ways.

I stare at the laughing woman, so real and without the current society's constraints. Where most ladies would titter, giggle and demurely bat their eyes, she just enjoys the moment with what comes naturally. Her loud joyful laughter is refreshing and the sound of it moves into a space in my chest that has been empty for so long. Once she gets control of herself, she picks up her cards, scans them quickly, and then she does bat those sparkling green eyes at Luca.

"Oh, Luca, I do so love the emeralds but I'm not sure even diamonds would win my... *heart!*"

The game devolves from there with the wolves trying to distract her with exaggerated flirting that comes with constant small touches. A hand on her arm, fingers captured for a kiss, and a curl swept behind her shoulder with fingers lingering on her skin has me tensing up with the need to be the one touching her. My hardened cock twitches painfully as it strains against the tight fabric of my breeches, forcing me to pick my book back up to rest it in front of my lap else my arousal be noticed. I finally reach my limit when the witch catches Cade, who has joined her on the floor, passing cards to Finn under the table. She throws her cards down and pretends to attack him while giggling threats. The wolf takes full advantage by wrapping his arms around her waist and dragging her to the floor until his back is flush with the rug and she is laying on top of him with her breasts pushed against him and their lips only inches apart. Her giggling stops with a soft gasp that sends an even more painful jolt to my straining cock.

Finn pushes to his feet and whines, "Not fair! I was cheating too. Come attack me, lass."

I can take no more and retire for the night.

Eden

By the time the guys escort me back to my room my cheeks hurt from smiling and laughing so much. It has been years since I had a night of just plain fun with good company. The emptiness and loneliness that I have lived with for so long has been beaten back by three charming, sexy as fuck men and I can't wait to see what tomorrow will bring. I'm also wound tight and ready to drag one of them into my room after their constant touching and flirting. I never knew that being kissed goodnight on the back of my hand could be so damn erotic and as I watch them walk away down the hall I try and find the courage to call one of them back to stay with me.

They turn the corner and disappear, leaving me disappointed in myself but I decide it's probably for the best not to get too attached and I'll just take matters into my own hands to soothe the throbbing need between my legs.

Pushing into my room I jump back, on guard as old habits come flooding back but Claudette is only a threat to my ribs and hair so I swallow down the fear that filled me for a moment and give her a smile. The room has been tidied up with all the gowns and undergarments put away and the bed has been turned down. It's late and I feel bad that she's been forced to wait up for me but when she goes to work getting me out of the gown and corset I'm grateful because there's no way I would have managed it myself. She slides a soft linen nightgown over my head before pushing me down on the stool so she can remove the combs and the thousand and one pins holding my hair up. We barely say a word to each other as she works and weariness takes over my body. I feel my eyes start to droop when she rubs my sore scalp before patting me on my shoulder to let me know she's finished. I reach up and clasp her hand giving it a small squeeze to let her know I appreciate her staying up to help me. When I let go, her hand smooths my hair back from my face with a soft, kind smile and she leads me to the bed tucking me in under the heavy blankets that cover it.

The door whispers closed letting me know she's gone and I'm asleep in seconds. My dreams are not filled with violence for a change but vivid scenes of Cade, Finn, and Luca caressing my body. Their hot mouths and strong hands claim every inch of my skin as I beg them to fill me where I need it most. They pleasure me with exquisite torture bringing me to the edge time and again but never take me over.

The tall, glaring man with the gold-flecked hungry eyes stares down at us from the end of the bed but won't allow the others to give me what I need most. It's not until I arch my back, offering my naked, flushed with pleasure body to him and beg for his touch that he finally nods regally and climbs up between my legs. His strong, long fingers land on my hips in a bruising grasp and lift them causing me to moan in anticipation. He leans over me and stares at me with hot angry eyes before with one hard thrust slams his cock into me as far as it will go causing me to...

BANG

My door slamming open has me shooting straight up in the bed with my heart pounding and my breath heaving. I swear I can still feel my pussy stretched and filled with Sebastian's hard cock as my eyes dart around the sun-drenched room to land on...UGH!

Fucking Bridgette and her best French resting bitch face. I let myself drop back against the pillows and curse the cow that just cock blocked one of the best sex dreams I've ever had. As she slams around the room doing whatever maid shit she thinks will annoy me the most my sad pussy clenches on emptiness and throbs as it begs me to take care of business. I would like nothing more than to close my eyes and get back to that dream while rubbing out an orgasm to the images but clearly the demon maid from hell is not going to go away.

I let out a sound of frustration that is half screech, half groan and sit back up pinning the back of her head with my best "gonna fuck you up" look but it's wasted as she's got her back to me.

When I see that it's my phone she's leaned over with a hand reaching out to touch I bark, "Hey!"

She spins around like I just hit her with a bolt of lightning with a touch of fear on her face but it quickly turns sour as she jabbers a bunch of French at me ending with her eyebrows raised and a small sneer on her lips. It's a petty power play on her part as she knows I don't speak or understand her language so I just point at the door for her to leave. When she lifts her hands and shrugs like she doesn't know what I want, I curse.

"For the sake of Fuck, get out!"

Her sneer turns into more of a smirk as she drops the most sarcastic curtsy and then sails out of the room like she has better things to do. Grumbling that I'm starting the day in a foul mood, I throw the blankets back and jump down from the bed so I can close the door the brat has left wide open. Turning back to the bed I consider crawling back into it to try and recapture the mood of my dream but know it's pointless so I start looking for something to wear. I find the gowns hanging in an armoire but as pretty as they are I'm not liking the idea of being tortured back into a corset. My ribs still feel like I took a couple of punches to them from wearing the one last night. The punches thing reminds me that Luca said I could train with them this morning which immediately brightens my mood. It's been a few days now since I last worked out and my body is more than ready to feel the burn of some hard activity. I feel my cheeks heat up at the hard activity my pussy would rather have so I fan at my face and turn away from the gowns.

Without any actual workout clothing to wear I start going through drawers until I find my leggings, tank top, bra, and underwear that I came to this time in. The black lace bra won't give the support of a sports bra but it's better than nothing or worse, a corset. I cringe as I use the chamber pot but a small evil part of me chuckles in glee knowing Bridgette will have to empty it. A quick wash with the fresh water she brought and I throw my clothes on ready to find some coffee. When I reach for the doorknob to leave and see my bare arm I stop with an annoyed sigh and grab my robe, throwing it on and sliding my phone into a pocket. It's ridiculous that it's acceptable for me to bare most of my chest in one of the fancy gowns but scandalous for me to walk around with only a tank top on. I would kill for a hoodie right now so I don't have to wear the robe and wonder if I can sweet-talk one of the guys into lending me one of their billowy shirts to use instead. As I shove my hands deep into the pockets of my robe my fingers brush against something that makes me close my eyes in happiness. I yank out the black fabric-covered circle and hold it up to my eyes and do a small happy dance. I'm not all that surprised to find the thick elastic band in my pocket. With the sheer amount of hair that I have I buy the damn things in bulk and usually have one around my wrist and in most of my clothing's pockets. I work quickly to gather my curls up into a high ponytail and give it a quick bouncy swish before leaving my room. Finding the hair elastic in my pocket reminds me of the lip balm Sebastian confiscated and never returned. I wonder if he will give it back or hold on to it out of pettiness.

When I reach the morning room we had breakfast in yesterday all of the men are already at the table. As soon as I'm spotted all four of them rise to their feet. A warm feeling fills my stomach at the respectful action. Don't get me wrong, I'm a total girl power feminist but there's just something about the old fashioned manners they use that makes me a little swoony. Looking at them all is a reminder of the naughty they got up to in my dreams but I do my best not to flush crimson as I walk to the table. They stay standing until I take my seat and then reseat themselves after offering up morning greetings towards me, well three of them do anyway. Sebastian just gives me a once over before dismissing me and goes back to reading from a pile of documents stacked next to his plate. An attendant is quick to fill my teacup with what looks like coffee made to my liking. The first sip confirms that the brew has been made just how I doctored it yesterday so I turn in my chair and call out an enthusiastic "Thank you!" The poor guy must not get thanked very often because he practically trips over his own feet as he moves away. With a shrug, I turn back to load up my plate.

"Good morning, Eden. Were the other gowns not to your liking or did they require alterations?" Luca asks with a slight frown that I swear has a hint of insecurity in it.

"Oh, no! They're gorgeous, Luca. It's just, um, you mentioned that I could train with you guys this morning. I'm pretty good but sparring in one of those gowns would be a bit of a challenge, even for me." I try and joke hoping I haven't hurt his feelings. When he just nods I bite my lower lip in nervousness. "Um, is it still ok if I join you guys? I mean, if you're not comfortable with that I could maybe use the space after you all are done. I, to be honest, I'm not used to not working out every day so it would be great if I can get some time in on it." When he still hesitates I focus my eyes down on my plate and move the eggs around on it in disappointment until Finn reaches over and places his hand on my arm.

"Lass, it's not a bother. We were more concerned that it would make you uncomfortable to be with us while we hone our skills. We can get pretty brutal with each other as we train. It may offend your more womanly sensibilities."

My eyes track to each one of them to see if they're serious or just pulling my leg but they are all practically cringing causing me to bark out a laugh. "Seriously?" I ask. "You mean the womanly sensibilities that brutally killed five men in front of you when we first met?" I feel myself cringe at the reminder of what I had done but push it away. "I appreciate your concern but the place I train in every day has way more men than woman in it and trust me when I say they don't take my gender into consideration when we're sparring in the ring."

I chew on a piece of toast as they all share a look before each one of them turns their eyes to Sebastian as if waiting for him to give his permission. I let out a deep sigh causing him to finally look up from his paper and nail me with a glacial look. I'm so over his intimidation tactics so I just roll my eyes so hard it would put a fourteen-year-old bratty girl to shame. One corner of his mouth lifts ever so slightly as he regally nods his approval.

"Let the wi…woman join us, then. If her sensibilities are scandalized by what she sees that will be her problem to deal with," he tells the others.

The look on his face says he's going to enjoy putting me in my place but the guy just doesn't get it. The only scandalous thoughts will be me objectifying their hot bodies as they fight and dreaming about what they could do to mine.

Cade

I share an excited look with Finn across the table as we finish the morning meal. We're both completely enamored by the lass and now we'll get to show off our fighting skills to her. Her beauty is the likes you would find in legend but it's her boldness, confidence, and the pull I feel in my chest when she laughs so freely that has me gobsmacked. Finn feels the pull as well. After our pack was massacred and we were forced to flee our home and territory we never believed we would ever find our mate or even someone who we felt a deep connection to. We've had many a toss with women and most likely broke a few hearts since then but neither of us has ever felt the pull like we do with the fiery lass at the table with us. I want her in a way that I've never wanted another and the scent of her arousal that we've caught a few times lets us know that there's a chance we might have her. Just the idea of getting my lips and teeth onto that smooth perfect skin has my cock growing. What she told us about women choosing their own lovers has me hoping she will be open to having both Finn and me as I know he wants her just as badly as I do.

The way she shows no fear of our Alpha and the battle skills she displayed when we first met only makes me feel like she would be an equal to us. I peer at Luca from the corner of my eye and see him watching her. The look in his eyes is one of intrigue and consideration. It's a bloody nice change from the dark depths of sadness and sorrow that have filled them since he and Bas took us in to form our own unique pack. Looking the other way to the vampire Finn and I consider our Alpha, I try and not grin at how hard he's working not to look at the woman beside him. I love my brothers all and I know they love us in their own way but between Bas's rigid control and Luca's martyr complex, Eden is just what our pack needs to shake off the dust of the long years we have lived.

When she swallows the last of her coffee and pushes her plate away, I can't contain my eagerness any longer and jump to my feet.

"Finn and I would be happy to escort you to the hall we train in, lass," I tell her as she accepts Finn's hand to rise from her chair.

She lets out a musical laugh and sends me a saucy wink.

"Don't be too eager, boys. I seriously plan to kick your asses in a match!"

As I move around the table I can't help but grin even larger. She can kick any part of me she wants if it means she's going to take off her cloak and I get to put my hands on her body. The lass makes us laugh as we lead her to the weapons hall when she asks us to draw her a map of the manor so she won't get lost but the laughter dries up when we take her into the weapons hall and her eyes widen — at first with surprise and then with delight.

"Do you like it then, lass?" Finn asks as she scans the large room with all the weapons of war hanging from the walls.

She shakes her head in wonder and says, "Fan-fucking-tastic!"

I don't know what that means but I'm taking it for her being happy with what she sees. She walks deeper into the room, going around the rugs that are spread out over the wood floor until she stops at a long, thick tube of tightly sewn leather filled with sand that's hanging from a chain attached to one of the wooden beams in the ceiling. She runs her hands over it like it's a lover's body and flashes us a tempting smile over her shoulder.

"This…is my favorite!" She laughs as she takes her robe off and hangs it on a nearby peg. My eyebrows shoot up as she slips her shoes off as well but I have an entirely different reaction when she takes a few hops back towards the bag and spins her body with one perfect leg kicking out above her head to snap into the bag with force. I feel my wolf surge forward hungrily in want at the display and have to clamp down on it. The choked noise Finn lets out beside me tells me he feels the same way.

"I would be grateful if you would instruct me on how to do that move, Eden. I believe it would be very effective in battle." Luca says in his calm voice as he walks past us.

She focuses on him with a happy smile and nod, giving Finn and me a chance to turn away and wrestle with control of our beasts. The sharp look Bas hits us with helps tamp down the primal desire flooding us a bit so that we can turn back to the main room.

"It takes some practice to control as well as a lot of flexibility but I'm sure it won't take you long to master." She tells Luca. "I'm just going to do some stretching to warm up and then I'll show you."

Luca frowns. "Are you cold? I can have the fireplaces lit to warm the room if you'd like."

Eden laughs again. "No, no, I mean warm my muscles up. You know, get limber so I don't strain them. At his look of understanding and nod, she drops down to the floor and begins a series of poses that twist and arch her body into positions that are borderline indecent. With the tight clothing she is wearing that cups every sweet curve the four of us just stand and watch her, entranced, and I know I'm not the only git in the room whose cock is weeping in desire. When she comes out of a stretch that has her biteable arse up in the air with her hands down on the floor and sees us all staring at her, she freezes and then quickly stands. In the dead silent hall I can hear her mutter under her breath, "Awk-ward" In a sort of sing-song tone.

Sebastian gives a half snarl and spins away to choose a sword from the many that are hanging on the wall. With another look at the rest of us, Eden laughs uncertainly.

"Um, do you guys mind if I put some music on? I have a kickass workout playlist on my phone."

When we just look at her in confusion she closes her eyes briefly and shakes her head.

"Right, my device will play music like…uh, never mind. I'll just show you."

She walks quickly over to where she hung her robe and removes the picture device from one of its pockets and swipes at the front a few times. She holds it up and gives us all a stern look with even Sebastian back to watching her. "NOT MAGIC!" She tells us loudly before she taps it again and music comes blaring from the device. But it's like no music I've ever heard before. I canna recognized most of the instruments being played but after the initial shock of it I find my head starting to nod along to the beat and a grin fills my face as a man sings about needing a spark to ignite, to light them up. It's loud and brash and the pounding beat of it makes me want to move my body. It's a braw tune to train to.

Seeing approval from Finn and I and a small nod from Luca, the lass leaves the device on a pedestal near the middle of the room and wanders back to the leather bag where she sets her feet and begins punching it in different combinations. I could stand and watch her every move until she tires but Bas smacks me in the back of the head with a glower.

"Pick your weapon." He motions to Finn. "You as well. I feel the need to go two on one today. While Luca learns her dance-like moves, we can spar."

Both Finn and I glance back over to where Eden's punishing the leather bag but another snarl from Bas has us turning away to pick out our own blunted training swords.

The effect Eden has on Bas is never clearer than when we begin to fight. He's a fierce opponent at the best of times but today he's more savage than usual. It's as if he's trying to fight a demon inside of himself instead of us. As Finn and I whirl, block and counter almost as one, I almost lose my head to Bas's sword slash when I catch sight of her standing next to Luca on one perfectly balanced leg. Her other leg is extended up above her head with one of her hands lightly holding it. I've seen dancers in such a pose before but seeing Eden in the pose has me thinking about spreading her wide in such a way while my cock pounds into what I'm sure will be a tight hot channel between her legs. I stumble back to avoid Bas's next slash and he follows up with a punch to my face barking out, "Focus!"

The strike has my head rocking back and my wolf surging forward to meet the challenge. While I have no fear of my Alpha killing me, he's not above inflicting injuries to make his point and it takes time and energy to heal even at the rapid pace we shifters heal at. I push the temptress from my mind and fully commit to the fight while a new song screams out from the device about doing whatever it takes. I lose myself to the music and movement as Finn and me, with eyes glowing gold, fight Bas to a draw. His own eyes have flared red and I catch sight of his elongated fangs when we finally separate to end the sparring match.

Panting from the exertion, I swipe the sweat from my eyes and spot Eden and Luca standing on the edge of the rug where they've been watching us. The excitement I see in the lass's eyes tells me we were eejits to think her sensibilities would be bothered at all by the violence conducted in this room. She claps her hands when she sees we are finished and steps onto the rug.

"I'm up for some of that action! Who wants to fight me next?" She asks with a big grin.

I wince when Bas scoffs from behind me. There's something about Eden that rides his arse and makes him say the dumbest things to get her back up.

"Little girls should not play with knives. Leave it for the men to handle such dangerous weapons."

I watch the grin slide off of her face and she just stares at him with a blank expression before she turns, walks a few feet to the next area that has a table with sets of perfectly balanced throwing knives. Ten feet away are four wooden effigies hanging from chains that have been carved into the shapes of men's bodies. She picks up a set of four knives, fans them out, and studies them with an intense expression on her face for a moment before looking up at Sebastian with big confused eyes. She blinks a few times and gives a tiny adorable shrug.

"You're supposed to stick the pointy end into the bad guys, right?"

She waits for a few beats so that a condescending look begins to form on Bas's face and then tosses one of the knives into the air, catches it, and snaps it towards the first wooden dummy where it lodges deeply into where a man's heart would be. She follows it with two more knives, each hitting the same spot on the next two wooden effigies. My mouth has dropped open in shock at her skill as I wait for her to throw the final knife but she pauses and hits Bas with a dark glare. Without ever taking her eyes from him she throws the final knife but this one lodges between the effigy's legs right where its manhood would be. She doesn't even look to see where it landed when a sweet satisfied smile crosses her face.

"Oops, I guess I missed that one's heart. My bad!"

I try not to howl with laughter when I see Sebastian pull his hips back away from her when he glances over and sees the knife lodged where a man's most tender spot would be. Luca doesn't hold back and lets out a large bellow of laughter. Finn and I spin towards him in shocked disbelief. It is the first truly joyful laugh we've ever heard from him since we joined him and Bas well over a hundred years ago. I send a quick look Finn's way and we both end up with matching grins. Aye, the lass is exactly what we all need.

I turn back to see Eden and Bas glaring at each other. If he was a mere mortal he would shatter his teeth at how hard he's clenching them.

"No swords, no knives. If you want to spare with a weapon it will only be a blunt staff." He tells her in a tone that lets me know he's seconds away from throttling her. I'll have to remember to get a bet going with Finn on when Bas will finally crack and bend the lass over the nearest hard surface. I have no fear that he will harm Eden with anything other than his sharp tongue and cold words but even those will end when he finally accepts that he's met his match. I've seen the way he looks at her when he thinks no one's watching. Aye, I'll place my money on no later than ten days from now.

I'm ready to intervene and break their stare down when Eden blinks, smiles and nods.

"I can work with that."

She turns her back on the vampire and shoots me a taunting look.

"What do you say, wolf boy? Wanna hit me with your staff?"

I bite my tongue to stop myself from telling her exactly what I want to do to her with my staff and instead guide her over to the wall where we pick out our weapons and then take them to the center of the fighting area. Eden sets herself a few feet away from me and gives me a small bow before launching into me. I block everything she throws at me but am unable to bring myself to strike at her. I can see she's getting frustrated that I won't fight back and I swear I hear a growl come from her mouth. I should have taken it as the warning it was because the next moment she drops down and sweeps my legs out from under me and I crash to the floor.

She glares down at me and shakes her head in disappointment but is distracted when Finn starts laughing at me. The lass stalks over to him and points her staff at him.

"What about you? Are you too afraid to fight a girl as well?" When he throws his hands up and backs away shaking his head, she spins away with a small frustrated screech and zeros in on Sebastian. "And you? I know you don't like me very much so you'd probably be happy to take a shot at me, right?" When he only raises an eyebrow in amusement, Eden throws her staff down. "What the hell is wrong with you all? Clearly, I know how to fight and it's not like I haven't taken many, many hits in the ring before. I promise not to cry if you somehow manage to get past my guard!"

Sebastian loses the amused expression and stalks over to her bending to pick up the staff at her feet. "We've all seen the picture on your device that shows just how many hits you've taken before. If you think any one of us would do such a thing to you, then you are a fool."

Her face pales at the reminder but she quickly recovers and spits back, "I train to fight so that will never happen to me again! I will never be defenseless ever again." She slides one hand over her hair and gives the gathered tail a hard pull before looking up at him with eyes that plead for him to understand. "Don't you get it? I need partners to spar with so that I can learn and practice how to stop the hits from getting through."

I see the moment his eyes soften towards her and curse under my breath when he holds out the staff for her to take.

"Alright," Bas tells her in a low voice causing Luca to step forward.

"Sebastian," he says in a warning tone but the Alpha merely holds up a hand to silence him without taking his eyes from Eden.

"I will spar with you and I will strike but it won't be at my full strength. If that's not enough for you, then this is over." He warns her.

Eden bites her lower lip but nods her agreement and goes back to the center to wait for him. Bas walks past me and snatches the staff from my hands and then sets himself a few feet away. She does that strange bow again but doesn't launch herself at him the way she had done with me. She hesitates long enough for the stiffness to leave Bas's stance and only then goes on the attack. He keeps his word and strikes as much as he blocks and I have to admire the lass for she doesn't react at all when a hit makes it through and lands on her body. I want to cheer her on when Bas tries to sweep her legs out from under her with his staff and she jumps in the air to avoid it and delivers a solid kick to his shoulder that causes him to stumble back a few feet. The more they fight the faster they both move and it's a kind of beautiful thing to watch them dance in such a violent way. Things change abruptly when Bas scores a hit to

Eden's ribs and her movements become jerky. She hacks and slashes with the staff and presses him hard in attack. He calls her name twice but she acts like she can't hear him. When I see his eyes flash red I'm one step away from pulling her away but he intercepts a hard slash with his palm instead of his staff and rips it from her hands, throwing it behind him. When she makes to hit him with her fists he pins her arms in place against her sides and holds tight with a furious expression as she thrashes in his arms.

Luca, Finn, and I have moved to encircle them, ready to take the lass away from him but he commands us with one look and we stay in place.

"She's not even here. The damn witch is lost in a berserker's rage."

The tension leaves my body as I remember seeing her get like this at the end of the fight with the assassins but I didn't think about it then. Now, that I know her better, I can see that this rage is the result of the trauma she went through. Lashing out blindly when lost to the hurt and pain is something both Finn and I can relate to and it's also something Sebastian broke us of.

Eden's thrashing comes to a stop as she freezes for a moment. She tilts her head back to look up at Bas's face and just asks, "What are you doing?"

He immediately lets her go and uses the motion to force her back away from him. His face and voice are cold when he tells her, "You are undisciplined. Letting the rage take over, control you like that will only work on the weakest of threats. You will be left blind to all attacks coming at you that are not right in front of your face. In short, witch, you will die." He pauses when she flinches back but then finishes with, "Focus, control, those are what you must master or all your skills and practice won't protect you from the next attack."

Her green eyes are huge and her mouth opens to speak but then she snaps it closed. I see the pain and desperation in them as well as a shine of tears before she spins away and runs from the room. I clench my fists. The lass promised she wouldn't cry from taking a physical hit but the hit she just took was to her heart.

We all stand and watch her go and then Bas uses his foot to toss the staff he dropped into the air. With reflexes almost too fast to see, he snatches it and launches it like a javelin at the closest wall where it buries itself halfway into the wood and plaster.

None of us make a move until he tosses an angry hand through his hair and turns to face us focusing on Finn and me.

"Go. Go and soothe her, for I cannot."

Eden

It only takes me a few strides down the hall away from the training room to regret running out. Embarrassment and a little bit of stubborn pride keep me from going back and apologizing. Now I'm wandering around the gardens with no shoes on in just my tank top and leggings, probably scandalizing the groundskeepers. I feel like an immature twit for reacting the way I did but even though every word Sebastian said was true, hearing it from him in his cold uppity accent was so much more devastating than when Diesel had basically said the same thing.

The guy just gets under my skin so bad and even though he drives me crazy with his Mr. Freeze thing, I can't help but want his approval for some reason. A sharp stone jabs into the tender arch of my foot breaking me out of my pity party of one. I need to pull up my big girl panties and go make it right no matter how much crow the Iceman makes me eat.

Thinking of Diesel makes me realize that I haven't thought about home or how I'm getting back since yesterday morning. What does that mean? Am I really just going to accept that I'm stuck here? Do I want to stay stuck here? It's not like there's a long list of reasons for me to go back to my life in the future. Shaking my head in exasperation at how fucked up I am, I start looking around to find my way back.

It takes me a while and three wrong turns but I finally make it out of the maze-like gardens and back to the house finding a set of French doors to get into it. The doors open to the formal dining room we had eaten in the night before. I don't know how to get to the training hall from here and of course, none of the army of servants are around to give me directions so I just head back to my room, remembering the way from the night before.

By the time I reach my door I'm feeling pretty despondent about the way I reacted, how I can't seem to control my rage, and not having one fucking clue on how to deal with the situation I've found myself in.

When I push open the door I'm not remotely surprised to see Cade and Finn waiting for me. Finn is lounging on my bed with his arms crossed behind his head and Cade's sitting on the small dressing table stool, staring intently at my phone. He jumps to his feet when I step into the room and quickly whips the hand holding my phone behind his back with an expression that screams naughty child guilt.

Without saying a word, I hold my hand out and wait. He shoots a nervous look toward Finn like he is looking for a rescue but all he gets from his friend is a shrug. With a deep sigh, he slowly pulls the phone from behind his back and places it in my hand.

"I'm truly sorry, lass! I think I've mashed it somehow. It just stopped in the middle of the music and I canna get it to light back up."

I have to bite my lip to keep from laughing at how devastated he looks but it's a really cute look on him so I give it a few beats before shaking my head.

"It's fine. You didn't do anything to it. The battery probably died. It just needs a recharge."

The look of relief and the gush of air that comes from him is so exaggerated, you'd think I just told him he wasn't going to die. He tucks his hands behind his back and leans over at the waist to look at the black screen before cocking an eyebrow at me. "Aye, and how do we do that then? Recharge it as you said. The music it makes is just grand and I'd like to hear more of it if I can."

I shoot him a tight smile. "You're lucky then, two years ago big tech finally pulled their head out of their asses and came up with a better option to charge these things." I flip the phone over and press down on the top of the case to unlatch it so that I can slide the back cover off and tap on the glass. "This part of the phone is a small, built-in solar panel. It captures the energy of the sun and turns it into power to recharge the battery. All you need to do is set it in a sunny spot like a window sill and leave it for a few hours. Takes longer than the rapid charger plug but there you go, no more being stranded with a dead battery if you don't have your charger."

I turn away from him and place the phone backside up in the sunniest window sill in the room and then just stand there staring out at the gardens. I wait for one of them to call me out on how I acted earlier, knowing I deserve it but not wanting to face the disappointments I'm sure I'll see on their faces. My shoulders tense when I hear Cade clear his throat.

"Lass - Eden, I'm sorry Bas was so harsh. He shouldn't have taken such a tone with you and I know he regrets it."

Huh? I turn slowly around with an incredulous look on my face.

"What? Why are you apologizing to me? I'm the one who acted like a child by running away. Everything he said was a hundred percent true! And he's not the first one to tell me that. Although he's the first one to say I would end up dead instead of me being the one to kill someone."

Finn sat up and swung his legs over the side of the bed closest to me with a cautious expression.

"Aye, what he said was true but he shouldn't have said it like that. We know he hurt your feelings and that's not right."

I look back and forth between them and see how seriously they feel about my hurt feelings and can't help the frustrated laugh that bubbles out. I throw my hands up into my hair and ruthlessly yank the band from my hair to ease the pull on my scalp.

"I have a trainer back home named Diesel. He's a beast of a man in size, easily a foot taller than you two and probably close to the size of you two combined. He's scary looking with tattoos covering his chest, arms, neck, and some of his shaved head. He once told me to quit being a little bitch and get off my ass when an opponent I was sparring with knocked me down. You know what I did? I got off my ass and won the match. Diesel patted me on the head after and told me to do better so I did. Sebastian didn't hurt my feelings and if you think his tone was harsh, well, I hope you never piss me off so you won't have to see what harsh really is!"

Finn barks out a laugh and points at Cade. "Remember when Bas beat you down and called you a mangy mutt that couldn't fetch a bone if it was between your paws? Ha! This Diesel fellow sounds like a direct descendant of Bas's. They have the same training style."

Cade sends Finn a sharp, pointed look that promises retribution for the reminder then turns back to me and takes my hands in his.

"Eden, I saw the tears in your eyes, love. I know he hurt you."

I snatch my hands back from him. "That wasn't hurt, it was frustration and embarrassment! I'm well aware that I can't control the rage that overtakes me. You have no idea what I've been through, what I've survived!" I spit at him but then I see what I think is a condescending look come into his eyes and it infuriates me.

"My whole family was wiped out in a blink of an eye. Everyone I loved just died and my husband, the person I thought I loved, he…arrgh! It doesn't matter what he did! I was alone in the world and just when I thought I was getting through it, getting back on my feet, Fate stepped in and decided I hadn't suffered enough so the bitch sent a gang of animals to attack me and kill not only my partner but my only friend. They beat me, broke me so bad I could barely function even after the bones, bruises, and scars healed. So don't fucking pretend you know what I'm going through!"

I'm practically snarling by the end of my rant and when I try and turn my back on him, he latches on to my upper arm and pulls me back to face him clamping on to both my biceps to hold me in place but the look on his face has me biting my lip. I've seen Cade sweet, charming, and amused but I've never seen him angry. Judging by the look on his face now though, he's seriously pissed.

"D'ye no ken that you're not the only one who's been damaged by the Fates? Aye, Finn and I well know how it feels to have such a monster inside and I'm no talking about our wolves, aye? It's a savage beast made up of grief, pain, and rage that makes you want to lash out. To rip and tear and claw at anyone in your way just to try and ease the agony of it. Aye, we know that beast well as we also saw our families slaughtered, our homes burnt and were forced to flee our home, our territory else we would be dead along with them. To not be strong enough to fight back, to save them? We were blinded by that beast of rage for years. We didn't just lose our families, we lost our pack, our Alpha, and any chance of finding our mate for a happy future. So yes, we do understand!"

We stand face to face as our chests heave with anger, not at each other but at the shit hand we've been dealt. I want to scream and rage that such tragedy happens to people who don't deserve it as my heart aches for all that we lost. I want to lash out like he said and bite, tear, rip and claw at something and I can see the restrained violence shimmering in his sea-blue eyes.

The snarl that comes out of him is the only warning I get before his lips crash down on mine.

His hands slide down my arms and go straight to my ass so he can yank my hips against him and my core hits flush with the hard bulge in his thin breeches. My mind blanks as heat spreads through me and the moan that leaves my mouth as his lips wage a relentless assault on mine is all the encouragement he needs to go further.

One hand goes up my back until it anchors into my hair and he pulls my head back, giving his mouth a better angle to deepen the kiss. As his tongue slides in to tangle with mine his other arm slides under my ass to lift my hips even closer to him. My pussy throbs as I grind it against his cock in search of the delicious friction it desperately craves. It's not enough. I'm no young girl that needs to be told what I want next. I'm a grown-ass woman and I want that cock in me, hard, fast, and deep.

I'm seconds away from climbing him like a tree so I can wrap my legs around his waist when he pulls his lips away from mine. A small whine of disappointment leaves my throat because I sure as hell am not done with his mouth but he spins me around to face the other side of the room and pulls me back against his chest so that his cock rubs between my ass cheeks making me arch back against him. His lips land on the sensitive skin behind my ear and trail fire down my neck as I feel his teeth scrape against it before his lips and tongue soothe the burn.

His other hand is splayed across my stomach as he slowly slides it up under my tank top to cup one of my breasts. His clever fingers find an aching nipple and rubs soft circles around it through the lace of my bra, making me want to beg him to strip me bare. When I thrust my tit against his hand and make a pleading noise, he stills and lifts his mouth back up to my ear. Cade's voice is low and husky with desire.

"Look, lass. Look what you do to him without a single touch."

My eyes are heavy and hazy with want as I see Finn across from us through my lashes. He's leaning against one of the bedposts without a shirt on and his bare chest has my gaze lingering on the smooth tanned skin that only showcases the firm pecs before trailing down to his defined abs and the glorious cut in V that disappears into his pants. When I see his hand stroking the hard outline straining against the fabric of his pants my pussy clenches and my eyes flash back up to meet the burning question in his.

Cade licks the shell of my ear and purrs, "Two will always be better than just one. What say you, lass?"

My knees almost give out on me when the idea of both of them at once has a bolt of heat and wetness drenching my core. I relax back against Cade and lift an arm behind my head to slide into his hair to tug his mouth back onto my skin before reaching out for Finn with a slow nod. He takes a few steps closer but stops just out of reach.

"You have to say it, lass. You have to say what you want."

His cobalt blue eyes dare me to lie and say no but why the fuck would I? I'm far from home and might not ever get back so why wouldn't I take every bit of pleasure I can. I let my lips form into a siren's smile of seduction.

I grind back against Cade's cock causing him to groan.

"I want you. I want you both," I tell him and that's all he needs to crush me between his hot, hard body and Cade's. His mouth angles against mine in a fierce rush of kissing, sucking, and small bites to my bottom lip as his hand slides up under my shirt and captures my other breast. With Cade's lips and tongue lavishing heat on my neck and both of them toying with my nipples through my bra, I'm overloaded with the need for more, for skin on skin.

There are too many fucking clothes in the way for me to get what I want so I yank my tank over my head. When I reach to push my leggings down, Finn pushes my hands away with a small chuckle and slowly lowers them with his body following until he's on his knees in front of me. His eyes blaze over my skin as I stand quivering in just the black lace panties and bra. His eyes zero in on the four moon tattoos under my left breast and his fingers reach out to trace them lightly, heated desire filling his eyes.

When he pulls back it takes everything I have in me not to grab the back of his head and pull his face to the hot, wet opening between my legs. As if reading my mind, he grasps my hips and pulls them forwards until his mouth and nose are pressed against me and takes a deep smell of my essence. When he eases back and looks up at me I see his eyes have that gold glow around the edges and it make my core pulse.

"You smell…fucking…divine." He growls and I swear I almost come right then and there.

Cade leaves my back to stand in front of me and beside Finn, taking in the modern bra and panties with a hungry look. "Fucking perfection."

Clearly, the wolves have taken to my favorite word and have mastered using it in the best way because I have never in my life felt so confident and turned on as in this moment.

I reach up between my breasts and flick open the front clasp of the bra, slowly sliding it off until it drops to the floor and then hook a thumb into the lace of my panties to gently slide them off. When both their eyes flare gold at the sight of my bare mound, I arch my back and drop my head back to pray thanks to all the gods of laser hair removal for causing that reaction. I have no time to think or even breathe after that as a pair of burning lips takes one of my tight nipples between them and sucks hard.

The hot tongue that slides between my folds licks me from bottom to top before circling my clit in an agonizing tease. I don't even try and hold back the panting or moaning as the two men work their greedy mouths over my most sensitive spots. My hips rock forward against Finn's mouth wanting more, needing to be filled. The wolf knows exactly what I need and slides one long thick finger into me and thrusts a few times before adding a second. I feel the sweet stretch of it but when he curls them slightly and drags them against that glorious spot inside where the magic happens, I buck wildly against his hand as his lips find my clit again.

Cade's fingers replace his lips and tongue on my nipple as he captures a handful of my hair, yanks it back so my head is tilted, and drops his mouth on mine just as Finn flicks my clit over and over again while fucking my pussy with his beautiful fingers. I shatter apart as the orgasm hits me like a truck after so many years of abstaining and sparks flicker behind my eyes as I ride wave after wave of it until I have to push Finn's mouth away from me, not able to take anymore. Cade swallows down all the loud moaning and ahhing I make until I slump against him bonelessly. We're not nearly done yet but I need a fucking minute to reattach my head to my body.

Cade runs his hands up and down my back and ass as if to soothe me as Finn gets to his feet, kissing a path up my body as he goes until his lips land on mine. I can taste myself on his lips and tongue as he kisses me softly but when he deepens it and I feel the passion and need in him my core responds by clenching in an aftershock.

My hands trail over his hard chest and down over his abs causing him to growl into my mouth. When they go lower and slide into his low-slung breeches he sucks in his stomach muscles but when my fingers encircle his silky smooth, rock hard cock he lets out a gasp that sounds almost painful in its pleasure. I stroke him gently and run my thumb over his crown, smearing the small drops of pre-cum until he backs away with a shudder and begins undoing his pants. I turn my back to him with a smoldering look of promise and bring my hands up to Cade's rock-hard chest.

I lean forward until my lips land on the heated skin and trail kisses, licks, and sucks across his chest stopping briefly to take his nipples into my mouth so I can swirl my tongue over them. I make my way down his body, tracing each ab with my tongue, and feel the thrill of womanly power when he jerks against my mouth. I kiss my way down until I reach the top of his breeches and don't waste time figuring out how they open and instead just tug on them until they pool at his feet.

His big, beautiful cock springs out at me and my mouth waters at the perfect size of it. The slight curve tells me it's going to hit all the right spots inside me when we get to that but first I look up at him and meet his eyes - showing him exactly how much I want him. He looks back at me like I'm a goddess at his feet, his hands clutched into fists at his side like he's afraid to touch me. When I lean forward and lick the small slit in the head of his cock he throws his head back and roars.

My lips are smug as I slide them over his shaft and take him deep into my mouth. I close my eyes and savor the feel and taste of him as I run my tongue up and down the shaft. His hands thread into my hair and make a fist as I lick and suck at him. My pussy is heating up again and the dull ache spreading through it makes me clench my thighs together searching for the friction it craves.

A whimper of want is forced out of me, escaping around the cock in my mouth when two strong hands latch onto my hips and lift me enough to slide my ass against Finn's lap leaving me at the perfect height to continue the sweet torture I'm inflicting on Cade.

I feel Finn's heat against my core as he slides between my legs and rubs the head of his cock between my folds and against my clit, sending bolts of pleasure through me with every pass. The intense feeling has me sucking Cade harder and his groans become louder as his grip on my hair tightens.

When Finn thrusts into me balls deep I almost gag on the cock in my mouth from wanting to scream my pleasure. It's been so fucking long, I feel like a virgin again but it's a humming burn that stretches me and I…want…more.

"Jesus wept, Eden. You're so goddamn tight!"

Finn gasps into my ear as he leans over me so his chest is pressed to my back. I make a humming noise against the hardness in my mouth and rock my hips back against him, begging him to move inside me. I'm burning up and desperate for him to fuck me hard and fast - to drown me in the rhythm of pleasure that will take me away from all the shit that's plagued me for the last few years. As he slowly slides out and back, I pull my mouth away from Cade. Keeping a firm grip on his shaft, I look over my shoulder to pin Finn with a commanding look.

"Hard, fast, and don't fucking stop!"

I see his eyes flare gold and am rewarded with a deep thrust that has me gasping my approval. As I go to turn back to Cade's delicious cock, I pause to take another thrust that has my eyes rolling back into my head for a moment in ecstasy but then turn my head back to see Finn with teeth bared and eyes squeezed shut as he pounds into me. I'm gasping in pleasure at each slide so when he opens his eyes and meets mine, my voice is stuttered but I manage to get out, "And pull...my...fucking...hair!"

Cade relinquishes his grip on my hair to Finn and it doesn't take long with me whimpering and groaning around his cock as I take him as deep as I can into my throat for him to start getting close to the edge. Using my hand to help keep a steady rhythm on his shaft I know the moment he's about to come as he tries to pull away from me but I use my free hand to hold him close as he jerks in my mouth and I feel, and then taste, the sweet evidence of his orgasm. I swallow it down and lick him clean before allowing him to move back from me.

When I look up at him I see an expression of awe on his face that quickly shifts to a sexy grin. He drops to his knees in front of me and then down to his chest but propped up on his elbows so his face is right in front of my pussy. Finn pulls me up so my back is against his chest. We're both on our knees with mine inside his that are spread on either side of me. The position change with my back arched against his chest has his thrusts hitting the exact right spot and the steady pounding has electric bolts shooting through my body as my orgasm builds. Finn has one hand anchoring me back by the hair that's wound around his fist and his other hand grips one of my hips hard enough that I'll probably have bruises tomorrow. I fucking love it as I lose myself in the sensations his hard cock is filling me with every time he thrusts deep into me. When Cade's tongue darts between my folds and targets my clit with fast hard flicks I'm dead as I explode clenching all around Finn's cock as my core milks him through the powerful waves. He follows me down with a roar of his own and I feel his hot seed fill me.

Finn clings to my back and wraps his arms around me from behind as Cade gets up to his knees and brushes my hair back from my face and then cups my cheek and rubs his thumb over my cheekbone. His voice is gentle and filled with sweetness when he asks, "Are you alright, lass?"

It takes me a minute to clear my throat as I'm bone dry with most of the moisture in my body between my legs but I finally nod and then smile. "Yeah, let's do *that* again!"

Sebastian

After the wolves leave to try and fix what I've broken I spend the next hour taking my anger out on every piece of equipment in the training hall. Luca leaves at some point when I'm hacking away at the third effigy with the first two reduced to splinters while trying to get the witch's tear-filled expression from my mind. I don't even know why it's bothering me so much that I was the cause of her misery. The damn woman has gotten under my skin and is like an itch I can't seem to scratch. As the wooden head flies off at my next savage slash, I snarl at the image of taking her into my arms to soothe and comfort her. I hack away at the wooden dummy as I try and ignore the overwhelming desire to promise her no one will ever lay another finger on her that would cause her pain. I've seen that type of rage madness before and I know it comes from deep trauma and pain. While I don't know the details of what happened to the witch, the picture the wolves showed me on her magic device of the aftermath had me wanting to rip whoever did that to her apart with my bare hands and teeth.

With the third effigy nothing more than scattered bark, I move on to the last one and shake my head at the throwing knife wedged deeply between its legs.

Why the witch has no fear of me, even after I showed her the monster that I am confounds me. It's also refreshing and enticing. It has only been a few days since she appeared in front of us but the impact she has had on all of us is nothing short of witchcraft. I've known many beautiful and charming women in my long sentence on this mortal plane but none of them compare to how this woman makes me feel. I bark out a sardonic laugh to the empty room that echoes back at me. Feel? I don't feel, have feelings that is, other than annoyance and occasionally impatience at the foolish mortals surrounding me year after year. But this witch, this woman – Eden - brings out long-forgotten emotions.

I've spent the last few days either wanting to throttle her or fuck her. One corner of my lips twitches at the new word that the wolves taught me. Such a simple four-letter word and yet extremely satisfying to use in all its versions.

I pull the throwing knife from the effigy and realize that I no longer wish to destroy it. I still don't know what to do about the vexing woman that has invaded our existence but a small nagging thought in the back of my mind has my stomach clenching at the idea that she might disappear at some point as quickly as she appeared. I tell myself that it would be best if she did but the gut clench tells me that is a lie.

I turn away from the wreckage I've caused in the room and spend a few moments collecting the scattered weapons to return them to their homes on the walls and then leave the rest for the servants to deal with. My gait is slow as I walk towards the library but it speeds up as I pass the entrance and find myself moving up the stairs and then down the hall that leads to her chambers. As I turn the corner to where her room is my feet freeze when I spot Luca. He's leaning with one hand against the frame of the closed door with his head hanging low but I can see enough of his face to make out the expression of sheer longing and loneliness covering it. The regret flashes through me hard and fast. I've done this to him. I turned him into the broken creature that he is when I gave him his second life.

Luca Soriano first came to my attention in the late fourteen hundreds when I discovered some of his sculptures in the Castile region of Spain. His work was breathtaking and stirred long-forgotten pleasure and awe in my mind and heart. His art captured both the tragedy and beauty of mortality and I was quick to seek him out.

I studied the young man from a distance trying to discover what it was that gave him such a spark of passion so that I might find some for myself once again. I stalked him through his life as he discussed books, poetry, and politics in salons and cafes with other like-minded young men.

His words were eloquent and passionate and full of conviction as he strove to educate others on the unbalanced scales of the class systems of the time. He was beautiful and it was plain for all to see how much he loved life, art, and his fellow man.

Of course, such a person would be considered a threat to those in power and it wasn't long before he was taken by the Inquisitors and charged as a heretic. It was a convenient and sweeping charge of those power-hungry madmen to use to subject the masses to their will and keep them cowering in fear.

I had long stopped interfering in the affairs of state and man but there was just something about Luca and his spark that I couldn't set aside and allow to be extinguished. I decided to intervene and free the man so that he could flee the area and continue his life somewhere he could be safe but I was too late in locating the deep dark cell he had been imprisoned in.

By the time I found him, the Inquisitors had ravaged his body with such torture that he was moments from death. Even then I offered him the choice of the change but as he was my first I didn't realize that there really wasn't a choice to be made.

No man would be capable of saying no to a chance at life when they are on the brink of death, consequences be damned. He was the first and only that I have sired and I fear that some part of him will always hate me for doing it. The bright passionate man that he was died under the tools of torture inflicted upon him in that dank cell. The two years of bloodlust and madness that followed his change forever altered the foundation of who he was and how he thought of himself. Luca believes himself to be the worst kind of monster and undeserving of any goodness or happiness.

I move slowly towards him and the sounds filtering through the door reach my ears. Moans and whimpers of pleasure from the woman inside ignite a maelstrom of want, need, and raging jealousy inside me. I want to rip the door from its hinges and snatch the witch from the wolves so clearly pleasuring her so that she would only make such sounds for me alone. I feel my fangs lengthening as the feeling intensifies but when Luca lifts his head to look my way, the agony of regret in his eyes cools my blood instantly. I stride over to him and take his arm to lead him away from her door and once we've turned the corner, speak softly.

"Let us go to the palace. I feel the need to thin the prisoner population from its dungeons. It has been too long since we have fed."

He follows me without a word and we ride halfway to the palace before he finally speaks but only briefly.

"She reminds me of what it was to be a man. The joy and passion of it and how I can never have that again."

His voice is low and hollow of life. There is nothing I can say to give comfort so I merely nod and look away. My own words are even lower and stolen by the wind as I whisper them.

"Me as well."

We reach the palace grounds with no more words spoken and leave our mounts at the stable to be cared for. As we make our way through the grounds and past the fountains, we both come to a stop as we spot the King and his entourage strolling on the other side of it.

When his head turns in our direction, both Luca and I make our bows to him. He studies us with interest for a few moments before his regal head nod lets us be on our way. As we continue towards the entrance of the palace closest to the underground levels, I muse on all the Kings and Queens I've had dealings with over the last millennia and a half. Some were excited by who and what I am and insisted I be a part of their court. Some wished to use me as a weapon to further their power. Others, like the current King of France, enjoy a respectful relationship with me where I and my brothers are allowed to live our lives out of the court's eye and are rarely called upon. Some monarchs liked to believe that they ruled and controlled us but the smart ones were very aware that they didn't and that we have no fear of them.

The scents of human misery reach us in an overpowering wave as we step through the door between us and the squalled cells where the prisoners live out their final days before execution. Pierre is in the outer room speaking with a guard but is alerted by the fear that crosses the guard's face when we enter. He glances towards us with a nod and then holds out his hand for the ring of keys, speaks a few words to the man and waves him away. With blank expressions on our faces, Luca and I step to the side so that the scared guard can rush past us. Once we are alone, Pierre opens a thick ledger and begins running his finger down the list of current prisoners. Finding the information he wants he stands up straight and addresses us.

"Your Grace, sir, there are currently six prisoners that meet your criteria but before I have them moved, a word on another matter, please."

At my nod, he sighs and shows the first sign of nervousness at our presence. The small French man clears his throat twice and fiddles with the ledger, clearly not wanting to broach the subject of whatever he needs to speak to us about. It finally takes a low hum of annoyance from me for him to square his shoulders and get on with it.

"Yes, well, there have been reports and rumors of…deaths and disappearances to the southeast. Um, the state of the bodies, well, they are familiar to me." He rushes out.

I lift one shoulder. "And what business is it of ours? Come, Pierre, say what you need to and be quick about it." I tell him impatiently.

The man wrings his hands a few times and shoots a nervous glance our way before finally blurting out, "The bodies, they are drained of blood and have had the heads removed!"

My brows shoot up at this and I send a quick look Luca's way before turning back to the sweating man.

"We follow the compact with the King to the letter. We do not sample the populace...ever. While the description of the remains sounds familiar, you can be sure that we are not responsible for them." I tell him sternly. "How many bodies have been found in such a manner?"

Pierre blinks quickly before a nervous, reassuring smile crosses his face to cover the unease he is feeling and he waves his hand in dismissal.

"There have been two noted but they were not of any consequence. Merely drifters traveling through the area. I'm sure it is nothing. You and yours have always been friends of the monarchy and I'm sorry to imply that you were responsible! I merely meant to convey the information so that you could be aware that there may be another of your...er...kind in the region."

My eyes narrow at the idea that there may be another vampire in the area. It's unusual for one of my kind to settle and nest where there is already a pack. More than likely, one was traveling through and got careless by leaving the evidence to be discovered. I pin Pierre with a hard look.

"I will be informed immediately if more bodies in such a state are discovered, yes?"

"Of course! I will send a runner to your estate should I hear of anything similar. You have my word, your Grace."

"Very well, tell us of these six prisoners," I demand, changing the subject and getting on with why we are here.

"Yes, yes! Two of them have murdered children and the other four have killed women. As you insist, each one is guilty with witnesses and confessions and all have been sentenced to execution. If you will but wait a moment, I will move them to the room you prefer for your…er…I will move them."

At my sharp nod, he practically runs from the room with the key ring clutched to his chest. I turn to Luca.

"Once we are finished here, send scouts to the southeast to see what they can find out. Hopefully, it's someone passing through and long gone but if not, we will have to delve deeper into the matter."

He nods with a grim expression. We both know how some of our kind can wreak havoc and terror if left unchecked. Pierre is back shortly and waves us towards the door with a bow. We move quickly past the sinking cells filled with human waste and despair before entering a final room at the very back. Inside we find the six prisoners shackled to the walls, eyes filled with a mix of defiance and fear. Before any of them have a chance to speak, my eyes flare red and my voice speaks low and commanding as I use my power to compel them.

"YOU WILL ONLY SPEAK THE TRUTH WHEN QUESTIONED!"

Their eyes glaze over and their heads all nod. Luca goes one way and I go the other as we begin to question the men to ensure they are guilty of the crimes they are sentenced to death for. When they begin to elaborate on the deprived pleasure they received from the pain they inflicted on innocent women and children we cut them off and begin to feed. We ignore their screams of terror as we drain them of blood. Our bites can give intense pleasure when welcomed or hellish pain when not. These men deserve the agony we give them. We might be monsters ourselves but one by one we cleanse the earth of a different kind of monster.

Eden

The three of us end up landing in my bed in a tangle of sweaty limbs as we work on catching our breaths. My body feels slow and deliciously heavy from the explosive pleasure these two men have given me. At the same time, I feel settled as if this is exactly where I'm supposed to be and I can't stop the smile that fills my face. Finn shifts on his side and props his head up on an elbow while using his free hand to trace soft tingling circles on the sensitive skin of my belly.

"You are a man's fantasy, Eden."

I huff out a small laugh. "Right back at you, wolf boy."

Cade's heavy thigh anchors both my legs in place as he nuzzles in the crook of my neck with his hot tongue licking my skin between kisses.

"We've never met anyone like you before, lass. It feels like we've been waiting our whole lives for you." He tells me in a whisper as his lips catch my earlobe between them and he sucks gently on it.

I practically purr at the attention they're giving me in our after lovemaking glow. When his teeth scrape against the delicate skin behind my ear and Finn's hand wanders lower to brush lightly over my bare mound my core clenches with a throb to be filled again. No matter what my greedy pussy wants, I need a few more moments to recover from the first round so I ask a question to try and slow things down.

"You grew up together? In the same family?"

Cade moves his head down and playfully nips at my shoulder before answering.

"Aye, we're cousins in a sense, yeah, not actually related by blood but raised together. Dinnae matter though, our whole clan, pack, lived in the same village so we were rolling around together since we were pups. We're the only family we have left."

"Mmm, it's nice that you have each other after what you said happened so you aren't completely alone. How long have you been with Sebastian and Luca?"

The back of Finn's fingers brush back and forth over my mound, making the heat there increase while his mouth dips down to run across the top of my breast, causing me to arch slightly towards it. I see the curve of his lips at my reaction when he lifts his head to meet my gaze.

"I'd say a hundred and fifty or so years now."

My pleasure-heavy eyes pop open at that. "What? How?" I sputter out, causing him to chuckle.

"Shifters live much longer than humans, lass. The longest I know of is around six hundred years but living with our brothers will likely increase that greatly."

I look back and forth between Finn and Cade with clear confusion on my face so Cade explains.

"We're bonded through blood. Bas' blood keeps us the same age and will prolong our lives as long as we stay together. We're a pack and he's our Alpha so short of a mortal wound we won't ever die." He tells me and then with a wicked gleam in his eyes, drops his head down to capture my nipple in his mouth.

The hard suck has me moaning and arching up to meet him as Finn takes that moment to slide one long, rough finger straight down my slit and deep into my opening with a sure thrust. As he adds a second finger to me and begins fucking me slowly with them, he moves his lips to capture my other nipple. The sucking, kissing, and tongue licking has my pussy clenching hard around Finn's fingers and when he curls them to drag against my g-spot the friction has me thrashing against his hand as waves of pleasure crash over me. He finger fucks me through the orgasm and slows as I begin to settle again before dragging his fingers from inside of me, swiping gently across my clit so I spasm again and bringing them up to his mouth to suck off the glistening arousal coating them.

"Like the sweetest nectar from the Gods." He whispers huskily as his lips crash down on mine in a savage kiss.

His tongue thrusts against mine and I can taste myself on his lips as his hard cock rides against my hip. Cade thrusts his hardness against my other hip and I reach down to slide my fingers over the hot throbbing length of him. He groans around my nipple and then bites down on it just enough that a small bolt of pain flashes and mixes with the pleasure in the best way possible. Finn drags his mouth from mine to glance down our bodies and watches me stroking Cade with hot eyes.

"Cousin, you've known the pleasure of her sweet lips on your cock but you won't know true heaven until you've buried yourself deep between her thighs."

Cade growls against my breast and latches onto my hips to roll me up onto his chest so that my thighs spread to either side of his. His strong hands slide down and squeeze my ass spreading me so when he thrusts up, his cock perfectly spears into my cunt in one balls-deep move. We both moan out loudly at the exquisite feel of him stretching me and my walls gripping him tightly. With my chest crushed against his, he thrusts up and into me over and over again with a perfect rhythm.

Finn slides his hand up my back and captures a handful of my hair using it to pull me up away from Cade's chest until I'm sitting up. He pulls my head back further so he has the perfect angle and lowers his mouth against mine. There's so much heat from the savage kiss as he bites my lips and then licks over them to soothe that I can barely breathe as Cade rocks slowly inside of me. When Finn finally pulls back from my mouth, I'm gasping for breath and feeling dizzy from want and need. He clutches my chin until I blink away the daze and meet his before saying,

"I want to see you ride his cock, mo chridhe."

I don't know what the last two words mean but I'm game for the first part so looking down at Cade under me, I rock my hips forward and then back until I find the perfect rolling rhythm. This position is perfect for soft, slow waves of pleasure as the hard cock inside of me slides against my tight walls with every roll of my hips. My head falls back with my hair brushing over Cade's thighs as I let myself get lost in the movements. My mind is blank to everything but the slow-building pleasure that's increasing with every rock against the man under me until I feel heated lips trail against my lower stomach. I let my head fall forward so I can look down and see Finn has laid his head on Cade's stomach inches from where we are joined together as I ride him.

I watch him through hooded eyes as he licks his lips at the sight of Cade's cock sliding in and out of me up close. When Cade lifts a hand and tangles it in the back of Finn's hair and pushes his face against me, my pussy spasms hard and clenches a tighter grip around the cock filling me. It's the most erotic fucking thing I've ever seen in my life.

"Aye, she likes that, Finn. Lick our girl good and drive her wild around my cock. Make her cum so hard she milks the seed from my body." He growls out, keeping his grip on Finn's hair and angling his head to the exact right spot for his tongue to go to work on my clit.

Finn's arm wraps around my hips to hold them in place, keeping me from rocking and rolling on this magical ride but Cade takes the opportunity to control the thrusts as he lifts his hips from below, proving the hard ridges of muscles on his stomach aren't just for show as he hammers into me. I want to throw my head back and lose myself in the motions of cock and tongue but I can't stop looking at Finn's head and face pressed against Cade's and my bodies. I've never been with two men at once before today and now I wonder how I can ever be satisfied again with just one. My whole body is tensing and clutching as the power of the pleasure they're giving me builds and builds until a long drawn out cry escapes from me as I plunge over the cliff as the waves of my orgasm wrack through me. My bones and muscles melt and I can barely keep myself up on Cade's lap when Finn quickly gets behind me and lifts me from Cade's pulsing cock so that he can scramble up to his knees in front of me. Finn leans me back against his chest while Cade grips my thighs and wraps my legs around him, plunging back into me hard and fast. My head falls to the side exposing my neck and Finn takes advantage to trail hot kisses down my neck until he reaches the juncture between it and my shoulder and his talented fingers find my mound and slip inside to pluck at the swollen bundle of nerves there.

"Again, Eden. Come for us again." He commands but I don't think I can. A whimper escapes from my throat and Cade leans in and licks at my lips until I grant him passage. After he's fucked my mouth with his tongue for a few minutes in tandem with the thrusts of his cock and Finn increases the pressure and motion on my clit, I feel the steady build hit me again in shock. He pulls back and his eyes are so intense as he adjusts himself under me and rolls his hips instead of thrusting. The smooth slide and different angle along with Finn's fingers rubbing my clit has the pleasure building faster than I thought possible after already orgasming so many times. Cade doesn't stop gazing into my eyes the entire time and I feel something shift inside me. A pull in my chest I don't understand. Finn is sucking and licking at the same spot over and over again between my neck and shoulder and it feels like he's branding me it's so hot.

My eyes begin to droop closed as I get close again but Cade's growl has me fluttering them open to see his blue-green eyes change to gold and start glowing as he snarls, "Together!" The word and eyes pull hard on me and I'm helpless to do anything but arch my back and thrust my core hard against his cock and Finn's fingers causing me to tip over once again into another orgasm. As soon as the first spasm clenches around him, Cade leans forward and clamps his teeth on the same spot on the other side of my neck that Finn has been sucking at and I feel Finn's teeth bite down on me as well causing me to scream at the combination of pain and pleasure crashing through me as Cade shoots his hot seed deep inside of me and I feel the hot wetness against my back as Finn finds his own release.

My mind shuts down at the overstimulation and without the two of them holding me up I would have slid boneless to the bed. They hold me in place as they kiss and lick at the spots where they bit me soothing the sharp pain that quickly turns to a low burn. I let them tend to me as I recover and then snuggle up to a hard chest as they lay me down on the bed with the heat of their bodies front and back. I feel so cared for and safe, connected to these men in a way I've never felt before that I let myself drift into sleep with a contented smile on my lips.

When I wake, the room is full of shadows. I'm so warm and comfortable but also sticky in many places. I try and ignore the feeling of it not wanting to leave the cozy nest of men and blankets but eventually I give up and squirm out from under a thigh and arm until I reach the end of the bed and hop down. I snag a billowy white shirt from the floor and toss it and a washcloth behind the privacy screen before grabbing a cloth bag of the crumbly soap and the water jug and bowl and take it all behind the screen to clean myself up. I'm sore and stretched in all the right places from the intense lovemaking we did but when I run the soapy cloth over my shoulder I hiss at the flare of pain. Craning my neck and dropping my shoulder forward lets me see part of the pink swollen bite mark. I wince as I gently wash it and then remember that they both bit me just as we came together so look to my other shoulder. My brow furrows as I see the identical matching mark there. I finish cleaning up and slide the borrowed shirt over my head, thankful for its looseness so it won't rub against the bites. I'm all for a few love nibbles during sex but the matching bites on my shoulders are deep and I'm almost positive they will take a long time to fade if they don't end up scarring.

My stomach takes that moment to rumble loudly reminding me that I had skipped lunch and it's close to or even after suppertime. I lay the washcloth over the screen to dry and step out from behind it to find my wolves waiting for me perched against the side of the bed. They both look me up and down as if checking me for injury but their expressions quickly fill with lust as they stare at my bare legs under the loose ends of whoever's shirt I'm wearing. Finn whistles in admiration.

"Now there's a bonny sight to see. Come here, lass."

I cross my arms over my chest and shake my head. "No! No more sex…right now. I'm sore and hungry and no more biting!"

It comes out way more whiny than I meant to say it but the sweet looks that fill their faces have me melting as they push off the bed and pull me towards them. Cade tugs the open neck of the shirt to the side and studies the mark he put on me with what I swear is smug satisfaction.

"Aye and I'm sure as sorry for the pain, lass. Let me ease it for you."

I don't have a chance to pull away before he dips his head down and swipes his tongue over the mark. I expect it to burn and tense against it but instead the pain eases immediately and a bolt of heat flashes between my legs. I start to shake my head at the greedy sex monster that has awakened inside of me but Finn tugs the shirt the other way and does the same thing with his tongue to the bite he put on me.

My eyes want to roll back into my head as my legs go weak. I can't believe how responsive I am to these two men but before I spread my legs like the hussy I'm becoming, my stomach growls loudly and both of them chuckle. Cade presses a soft kiss to my temple and lets me go.

"Alright then, lass. I'll fetch us a feast to tame the beast in your belly as I'm not ready to end our time together and share you with the others yet."

I feel the heat of a blush climb my neck and fill my face at the reminder that I will have to face Sebastian and Luca. Not only do I have to apologize for running out of the training room earlier but I'm sure they will have an idea of what I've been up to with Cade and Finn all day and probably will be tonight, judging by the way Finn is looking at my bare legs.

I let out a deep sigh as Cade leaves to get us food and resign myself to facing them over breakfast. It's not like I can hide in this room forever and I really do want to try and convince Sebastian to help me get control when fighting. Finn breaks me from my thoughts as he pulls me closer and strokes my tousled hair.

"Ease yourself, Eden. All will be well. Cade and I will take care of you and keep you from harm."

I snuggle against his chest and close my eyes and just let myself enjoy being cared for after so long being alone but I could have sworn I heard him whisper into my hair, "Forevermore."

Eden

When I wake in the morning my wolves are gone but I can still smell them on the pillows and feel the residual heat of them next to me. A large smile crosses my face when I stretch and feel the aches in various parts from being so well-loved the day and night before. I close my eyes and do a replay of some of the things we got up to together and hum in happiness. I find myself laughing out loud in the empty room. I'm happy? Somehow I managed to travel back in time almost four hundred years, I have no way to get home and I'm at the complete mercy of vampires and wolf shifters and I'm happy? Hell yes, I am! I mean, let's face it - home wasn't so great anyway. I literally had no one left in my life that really meant anything to me. Dealing with my anxiety and PTSD was a full-time job and it's not like those issues have now been fucked out of me after one amazing day and night but this is the first time in as long as I can remember that I feel peaceful, safe, and cared for. If these men will have me, I don't care if I ever go home.

I wrap my arms around my bare chest and hug the memory of how Finn and Cade took care of me by having steaming buckets of water brought in to fill the tub where they washed every part of me with tenderness like I was so delicate and special to them. The way they dried me off and laid me out on the bed so that they could rub perfumed oil into my skin in the most erotic massage I've ever had and then held me pressed between them as we slept. I fling my arms back out and gather the pillows with their scent and press them to my chest missing them already.

The thought makes me laugh in giddiness and I roll off the bed in search of clothes so I can go find them. Even knowing I'll be facing Sebastian and Luca this morning doesn't dim the glow I'm feeling. I shimmy into my panties and bra and lift one of their shirts that they left for me bringing it to my nose to take a deep breath of their scent before shaking it out and lifting it to slide over my head.

There's a sharp knock against the door a half a second before it's shoved open and Bridgette stomps in only to freeze in her tracks as her eyes catch sight of my nearly naked body. She sniffs in disdain, causing her eyes to narrow. I know exactly what the room smells like after multiple rounds of lovemaking from the night before. It definitely needs a good airing out.

Her narrowed eyes flick to the rumpled bed before coming back to me with a slight sneer but when she catches sight of the shirt tangled above my head the sneer turns to pure female outrage. She takes two hard steps towards me looking like she's going to scratch out my eyes and spits something in French at me but all I understand is Cade's name so I'm guessing she's got history there with him. As she reaches to snatch the shirt from me her eyes drop down my body and she freezes again but this time her eyes widen with a hint of fear. I look down my body to see what she's looking at, fearing I'm bleeding or something, and realize she's staring at the four moon tattoos clearly visible with my arms up this way. I open my mouth to tell her that they're just tattoos but my phone chimes out from across the room and Siri announces, *"Reminder, you have a lawyer's appointment today at two o'clock. Reminder!"*

Bridgette almost gives herself whiplash from the head jerk in its direction and I would have laughed out loud at the scene but she's in a panic now. She stumbles back towards the door almost tripping over her feet in her haste but before she leaves, her pale arms come up and she makes the sign of the cross with two shaking fingers. I take a step towards her to try and calm her down and explain but the hate I see radiating out of her blazing eyes tells me it's pointless. As she steps out into the hall she hisses at me.

"Sorcière!" Then runs away down the hall.

I stand in the doorway with Cade's shirt clutched in my fist for a moment. I might not be fluent in French but I'm pretty confident she just called me a sorcerer, also known as a witch. I want to roll my eyes at the girl's dramatics. I mean, bitch, please! You work in a house owned by vampires and shifters, how scary can a witch be, even if I'm not one but a sour feeling in my belly tells me she might cause some trouble for me in some way if I can't talk her down from it. As I step back into the room and close the door to finish dressing I grumble a little in pettiness. The French tart probably hates me more for being with Cade than any witchy powers she thinks I have. She either has or had a thing with my wolf and a woman scorned and all that can be pretty fucking dangerous if not handled properly.

I go silence the reminder alert on the phone and then flip it the bird for good measure. I'm beyond happy that I won't be facing off against my ex, Troy today as our lawyers dig for blood. Every appointment I've had in the past has left me a quivering mess of anxiety. As I turn away I pause and look inside for tendrils of that anxiety but I find none. Hmm, maybe that means I'm healing. I shrug and pull the shirt over my head and work my leggings up over my hips. Doesn't matter. If luck is on my side, I won't ever have to see Troy or a lawyer again. I slide my shoes on, stick my phone in the bra band on my side and go in search of coffee, food, and my men.

As I walk towards the dining room we have been having breakfast in a few servants do double-takes at what I'm wearing, but really? The shirt hits me mid-thigh and if they're having scandalized spasms over my black body-hugging leggings they can get bent for all I care. The dresses Luca got for me are gorgeous but there's just no way I can wear them every day.

When I reach the door to the dining room I slow as nerves hit me. I'm embarrassed by the way I acted yesterday but I'm also nervous about how Finn and Cade will treat me in front of Luca and Sebastian. Not that I plan on hiding what happened with them but…yeah nervous. I step through the doors with a tentative smile on my lips that only wobbles a bit and walk to the table where all four are seated.

"Good morning, everyone."

I try for casual and square up my shoulders to give myself more confidence.

Four heads turn my way and three of them rise to their feet. Good mornings ringing out from them but the fourth arches an eyebrow with a cold look and takes a few minutes before he too finally stands. I can feel the heat filling my cheeks but just turn away from him and send a tight smile to Cade and Finn and a quick shake of my head as they move to come to me before taking my seat. I look towards Luca and when he nods with a small smile at me let out the breath I'm holding. Ok, best to just dive right in.

"I would like to apologize to all of you for the way I reacted yesterday in the training room. You were kind enough to allow me to join you in training and I…I…" Turning to Sebastian, I swallow the lump in my throat and plow ahead. "I'm sorry! Everything you said was true. I don't have control or discipline and it will get me into trouble someday when I blank out like that." I let out a deep sigh. "I'm sorry. I can't seem to control it and I don't want to be a danger to anyone else or myself. I was frustrated and well, embarrassed that it happened after you agreed to train with me. I can't promise it won't happen again but if you would work with me then maybe I can overcome it."

I chew on my bottom lip as he stares coldly at me and when he tosses his napkin over his plate and leans back in his chair I see a flash of something not nice in his eyes that immediately puts me further on edge.

"It seems you have two willing males to tend to **all** your needs so I don't see why I should waste my time with that."

There's a beat of stunned silence around the table as my mouth drops open and I blink at him a few times. Cade and Finn shove to their feet with growls and even Luca makes an outraged noise but I just sit staring at him. I can't fucking believe the asshole went there with me. It takes a minute for my temper to surge but once it's roaring I throw up a hand towards the others to quiet them without ever taking my eyes from Sebastian's.

Once there is silence I ask in a deadly calm voice with just a hint of snap in it, "Did you just try to slut shame me?"

His eyes widen slightly and then slide away from mine and I wonder if the word slut is around in this time so I ask again with a word I know he will understand and this time I say it with a lot of snap.

"Whore! You basically just called me a whore, didn't you?"

I see his features tighten but he keeps his eyes down on his plate. I give him a moment to reply but I'm met with silence so I shove to my feet, knocking my chair over behind me in the process which finally has him looking up and I put him on blast. Not with heat but with the ice he likes so fucking much.

"Don't trouble yourself, Sebastian. I don't need your help. Besides, that giant stick you have shoved up your ass would probably get in the way anyways."

I make to turn and leave it at that but nope, not done yet, and here comes the heat.

"Also, go fuck yourself sideways, you narrow-minded prick!"

Now I'm done. I spin away and stalk towards the door but I only make it halfway when his hard voice barks out, "Wait!"

I desperately want to shoot him the finger over my shoulder and sail on out of the room but for some reason I can't fucking move a muscle. I'm frozen in place with muscles quivering to move when his hand lands on my shoulder and he gently turns me to face him. His expression flashes between shame, sadness, and frustration, finally settling on exasperation as he holds me in place.

"I apologize. I shouldn't have implied that. I didn't mean it. I would…please, allow me to help you to overcome your affliction."

When I just glare at him in answer, he nods slowly and looks a little bit lost.

"Please, stay. Enjoy your breakfast and if you wish to join me after, I will be waiting in the training hall."

As soon as he drops his hand from my shoulder I'm able to move again and I find myself sagging slightly as he slides past me and leaves the room. My eyes dart between Cade, Finn, and Luca as I heave out a breath.

"What the fuck was that? I couldn't move!"

Cade comes to me and places a soft kiss on the top of my head before guiding me to my seat that he rights and then sits back into his own. Finn is the one to answer me.

"He compelled you."

I throw up my hands. "He what now?"

Cade reaches over and wraps one of my curls around his finger. "It's one of his powers. He can compel you to do as he wishes."

I send a big-eyed inquiring look Luca's way and his lips twitch in a smile before nodding that it's true. I shake my head and reach for my coffee that's never been needed more.

"Huh, neat flex," I say, slightly awed.

I fill my plate and think about if I even want to train with the Iceman anymore as I eat. The guys had told me last night that they were in a similar state but barely functional when they first met Sebastian and Luca. They said they were close to feral and would lash out blindly at anything and anyone when he first started working with them. I wrinkle my nose in annoyance because I know I need to try and get this rage issue under control and as much as he's an Alpha-hole that makes me want to claw at, he's the guy I need. Learning he can freeze me any time he wants doesn't scare me, it actually would be a great tool to stop me in my tracks when I go all red ragey. Ugh, as much as I might not like the fucker, I think I need him.

"What has your head spinning, lass?" Finn asks causing me to look up from my plate and see that Luca has left at some point and it's just the three of us plus all the servants against the wall in the room. "We're sorry Bas was such a bastard to you. Some days, I don't understand him at all. He needs to…uh, get his head on straight, yeah?"

I grin because I just know if it was in my time frame Finn would have said something like, he needs to get laid. I wave his words away and change the subject.

"So, I had a little dust-up with Bridgette this morning." I catch the quick looks they send towards each other and it confirms they hit that. "She was pretty pissed when she saw me with your shirt. I thought she was going to go all catfight on me and try and pull my hair. That was before she spotted my tattoos and my alarm went off. Then she was full-on witch, witch, witch! Grab the stake and the torches kind of thing - so that might be an issue."

I almost burst out laughing at the dog with its tail between his legs looks they're giving me at being caught out so I roll my eyes and shake my head.

"Guys, it's not a big deal, I mean the sexing up the French tart part. The witch thing probably isn't great, though. We're all adults here and we've all been with other sex partners before. Just, you know, maybe let anyone current know there's a new sheriff in town that doesn't share." As soon as I say it my stomach rolls. Shit, we didn't exactly chat about the whole exclusive thing. I may have just gotten way ahead of myself here so I stutter out, "Uh, I mean, only if you want to continue uh, you know with uh, me?"

They both laugh which doesn't make me feel any better but when Cade reaches over and snatches me from my chair to sit on his lap I swallow back some of the nerves I'm feeling. He tugs the neck of my shirt to the side and puts his hot lips and tongue on where he bit me causing me to squirm as heat pools between my legs. Finn comes around the table and does the same on the other side of my neck and I have visions of us clearing the table with an arm sweep, sending plates and glasses to shatter on the floor so we can fuck right here and now but when my head tilts back my hooded eyes catch sight of the servants lining the walls and it snaps me out of it. I push them away with a flaming red face and nod towards the nearest ones who stand with blank expressions and eyes averted.

Finn chuckles and kneels beside us taking my chin between his fingers so I will look into his deep cobalt blue eyes. "Lass, Eden, there will be no other women for either of us now that we have you." He says it so seriously that I feel that pull in my chest again and I can't help but drop my lips to his. After a few moments, Cade pulls me away from Finn and turns me to face him.

"You're part of our pack now, Eden. You're ours and I know you said in your time that you choose who you mate with but it would devastate us if you chose to mate with someone outside of our pack. The bond goes both ways, love."

My heart surges in my chest at these beautiful men's words. They only want to be with me and they only want me to be with them. It's only been four days since I landed at their feet but I can already feel myself sliding into a love I've never felt before. I'm so fucked.

Sebastian

Stop!" I command as I see her eyes begin to blank. "Breathe, focus, control." When Eden exhales and nods, I bark, "Again!"

I block the strike she launches at me as we continue sparring with the staves we've been using for the last week. As we move through the moves I keep my face blank even though inside I'm impressed and even a little proud of how quickly she's progressed. I haven't needed to compel her at all in the last few days as she's been able to bring herself back from losing control with just a word. I would like to be able to take all the credit due to our daily training but I know it's a combination of it and the time she spends with the others. The long walks through the gardens and conversations she shares with Luca and the passions she shares with the wolves as well as my thaw and training with her have brought about a change in her. If I was poetic at all I would say it was like seeing a flower bloom. When she first arrived there was a constant tension riding her body at all times even when she seemed to be relaxed and joking. The shadows in her eyes spoke of pain, anxiety, and deep sadness. She held herself stiffly as if always waiting for a blow. Over the last week she has truly relaxed and brightened and while I still catch the shadows in her eyes occasionally it's not constant as it was before.

"Umph…" escapes me when her staff makes it through my guard in my distraction and lands solidly against my left hip. The noise I make has her lips twitching in a smug grin so I speed up my movements to keep her focused. I swing a fast swipe towards her thighs and she surprises me by diving over the staff into a roll that has her coming up onto her knees behind me and spinning around to face my back. I've only managed to turn halfway towards her when she strikes out and sweeps my legs from under me causing me to land flat on my back on the rug. Quick as a cat, she has the end of her staff at my throat and a giddy laugh trills out from between her lips, eyes dancing with happiness.

"I believe your life is mine, your Grace!" She teases and it takes all my control not to knock the staff from her hand and yank her down onto my chest so that I may ravish her smiling mouth. Instead, I arch an eyebrow. While I don't want to take this small victory from her, I also don't want her to be overconfident.

"It would appear so, wouldn't it?" I tell her before using my supernatural speed to roll out from under the staff and launch myself to my feet, moving behind her to grip her throat.

My movements are too fast for a mortal eye to see so it appears as though I disappeared in front of her eyes. My chest is tight against her back with my arm resting in between her breasts so that my hand can lightly grip her entire throat.

I whisper into her ear, "Appearances can be deceiving as now it's your life that is mine."

Pressed so close to her I feel the shudder that runs through her body as my hot breath washes over her sensitive flesh. I curse myself for causing her fear but before I can move away she surprises me by relaxing against me and letting her head fall back against my shoulder so she can look up at me. I feel her swallow against my hand as she looks up at me with hooded eyes. Her tiny pink tongue darts out to lick her pouty lower lip causing my eyes to drop to a mouth I want to possess more than I've ever wanted anything in my long life.

Her voice is low and thick when she asks, "And what would you do with it if it was yours?"

A low growl rumbles in my chest at the loaded question and I'm seconds away from dragging her down to the rug to cover her body with mine when a throat clears from across the room. My eyes flash red and I force down a snarl at the interruption when I spot Luca standing at the edge of the rug with a perfectly blank expression except for the pointed look in his eyes. I quickly release the witch and step away from her, schooling my features into their customary cold state.

"Luca, what is it?" I ask as I busy myself gathering our fallen staves to return them to their place on the wall. Training is over as I will need space from her to regain my control.

"A runner has arrived from the palace with a missive from Pierre." He tells me before turning to Eden. "As well, the seamstress has arrived to take your measurements, Eden."

She glances between the two of us briefly before beaming a smile at him. "Oh, Luca, you've already given me so many gowns. I don't need anymore!"

He smiles indulgently at her. "It is my pleasure to offer you the finest gowns but this is for something I think you will enjoy much more. While you look enchanting wearing the gowns in the evenings I've noticed you choose to be more casual in your dress during the day. It's not right that you must wear the same leg coverings repeatedly and one of Cade or Finn's shirts so I have instructed her to create a more casual wardrobe for you to wear during the days. She will make you anything you wish so that you may be more comfortable."

I turn away as she claps her hands in delight and rushes towards him but checks herself before she actually touches him when he pulls back slightly.

I had also noticed that she chose to wear the tight black leg coverings she arrived in daily but hadn't thought to hire anyone to replicate them so she had more options in what she wore. As for the wolves' shirts she wears every day, I try hard not to notice how appealing they look on her. When I turn back the two are walking side by side toward the doors. I watch them go with a slight frown, sad to see her go, even though I need the space and distance from her right now. When she looks back at me over her shoulder with a questioning look in her eyes I turn away once again so she won't see the regret that we were interrupted there. The witch belongs to the wolves in that way and I will do nothing to jeopardize the relationship I have with them. They and Luca are my only family, my pack as they call it, and I can't imagine living out the long years without them. The witch must remain off-limits for me.

I leave the training room and locate the runner in the entrance hall, bid him wait for any reply I wish to send back, and take the wax-sealed message to my desk in the library to read. My fingers almost shred the delicate parchment as I read of more bloodless, headless bodies found and missing villagers. Pierre writes that it's all concentrate in the woodlands that border the Marquis du Corbeil's estate southeast of the palace. This is not the work of a passing fiend as I hoped. The Marquis is well known for his deviance and debauchery. The King turns a blind eye to the rumors and gossip of the scoundrel's reputation due to the man's high contacts in the King's military but it is well known that there is no love or respect between them.

I toss the missive down and clench my fists. He is just such a man who would welcome one of my kind of lesser repute to dine at his table or on his vassals, either for entertainment or to further any nefarious schemes he might have in play. I quickly scratch out a reply on fresh parchment to tell Pierre that I will deal with the issue and for him to gather information on all of the Marquis dealings, fold it before sealing it with melted wax stamped with my crest symbol then return it to the runner to be on his way. This cannot stand. If there is a rogue vampire or even a nest preying on the innocents in our territory we will wipe them out, invited or not. Their carelessness of leaving victims to be so easily discovered puts all of my kind at risk and goes directly against the compact we have with the Monarchy. I send a footman to find the rest of my pack and wait for them in the library where I unroll a large map of the region to study. Once they've all joined me and read the missive for themselves, Cade throws it down with a growl.

"Fucking eejits, yeah? They had to know we wouldn't stand for such and I dinnae believe for a moment that they're unaware this is our territory. How do you want to handle it, then?"

I nod. "Indeed, my concern is the missing villagers. Either their bodies have yet to be discovered or someone is creating new vampires. You all know that a newly turned vampire is close to feral in their insatiable bloodlust. If they aren't under a strong-willed sire they are capable of draining an entire village in one night and will still want more. If there is a nest, we must find it and eradicate it. We will travel to the woods where the bodies have been discovered and try to find their scent. We will also speak to the villagers and see if we can find any information that ties these disappearances and deaths to the Marquis. Finn, Cade, gather the silvered weapons. Luca and I will have the horses made ready and the kitchen prepare food to take as we may need to stay in the woods overnight."

Cade and Finn exchange a loaded look with each other instead of leaving to gather the weapons we will need.

"What? What is the problem?" I ask in annoyance.

They both cross their arms over their chests in a stubborn stance with Cade answering.

"It's Eden. We're not comfortable leaving her here alone unprotected for so long."

I can't help but scoff at how ridiculous that sounds. "I'm positive your cocks won't fall off from a mere day of want."

The shock I get to Finn's reaction has me taking a step back as his eyes flare gold and he bares his teeth at me and snaps out, "Mind yourself!"

Not since the very beginning of our journey together has either one of the wolves challenged me in such a way and it dawns on me for the first time that the witch isn't just a plaything to them and that there's something deeper between them. The realization has an ache of envy filling my chest that I ignore and instead give a sharp nod of apology to them.

"What is it that has you worried? She will hardly be alone in our home with so many servants and it's not like she isn't capable of defending herself." I ask in a more neutral tone.

Cade lifts his chin in defiance. "We aren't leaving her alone for that long especially now that we know there are vampires in our area." He glances at Finn again and frowns. "It's not just that, yeah? We still don't know how she traveled here in the first place from her own time. We…we worry that she may go back as suddenly as she came. We just don't want her to be alone in case we can stop it somehow. One of us will need to stay here with her."

I rake my fingers through my hair in frustration. "I understand your concern but we need both of you. Luca and I can't track scent the way you two can in your wolf forms. If only one of you comes, we could be in that forest for days searching."

"I will stay with her," Luca says softly causing all of us to turn his way with surprised looks. He shrugs one shoulder. "Sebastian is correct. It would take too long with just one of you trying to find the scent."

He tells the wolves before turning to me. "I'm sure the three of you will be able to handle taking out anything you find. If it is a nest of newly turned, they won't be much of a threat to you. I will stay and keep Eden safe."

Finn and Cade share a look as if they are having a silent conversation before they both nod in agreement. Cade crosses his arms like he doesn't like it but will go along. "Fine. Let's get going then. It's early enough that if we get lucky we can be back just after dark if we get moving right away."

I nod as well keeping my face blank so they don't see the concern coursing through me. Now that the two wolves have invested emotion into the situation with the witch, things will become much more complicated.

Eden

The seamstress and her assistants can barely speak English but between them all we manage to convey what I would like to have made. I stripped off my leggings, tank top, and underwear leaving me naked under my robe so she could create a pattern for them to replicate but I'm pretty sure without elastic and other modern materials it's going to fall pretty short. I don't care. I'm just happy I will have a few more options to wear that aren't ball gowns. Luca must have given the woman an idea of what I like wearing because she came with three pairs of pants. At first I thought they were skirts because of how much fabric there was but when I tried the first pair on I realized that they were more like palazzo pants just with much wider legs so that they looked like a skirt. As well as the pants she had brought three blouses similar to the dress shirts the guys all wear but more fitted to flatter my size. A few wide leather belts with decorative markings tooled into the leather gave me three new casual outfits. Now if only I could explain to her how to make an oversized, slouchy hoodie, I grumble under my breath as they start packing up to leave.

Finn and Cade come into my room with grim expressions immediately making me nervous. They wait for the seamstress and her team to leave before shutting the door behind them and then turn to face me. I chew on my bottom lip waiting for whatever bomb they need to drop on me as Finn clears his throat.

"Something's come up, lass and we're truly sorry but we have to leave you."

He says it so solemnly and Cade's jaw twitches as he holds it so tightly that I feel tears spring up into my eyes. I'm such an idiot. Of course they're leaving. They had their fun with me and now it's time to move on. I mean, what did I think was going to happen? Just because I fell down the rabbit hole doesn't mean fairy tales are fucking true. After all the shit that's been handed to me in my life, I should know that better than most. I spin my back to them so they won't see how much it hurts and try to keep the little bit of pride that I have left. I have to swallow twice to be sure my voice doesn't betray me before I can speak.

"I understand. I'll gather my things and go." I say, wincing at the tremble in my voice. I don't know where I can go but I'll figure it out somehow.

"Go? Go where?" Cade asks in confusion.

I square my shoulders and take a steadying breath before turning back to them but keep my gaze averted. "I…I don't know. Maybe there's a tavern or Inn I could find a job at. Don't worry about it. It's not your problem." I say, blinking back my tears.

I catch them exchanging looks out of the corner of my eye and flinch back when Finn reaches for me. He's quick to pull his hand back when he sees my reaction though.

"Eden, what the hell are you talking about? Why would you want to go?" He asks in a shocked tone, causing me to look up at him just as his expression changes to frustration. "Luca will be here to take care of you. You don't need to go anywhere or worry about getting a job!"

My mouth drops open as anger floods my stomach. "Are you for real?" I yell. "You think you can just play with me like a toy and then pass me on to your buddy once you're done with me? Fuck you! Fuck you both!"

My voice breaks on the last word and I'm forced to swipe away at the hot tears that spill over.

"Oh, no, no mo ghràdh. We aren't done with you! We are only just getting started." Cade says as he yanks me against him. I look up into his heated eyes as another tear spills down my cheek.

"I don't understand. You said you were leaving me." I ask in a choked voice. My brow furrows when a grin forms on his lips.

"For the day, possibly overnight. Bas, Finn, and I have some business to take care of but Luca will be here if you need anything." He tells me, amusement thick in his tone.

I push away from him and glare at both of them as I feel my face going red in embarrassment.

"Oh my God! You assholes! Why didn't you just say that? The way Finn said you were leaving and the expressions on your face?" I shove a hand through my hair so I don't punch them. "You jerks made it sound like you were leaving me for good!"

Both Finn and Cade move at the same time until they have me sandwiched between them. Finn is behind me and his mouth drops to my neck as Cade captures my mouth in a searing kiss that has me forgetting why I'm mad at them in an instant. Finn's clever fingers find the gap in my robe so he can trace circles against my skin slowly lowering them until I want to force them down the rest of the way where heat and wetness have bloomed. My hips rock forward against his fingers to try and get them to lower causing him to chuckle against my neck and then nip my skin lightly. I don't mean to whimper when they both lift their lips from me but it comes out anyway. Finn cups my cheek and all amusement is gone from his eyes when he tells me,

"Eden, a day away from you will feel like an eternity to us. You never have to doubt our intentions towards you. We will never leave you."

"Ever," Cade whispers in my ear before pulling away and moving towards the door with Finn right behind him. He looks back at me and my breath catches in my throat at the depth of the feelings I see in his eyes before he nods and disappears. Finn turns to look at me over his shoulder and his eyes smolder with desire.

"We would never toy with you and then pass you on to Luca but if you were open to it, we would share you with him."

My pussy clenches hard when his words hit me and an image of the three of them on me at once flashes through my brain. I'm stunned stupid and can't get words to form but he's already gone so it doesn't matter. My knees feel weak at the up and downs of the last ten minutes so I climb up on the bed and flop down onto it in a heap and try and ignore the ache between my legs as I process that bomb.

Fuck me sideways! How did I go from a lonely, scared, traumatized, pathetic life to this? And how am I not a complete wreck? Time travel, vampires, shifters, and a threesome in ten days and now a possible foursome? I should be a quivering ball of a mess huddled in a corner but instead…instead, I'm fucking happier than I've ever been in my life. There is literally nowhere that I'd rather be than in this time and place with these men.

I must doze off for quite a while because when I wake up it's later in the afternoon. It's crazy how many naps I end up having since I landed here. I can only assume it's because I feel safe and my body is making up for the many years that I would barely sleep through the night.

As I get dressed in one of the new outfits I think about that. I feel safe here. Not once have I twitched for my knife or gun that I always carry back home. Not only that but I wasn't scared of the four men right from the start. Usually, I would flinch when anyone tried to touch me and I certainly don't trust any men other than Diesel and a few old coworkers.

From the time I landed here though, I didn't fear them or flinch away from them. I just climbed onto that horse and left my fate in their hands. As I study my new look in the mirror I shake my head. Maybe, just maybe, there's something bigger playing a hand in my life. Maybe there is fate or karma or God and they decided I needed a break in life. I don't know how it happened but I'm incredibly grateful that it did.

I leave my room with a bounce in my step and wander around the huge house peeking into rooms I haven't been in yet to kill some time. I'm not really in the mood to go to the library and read or to work out in the training hall again. I turn down a hallway I haven't been down before and hear the faint notes of a song playing that definitely doesn't belong in this era so I keep going as the music gets clearer. I've kind of lost custody of my phone as the wolves are obsessed with the music and pictures on it. A smile spreads across my face when I remember how amazed and then addicted they became when I let them read one of my paranormal romance ebooks downloaded on the Kindle app and then how they re-enacted one of the steamy scenes with me. I'm waiting for a quiet night to share some of the movies I have downloaded on my phone to really blow their minds.

There's a set of double doors at the end of the hall that are firmly closed but I can hear Wicked Games by Chris Isaak clearly through them. I frown at the choice of song as I knock on the door. It's a sad, sad song that is hauntingly beautiful but I hope it's not how Luca feels. I've picked up a few things from him and the others that tell me he has had a tragic past that haunts him. I knock again but after a few moments I crack the door open and stick my head in to call out thinking he can't hear my knocking over the music.

His back is to me and his hands are a blur as they move over a half-formed statue. When my eyes slide away from him and take in the rest of the room my mouth O's in surprise and my feet move deeper into the room without conscious thought. The large room's walls and ceiling are made up of glass so it is very bright but it's what fills the space that sucker punches me right in the heart.

There are at least fifty finished statues shoved against the glass walls and every one of them is of a man in agony. They're so lifelike that I can feel the pain radiating off them. The worst part is that I can see the resemblance to Luca in every face that stares back at me. My heart hurts that he has such pain trapped inside of him. I know what that feels like but this, this is a whole different level of pain. I turn to look at him just as the song comes to an end and the words just slip out of me in a choked gasp.

"Oh, Luca…"

His reaction is instant. His body is almost blurred as he swings my way with a snarl, his arm cocked as if to hit out with a clay-covered fist. I'm shocked that I don't flinch away but instead take a step towards him. I see the moment he realizes what he's done as shame flashes across his face and his arm drops to his side. Cindy Lauper's Time After Time starts playing from my phone and I realize he's got my retro love song playlist going.

He makes a move towards the phone to shut it off but I stop him by calling out, "Siri, pause music."

The silence in the room is thick for a few moments before he clears his throat.

"I apologize. I was lost in the clay and didn't hear you come in. Please know, I would never hurt you."

He looks absolutely miserable and he won't meet my eyes so I take a few steps closer.

"Luca – Luca, look at me," I tell him and have to swallow the gasp at the shame I see in his eyes when he finally lifts them to me.

I want to rush the last few feet between us and throw my arms around him to try and ease his mind but I know from my own trauma that the last thing I ever wanted was to be touched. Instead, I let out a deep breath and start to speak.

"The day I traveled here, a friend called out to me. A bunch of times he said, but I was lost in my head and didn't hear him so when he put his hand on my shoulder to get my attention I almost broke his face with my fist." I take another step toward him and try and convey my understanding of what just happened. "I understand your reaction because that's how I reacted most of the time before coming here. I know you wouldn't hurt me, Luca."

His brow furrows and he sucks in his lower lip before turning away from me to pick up a rag and clean the clay from his hands.

"I'm sorry I took your device. The music, the music on it is like nothing I've ever heard before. Some of the songs, I feel them so deeply. They make me feel and remember things long forgotten."

I smile. "Then I'm glad. Music is supposed to touch and fuel your soul just like art." I turn and gesture towards the many statues. "This art, is it what's in your soul? Do you live with such pain, Luca?" I ask quietly.

His eyes drop once again and he scrubs harder at the clay clinging to his fingers. I feel terrible for asking him such a prying question so I shift away from it. "Tell me something happy from your life - something from before. You're originally from Spain? I've always wanted to travel there to see its beauty."

At first, I don't think he'll answer me as he goes to a basin of water and properly washes the clay off. We've had so many conversations on our daily walks but they've almost all been about what happens in the future. What strides mankind makes between now and my time. He's always full of questions but he's never really told me anything about himself or his own history. When he finally starts to talk I almost have to strain to hear him so I move closer.

"I was born the youngest son of five. My family were simple farmers. We grew many crops but olives were my papa's passion. He had dreams of building an empire with his liquid gold, as he called it. My two oldest brothers were content to follow along in his footsteps and my middle brothers both joined the military. I had no interest in either. I was content to create with the clay I would dig up from one spot on our land. I was only seventeen when my father took me with him to Seville to sell casks of pressed oil. He was fast losing patience with me not contributing to the family's wealth so he set an ultimatum on me. I was to bring my best creations to Seville and try to sell them. If no one wanted them then I would leave my childish art dreams behind and get to work, either working the farm or joining the military like my brothers."

Luca turns to me with a small smile of remembrance on his face.

"Imagine his surprise when all my pieces sold the first day at the market. When patrons began asking if I would take commissions we both knew I would not be returning to the farm with him." The smile drops away and a look of sadness washes across his face. "That was the last time I saw him or any of my family. I always meant to go back to visit but there always seemed to be a new piece to be created."

He shakes his head and sends me a wistful look before turning away again as he continues.

"Seville was full of artists of every kind and we were all so passionate about everything. We would lose hours debating when we weren't creating our masterpieces. We were so wrapped up in being young and free that we didn't see what was forming right in front of us. When the Inquisition began, most of us laughed it off even as some of our friends disappeared. With the naiveté of youth, we believed ourselves to be untouchable. By the time we saw what was really happening, it was too late to run."

He sits down on a stool and looks over at his half-completed work and sighs.

"There wasn't much that was fun after that I'm afraid."

I instinctively know that's all he will tell me so I smile in understanding and wander around his studio, now and then reaching out to run a hand over some of his work. I wish I could help him the way he has helped me. He's only ever shown kindness and patience to me and I hate the pain I see in his beautiful grey eyes. Deciding to try and push a little bit, I turn back to him.

"Do you know what Post Traumatic Stress Disorder is?"

Luca

I frown at the question even as I shake my head. The things I've shared with her surprise me. I never talk about my past, with anyone. Not even Sebastian. It has been decades since I've even thought about my family, let alone spoke to another about them.

Eden pulls at something inside of me that has been long dormant. I'm helpless to stop it even though I know it will only cause me fresh pain. I've worked so hard to block off all my emotions, convinced I would surely go mad if I allowed myself to feel as I once did. The only time I allow them to escape is when I'm creating. I let them flow out of me into the piece I'm working on and it helps ease the pressure of repressing them.

"It's a mental affliction that happens to even the strongest people after a trauma or series of traumas in my case. My parents and sister died in a horrific accident. It broke me, at least it felt like it did at the time. As I was trying to deal with the grief of it, the man I was married to betrayed me in so many ways. He used my pain against me like a weapon and I had no defenses to stop him. I was lucky, my Aunt Adera got me away from him and I slowly started to heal, to take back control of my life. Things were getting better for me but then my partner, Sam, and I were attacked by a gang. They killed him in front of me and then toyed and taunted me as they beat me almost to death. It would have been much worse but the police showed up, late to the call but they showed up and the gang ran away. It was three days later when I woke up in the hospital. That's when I knew what broken really meant."

She meets my eyes and I see the shadows there that have slowly been disappearing come flaring back. I want nothing more than to take her in my arms and promise that no one will ever harm her again but I know the monster inside me makes me unworthy of touching her or any return kindness so I stay in place and just listen as she continues.

"I don't sleep very well. I have terrible nightmares that force me to relive not only the attack but the aftermath of my family's deaths. I can't stand to be touched unless it's during a sparring match. I flinch and react badly when I'm surprised and I lose myself to a rage haze when I feel threatened."

She takes a step towards me and her face crumples just for a moment before she gets control.

Her next words have an incredible ache filling my chest.

"I was so damn lonely, broken, and tired that I just wanted it to end. I wanted to die and I've been working up the courage to end my life so the pain will stop. And then, I came here."

She takes a few more steps towards me so that her skirts brush against my leg and I'm pinned in place by her shadowed green eyes.

"I came here and everything changed. Cade, Finn, and you…" She rolls her eyes and huffs out a laugh. "Even Sebastian in his way started to heal me. I wasn't alone anymore. Here were four men that took me in and kept me safe. Four men who showed me kindness and caring when I so desperately needed it. Cade and Finn sped that healing up even more with our, well, what's between us now. Spending time with you, our chats during our walks, and the games we play together after supper. The way you went out of your way to give me gowns and comfortable clothing, me a total stranger to you, makes me feel…wanted? Included? I don't know the right word except to say you help to heal me, Luca, and I wish I could do the same for you."

My fingers itch to pull her close to me, to pour my damaged broken soul out to her in the hopes that she could heal me too but I know that's not possible. She thinks I'm broken because of what's been done to me but the truth is so much worse. I can't let her keep trying and I know the way she looks at me will change once she knows but it's better for her to keep her distance. It's better to keep her safe from what's inside of me. I lean towards her and let my monster out enough so that my eyes flare red. Her own grow wide but she doesn't flinch or step back as she should.

"I slaughtered hundreds, many who were innocent, in the first two years after Sebastian changed me. I drained them dry and ignored their pleas for mercy. There is no help for me."

The stubborn woman keeps a steady gaze with me not reacting at all to my confession. I'm about to snarl at her to get her to understand I am no man to be fixed when she says the one word I don't expect.

"Why?"

I lean back and shake my head. "What do you mean, why?"

"Why did you kill so many?" She asks in a maddeningly steady voice like she's asking why the sky is blue instead of why I ruthlessly killed so many.

I shove a hand through my hair to keep from shaking her and now it's my voice that's unsteady.

"The first few years after a vampire is turned they have extreme bloodlust that is hard to satisfy. It is a constant need that burns through you and nothing will ease it except feeding. It was all-consuming. The need strips everything good and moral away. The only thing left is the need to satisfy the thirst."

She arches one of her perfect dark red eyebrows.

"So what you're saying is you had absolutely no control of your actions, then?"

When my face shows my frustration of her simplifying the horrors I committed, she throws up a hand to stop me from speaking.

"Answer me this, if you could have stopped yourself from doing it, would you have?"

This time both my hands sink into my hair as I pull on it and grind out, "Of course I would have stopped myself if I could have!"

She keeps her expression neutral as she slowly nods. "So you had no control and you couldn't stop yourself but you blame yourself anyway." Her eyes narrow. "You aren't punishing yourself for what you did to those people. You're punishing yourself for choosing to say yes to Sebastian. You're punishing yourself for not choosing to die instead. You chose to live, the most basic human instinct, and you've been punishing yourself for it ever since."

She reaches out slowly as if to a frightened animal and gently caresses my cheek with the back of her fingers before whispering, "I'm so sorry for all the terrible things that happened to you, Luca but I'm glad you chose to live."

My eyes drop closed and I allow myself to lean into her touch for the briefest moment before pulling back. I push the stool away from her so I can stand and move away. It's has been so long since anyone has touched me in kindness that even her simple caress has my entire body aching in need of more. She stays silent as I work at cleaning my tools to give my hands something to do as my mind processes all that she's said. I've spent two hundred years blaming myself for all the lives I took during the bloodlust years and that won't change but put as bluntly and plainly as she put it shifts my view of it slightly. I do hate myself for not dying. I was pathetically weak when the red-eyed demon offered me the chance to live. In the moment, I barely gave a thought to the consequences of the choice. The sad truth is that had I fully understood what I would become and the atrocities I would commit, I can't say that I would have been strong enough to choose death instead.

These thoughts and feelings that I've long suppressed are like a smothering weight on me. My skin feels too tight and the room feels too small. I need to leave, go outside where there is more room, more air but I don't want to leave her. She has shifted something in me and even though I don't want to talk about this anymore, I still want to have her by my side. I lift the sack of clay to put it away and when I feel how little is left in it, inspiration hits. I lift my gaze to her and find her standing in the same spot quietly watching me with her head tilted to the side as if she's waiting for what comes next.

"Eden, would you like to go for a ride with me? I need to place another order for more clay. It's not far, just to a nearby village."

Excitement flashes across her face as she replies. "I would love that! It's been ten days since I got here and as much as I love being here with all of you, it'd be great to get out and see some different places and faces."

"Good. I think some fresh air is just what we need."

The sun is bright and the air warm so we don't bother fetching cloaks for the short ride. I have our gentlest mount saddled for her and we are soon riding towards the small village where I get my clay supplies from. We don't speak as we ride but it's a comfortable silence. After the heavy topic we spoke of in my studio I'm glad she doesn't push further and just seems to enjoy being in my company still. I wish I could have more with her but I'm resigned to just enjoying having her near in any capacity. I find myself watching her face as she studies the landscape and my lips twitch with a smile when the village comes into view and she perks up with a look of delight. I've seen the pictures of the city she lives in so I imagine that she would find the small village quaint as it's so different from what she's used to.

We've only passed the first few cottages when a trickle of unease skates along my senses. I've traveled through this village hundreds of times in the past and always received respected nods and even some smiles on occasion but today as we ride past the residents all stop what they are doing and stare, some with hostility, some with fear and some quickly gather their children and rush into their homes. As a good friend of Sebastian, the Duc de Gaul who manages these lands I'm well known to these people and this isn't the response my presence should provoke. My right hand drops to my side where I normally would have my sword strapped. I curse under my breath to find it missing. I was in such a rush to get out into the open that I did not think to arm myself. I glance over at Eden and see the delight she had has changed to confused nervousness at the way the villagers are staring at her.

I'm just about to suggest to her that we should turn around and leave when an arrow flies out and hits her horse's flank causing it to whinny loudly and launch itself into a series of hopping bucks away from me. I catch a glimpse of her shocked face but she is already too far for me to reach. My heel is a split second from striking my own mount's side to lunge after her when I'm ripped sideways from the horse's back to land hard on the dirt-packed road.

I'm on my feet in an instant and it takes barely any effort to rip the thick rope from around my upper body that was used to haul me off my horse. My eyes never leave Eden so I see the group of men that rush out and surround her horse. When one of the tallest reaches up and grabs a thick handful of her hair, using it to jerk her out of the saddle and onto the ground, my bellow of rage echoes through the village, causing many to duck and cringe including a few of the men that have quickly formed a barrier between her and me.

"My Lord! Please know that we have no quarrel with you or Duc de Gaul, but we cannot stand a witch to live, especially so close to our families!" One of the men calls out, desperation and fear thick in his voice.

My own voice is a snarl as I reply but I never take my eyes from the struggling woman ahead of me.

"She is no witch! If you harm her in any way I will slaughter every man, woman, and child in this village and then the Duc will burn it all to the ground!"

I rage at him as I move to push through the group of men. I don't know why I'm surprised when I feel knives slide into my back from behind in two different places. I know how people become the worst versions of themselves when irrational fear is involved. Eden's eyes are latched on to me as she screams my name so I keep my monster in check, clinging to the hope that I can keep her from seeing the worst of me and hating me for it. Too many blades slide into my body as I fight them off and at least one has a hint of silver in it that burns my flesh like a fiery brand but still I hold back so as to not have her witness my monster. Half the men are down when an ax buries into my side sending me staggering. I keep my eyes on Eden and see her fighting off the men holding her as my sight begins to blur. She's free of them and begins running my way when a man rushes out and swipes at her with a sword catching her in the upper arm as she spins away from him. The scent of her blood hits the air and all control I had over my monster is ripped from me as it takes over in the fury that floods through me.

Eden

I'm still trying to make sense of what the fuck is happening as two burly men drag me by the arms backwards and away from Luca who is surrounded by his own group of men. It's all happening so fast. First, my horse goes nuts under me and then some jackass rips me off it by my hair. My scalp is screaming and my hip is numb from where I landed painfully on it when I hit the ground. I don't have the first fucking clue what they want but based on how many men are surrounding Luca, I assume that they are after him for some reason. I don't panic yet because, hello, he's a goddamned vampire so any minute now he's going to start knocking some heads together. That all changes when I see blood blooming on his white billowy shirt as some motherfucker stabs him in the back right through his body. That's when I completely lose my shit and start struggling while screaming his name.

The man pulling on my right arm wrenches it so hard I'm afraid it's been dislocated. He spits at me. He literally spits on me and I feel a nasty trail of saliva drip down my cheek. His eyes are manic as he yells some shit in French at me that I don't understand until the last word he says…sorcière.

That word, that one I fucking know! I look past him and sure enough, standing with a smug fucking expression on her French bitch face is Bridgette. She gives me a sarcastic little finger wave and it's all I need to see to know that I'm going to be burned as a witch.

My eyes shoot in every direction and see a bunch of villagers staring back at me with eyes filled with fear and hate. Some stupid part of my brain wonders where the pitchforks and torches are until I crane my neck around to see where these fuckers are dragging me to and yup, there they are. A group holding torches stand in a ring around a post with ropes hanging from it and wood surrounding it. The priest glaring at me with a bible clutched in front of him like a shield is a nice touch but hell no! Not today Satan! Not today!

I manage to get my feet under me as I'm being dragged and that's enough to give me the balance I need to kick out sideways. My foot connects with the side of Spitty McSpitterton's knee and the crunch it makes when it bends to the side like no knee should ever do has a feral grin stretching across my face showing plenty of teeth. He drops down to the side releasing my arm so that I can curl myself towards the guy holding my left arm. He's not expecting me to curl right up to his chest so it's easy to swipe the dagger he has sheathed at his side and flip it as I ram it straight up under his chin. His eyes are the size of saucers and I make a grossed out face at the huge skin tag hanging from one of his eyelids and the massive wave of body odor that hits my nose while I'm pressed against him. I gag but swallow down the bile that fills my throat as he topples leaving me a clear view of the shocked lynch mob waiting for me. I can't help myself when my eyes land on the priest. I shoot him the middle finger and a saucy wink before spinning and running back towards Luca.

What I see has me screaming his name again in terror. An ax lands deep in his side sending a spray of blood out and he staggers and almost goes down.

What is he doing? Why isn't he all red-eyed and fangy to put a stop to this? His whole body is painted with blood and only half the men that surround him are down. I don't understand why he's holding back or am I seriously wrong about just how badass vampires are? Either way, I need to get to him to help because he's swaying on his feet.

I pick up the pace but movement from the corner of my eye has me spinning away from another attack.

A pained hiss comes from between my teeth as the edge of a sword catches my upper arm and slices into it. I feel the hot blood pour down my arm even as I keep spinning to deliver a roundhouse kick to Mr. Slicy, sending him to the ground. Hmm, this split skirt/pants combo isn't the worst to fight in slides across my weird-ass brain as I snatch the guy's sword up and turn back to rush to Luca's aid.

My feet slow to a stop and I decide it's best to just slow my roll and let him do his thing without getting in the way because Luca has finally put his big boy vamp pants on and he's ripping off heads...literally. I step to the side as one goes rolling past me like a demented bowling ball and take a beat to one, admire just how fucking gloriously savage the vampire is, and two, wonder why I'm not cracking up in hysterical terror at the very messy slaughter happening right in front of my eyes. I mean, I know I'm damaged but come on, most sane women would be a quivering puddle of hysteria right about now, right? Shaking my head at how messed up I am causes me to wince when a flare of pain streaks down my arm. I turn away from Luca who is finishing off the last of the dumb fucks who thought they could take him to look down and see just how bad my wound is but my eyes meet that fucking bitch Bridgette's, she is still standing between two huts but she's no longer smirking. Her eyes are huge and filled with fear as I slowly switch the sword to my injured arm and take the dagger in my right hand. It's longer and heavier than what I would normally use to throw but I'm more about making a point than scoring a death hit.

Sure enough, when the dagger reaches the halfway point in its trajectory towards her it starts to dip meaning it lands embedded in her thigh instead of her chest. She goes down with a squeal of pained surprise but freezes when I take a hard step in her direction.

"You should run," I tell her in a bland tone. "If he doesn't kill you, I probably will."

Bridgette's eyes fill with desperation as she starts crabbing her way back away from me. I leave the petty bitch to it and turn back to see Luca is the last man, or vampire rather, standing surrounded by a ring of bloody bodies. His red eyes are latched on to me and his fangs are on full display as his chest heaves. I take in the blood that's soaked his body from head to toe and pray that the majority isn't his.

I move toward him and I see him flinch back before his eyes return to their normal grey, his fangs retract and his head drops on his neck as he begins to sway on his feet. I manage to reach him just as he's about to go over and duck under one of his arms to keep him upright.

"Luca! Are you alright? Luca, open your eyes!" I beg him as I see the lynch mob from around the pyre heading our way with anger and rage in every step. I look around frantically for a way out and spot his horse not too far away so I start dragging him over towards it. My sliced arm screams in protest and I have no idea how I'm going to get him up on it but I don't know what else to do.

"Luca! Wake the fuck up! There's more coming and I won't be able to fight them all off. Luca! Please, please, I need you!" I yell into his ear.

My knees go weak when his head lifts slightly and dazed grey eyes meet mine.

"Yes! That's it, baby, wake up. We need to get out of here or we're both going to die in the next few minutes." I plead with him.

My words seem to reach him as his legs get steadier as we reach the horse. He pulls himself up into the saddle and my desperation and adrenaline give me the strength to quickly climb up behind him as he sways and almost goes over the other side after sliding the sword into a loop connected to the saddle. I'm not willing to leave it in case we need to defend ourselves again. I wrap my arms around his waist to try and keep him upright as I grasp the reins and get the horse's head turned back in the direction we came from and then jab my heel into its side to get it moving at a fast trot.

My arm is screaming in pain and I can still feel the hot blood sliding down it so I know I need to tend to it soon but all I care about is the man in front of me that I'm pressed against. I can feel his blood soaking through my shirt. I need to get us back to the house so the servants can help me get the bleeding stopped. I don't know enough about vampires to know if he's just weakened or if this is something he can die from. All the pop culture lore about vampires that I know doesn't mean shit in reality and I'm terrified he's going to die on me.

I judge we are halfway back to the house when I feel him start to tilt to the side. I clutch at him to keep him up, knowing that I won't be able to get him back on the horse if he falls but I'm barely hanging on to his heavy weight and it's just a matter of time.

Hot tears run down my cheeks as I risk a glance behind us, terrified that the lynch mob is coming after us but all I see is an empty track. That doesn't mean they're not on their way, though. I whimper at the thought of them catching up to us with Luca unconscious in the middle of the trail with nothing but me to protect him so I nudge the horse off of the trail and try and steer it into the thick trees that line it hoping we can get far enough to hide if they do pass by. Branches scratch against us and snag on our clothes but we only make it twenty feet into the woods before Luca finally tilts too far and topples from the back of the horse, hitting the ground with a thud.

I look back towards the track and pray we've gotten far enough away so we won't be found if the mob does come after us and then slide down off the horse. I lead it a little further away and tie its reins to a branch before moving back to Luca. I crash down next to him on my knees and hear a pained whimper escape my mouth at the sheer amount of blood that's pooling on his back. I bite my lip hard and shake out my arms causing my own injury to spike but I ignore it and get my head straight so I can treat my patient. That's who he needs to be to me right now. I'm a trained EMT, I can do this but not if I'm panicking so I take a deep fortifying breath and get to work. His shirt has so many holes in it from the many stab wounds that it easily shreds in my hands when I pull it off him. I toss it to the side as it's too ragged and saturated to be any help. I need to clear the blood and start applying pressure to the worst injuries so I use the only thing I have that's not already covered in blood. I quickly push to my feet and unbuckle the wide belt around my waist and then shimmy out of the full skirt. I race back to the horse and yank the sword from the loop and then back again where I go to work tearing into the fabric to make long wide strips to use as bindings. Once all the fabric has been cut down, I use a wadded-up piece to clean away as much of the blood as I can from his back. My eyes widen as I see just how many times he's been stabbed but I shove it away and focus on the deepest, widest wounds. I blink a few times in disbelief thinking that my own blood loss is fucking with my head when I see some of the smaller wounds start knitting together in front of my eyes. It takes me a minute to process that this is probably normal for a vampire but I also see that the largest gaping wounds aren't healing at all and are still bleeding freely. The worse one by far is the ax wound in his side. It's so deep I swear I can see the white of his rib bones. I'm making a tortured humming noise in my throat as I fold one of the long strips into a pad and press it against the deep gash and then work a second strip under and around him so that I can bind the pad in place.

I feel myself baring my teeth in anger that I don't have my modern kit to tend to these wounds properly. I would sell my soul right now for a few clamps and some quick clot powder. Once I have his back mostly tended to I lean back and crack my neck to the side. Now's the time to roll him so I can go to work on his front. This is going to be so much harder for me. It made it easier to focus on my work when I could pretend he was just a patient but once I turn him over I'll be able to see his face and that will go out the window. I feel tears dripping off my chin that I didn't even realize were falling and lift a hand to wipe them away but both of my hands are completely gloved in his blood so I settle for wiping my face against my shoulders. The pain in my arm is shoved to the background as I lever his body up and over onto his back. Peeling the last of his destroyed shirt away from his body, my breath whooshes out of me when I can only see three deep wounds. Fucking cowards did most of the damage by stabbing him in the back.

I blink away a wave of dizziness as I make padded dressings for the wounds and use the last of the cloth strips to bind them in place. I'm leaning over him chanting, "Please, please be ok." Softly and reach out a shaking hand to push some of his sweet chestnut curls from his face with my left hand. A small sob leaves me when a few drops of my blood that's still running down my arm trickles onto his face. It turns into a gasp when his eyes spring open and his hand comes up and locks onto my wrist with more strength than someone with his many wounds should have. His eyes pin me in place as he turns his head slightly and takes a deep sniff from my arm. The red flames start in his pupils and spread outward until all the grey of his irises and white of his sclera are a solid red. His fangs grow until they overlap his bottom lip and he growls at me. I should be terrified. This is a wounded animal at his most dangerous and he can tear me to shreds but I know with the utmost certainty that Luca will never harm me so I stay perfectly still as the tears stream down my face.

"Get away from me!" He growls out in a weak voice. "Eden, you need to run as fast as you can away from me. Right now!"

I shake my head violently. "No! No, Luca. I won't leave you. You have so many wounds and you've lost so much blood. I don't know what to do! Please, tell me how I can help you!"

He batters my wrist away from him and turns his face away from me. "You can help me by leaving. You need to start running now. I don't know how much longer I can hold it back in my weakened state. Your blood…it's driving me wild with need!"

I sob as I pull his face back towards me. "Shut up! I don't care about me. Please, please Luca tell me how I can help you. I can't lose you. Please, Luca, please don't die." I beg as my tears drip down onto his bloody chest.

His hand comes up and grips my chin tightly. "You would cry for a monster? Beg me to live? You saw what I am, what I'm capable of, and yet you don't flee for your life?"

I choke out a sad laugh through my sobs. "You idiot! You aren't a monster. I've been attacked by monsters, hurt by them. That's not who you are."

The red in his eyes dims slightly and he closes them briefly but when he opens them again they are just as bright and fierce as before. I can see how tight he's holding his jaw when he grits out, "Then don't make me one! Your blood is too close. You need to get away before I lose control and take it."

I lean back away from him and scan his body and the many wounds. Some of them are already closed up but the worst wounds are not healing at all and that's when it penetrates the fog I've been thinking through since we were attacked. He's lost too much blood to heal properly. He needs blood. He needs me.

"Take it!" I tell him in a firm tone. "Take my blood. Drink from me and heal. You aren't a monster stealing it from me because I'm giving it to you freely. Please, Luca, let me help you!" I command him and then thrust my wrist in front of his mouth.

He makes a savage snarl and I think he's going to refuse once again until his hands snap up and lock onto my wrist a few inches apart and then pulls it to his mouth. The pain barely registers before my whole body clenches and a powerful orgasm rocks through me. My head drops back as an obscene moan rings out from between my lips as wave after wave of pleasure thrums through me. I can't think, I can't speak, I can't move. All I can do is feel the fireworks that go off nonstop in my body. The only thing that would make this experience better is if his cock was deep inside of me to clench around. It goes on for what feels like a lifetime and I'm only vaguely aware of dropping bonelessly down onto his chest as my head swims through a sea of shimmering colored pleasure.

Luca

When I release her wrist and lick the puncture wounds to seal them Eden makes a small mewling sound like she's disappointed I've stopped. She's crumpled against my chest and her green cat eyes stare up at me with her pupils completely blown and hazy from the pleasure she just experienced. Conflicting emotions war inside of me as I feel the deepest of my wounds begin to knit closed. I hate this woman who pushed herself on me and gave me the same orgasmic pleasure she just had. It's been forever since I've taken another's blood offered willingly. The pleasure is so extreme that I will ache for it for decades before it finally fades again. I pull her closer and revel in the feel of another's, her body close to mine. It makes me want to weep at the love I have surging inside of me for her. I want her to be mine so badly but it will kill me to see her age and wither away as the cruel years finally take her from me.

Her arm moves slowly up her body and flops beside my head. She uses clumsy fingers to brush across my lips as a soft smile forms on her lips.

"My monster. Mine." She slurs, causing me to frown. She shouldn't be this affected by the amount of blood I took from her. I sit up quickly as I hear her heart start to slow and she tumbles down into my lap.

"Eden? Eden!"

I give her a soft shake but she's gone, sliding closer and closer to death as her heartbeat slows. This doesn't make sense. I didn't come close to draining her. Her skin is so pale it's almost translucent and her lips have a hint of blue to them. All of my strength is back thanks to the blood she fed me so I pull her up quickly, strip the bloody shirt from her body and search for a wound I didn't see before. My hand comes away wet from her upper arm where I've been holding her and I see just how deep the sword sliced into her. If she's been bleeding this whole time and add the blood I took from her, then it's not a surprise that she's close to death from blood loss.

I curse the fools that we are. Me for being too weak to refuse her and her for not tending to herself before she worked on my wounds. I lay her back down on my lap and use my fangs to cut open the skin on my wrist. I use my other hand on her jaw to force her mouth open and let the blood trickle down over her lips and into her throat. It seems to take an eternity before I hear her heartbeat pick up into a faster rhythm. Seconds later her eyes fly open and she gasps before pulling my wrist closer so she can suck at the punctures. When her eyes begin to tinge red I gently force her mouth off my wrist and lick the holes to seal them. My nerves are strung tight as I wait to see if I was in time. If she had died before my blood entered her system then she will be transitioning into one of my kind but if she was still alive then my tainted blood will replicate and spread as it works to heal her in minutes and she will only feel its intoxicating effects that will wear off eventually. If I was in time, Eden will be on a high for a few days but will eventually go back to being human but with a slightly prolonged life.

I closed the door on believing in any God while I was being tortured on the Inquisitor's rack but for this woman, I throw the door open and pray that I haven't sentenced her to an eternity of the hell I live with.

Her soft, cold fingers bring me out of my trance of pleading with God to spare her when she gently rubs them across my lips. A moan of thanks and relief leaves me when I see her clear green eyes without a hint of red in them. My lips kiss her fingertips causing her to smile a soft dreamy smile and her voice is a thick whisper when she asks,

"You're ok? You're going to be ok?"

This woman, this reckless, beautiful woman who was just moments from dying's first thought when coming back is for me and my welfare. How did I ever think I could be strong enough to resist her? I'm not and I won't. I need her in so many ways. I pull her up from my lap and crush her lips to mine. The first kiss I've had in two hundred years sends an explosion of fire through my veins and it feels like all the love, care, and kindness I've denied myself for so long fill every aching part of my heart when she moans sweetly and opens her soft lips to me and kisses me back. My hands slide down her smooth back reveling at the feel of her bare skin against my fingers and land on her hips to pull her even closer. Our lips never part as my tongue duels with hers as she wiggles and squirms until she's straddled me. Her fingers slide up into my hair and thread through it until she can use her grip to angle my head to deepen the kiss further with a whimper of need.

With her skirt and blouse gone, Eden clings and grinds against me in nothing but the thin scraps of lace that cover her mound and breasts. Her hips rock against mine, pressing her heated core against my engorged cock and sending a shudder through me. I want to consume every inch of her as she grinds us together and makes small mewling noises against my mouth. A saner piece of my brain tells me her actions are a result of the blood intoxication and that I'm taking advantage of her but I can't will myself to care when she nips at my bottom lip. With a choked snarl of lust, I thrust her to her feet so she's standing with her feet on either side of my thighs and peel the lace down her legs exposing her wet glistening Venus mound. My teeth bare at the sight and smell of her arousal and my cock throbs painfully against my breeches. When she tries to lower herself back down onto my lap I hold her thighs in a steely grip so that I can dart my face against her and swipe my tongue against her slit parting her pouty lips and across the heated core of her. She tastes like heaven as I lick up her cream. Her fingers are buried in my hair in a tight grip as she rocks her hips to grind against my mouth while making the sexiest little whimpers filled with pleasure. I could live thousands of years and nothing will ever taste as sweet as her arousal on my tongue. I trace swirls around the swollen nub of her clit and slide one of my hands up between her thighs until my fingers find her entrance. She's so wet that I easily thrust two fingers deep inside of her causing her to yell my name as her heated inside walls clench tightly around them in orgasm.

I can't wait anymore, I need to be inside of her, to feel her clamp down around my cock the way she's doing to my fingers. Keeping my tongue moving over her quivering flesh I use my free hand to open my breaches and prepare myself for her. I slide my fingers from the depths of her body causing her to gasp a sad moan of need and I smile against her core at how responsive she is to my touch. My hands on her hips guide her back down and as her knees land on cither side of my thighs I thrust my throbbing cock up into her to the hilt. Her back arches as the hot, wet velvet of her channel clamps around me like a vise. The sound that rips from me and echoes through the woods could be mistaken for an animal's it's so primal. The pleasure is so exquisite that my sight dims and my monster surges to the surface. When she rolls her hips searching for more movement, more friction my fangs elongate, eyes flare red and I thrust into her again and again. Her hands clutch at my shoulders with her nails digging into my skin as she pants my name over and over again begging me to push her over the edge of the pleasure wave she's riding. As my cock slides out of her only to slam back in my head dips down to her breasts that I've freed from the lace that was covering them. I capture one of her taut rosebud nipples between my lips and suck hard feeling her womb spasm against my cock as it feels the pull. It's so goddamn delicious that I bite down into her soft flesh with my fangs to taste her sweet blood again. It sets off an instant orgasm for her and the way her heat squeezes and milks my cock as she comes apart around me in pleasure has me tumbling over the edge with her and my hot seed fills her.

Night descends over us as I hold her tightly against me and just marvel at this incredible woman that I never want to let go of. Her sweet lips trail small kisses over my chest and up my neck until she finds my mouth. As she nibbles and sucks delicately on my lips I pray that when the drugging effects of my blood in her system wear off she'll still want me. Her green eyes slowly open and are filled with the soft haze of pleasure we shared as she stares into my eyes.

"You are so fucking beautiful." She whispers against my mouth causing me to groan in wonder at her sweetness as my cock begins to swell inside her again. I want to flip her onto her back and drive deep inside her over and over again but I won't risk her tender bare flesh against the cold rough ground of the forest. I would kill for a blanket or even a cloak to wrap her in. Our clothes are mostly shredded or saturated in blood and when she shivers in my arms I know it's not just from the hard cock inside of her. I have to get her back to the manor. Even fortified with my blood running through her veins she's susceptible to the elements and with night fallen the temperature will only continue to drop.

I wish with all my being that we could stay right here just the two of us alone in this perfect moment. I know once we return to the manor I will have to explain my actions to my brothers and Finn and Cade will be furious at how I put her in jeopardy and brought harm to her. I can only hope they will forgive me and allow me a small part of her attention in the future. I rub my thumbs gently over the bite marks they've left on her shoulders that claim her as their mate and feel a pang of guilt and sorrow that my actions this day might sever the bond we have.

As if she can read my mind, Eden dips her head down, places a hot kiss between my thumb and forefinger and murmurs huskily, "It will be fine."

Her head lifts so she can meet my gaze and she rolls her hips slightly to send me deeper inside her.

"They said they would share me with you."

My hands drop to her hips to hold her steady against me knowing we need to leave as her words penetrate my brain. Another overwhelming wave of love crashes through me that my brothers would gift me such a priceless treasure. One arm wraps around her hips and the other slides up her back so I can anchor my fingers through her hair to cup the back of her head and devour her mouth. My tongue slides between her lips and tangles with hers as she wiggles in my lap. When she breaks the kiss with a gasp it's to plead with me.

"Please, please Luca! I need you. I need you to move inside of me!" She begs.

A small smile lifts my lips at her pretty begging. "You will be insatiable for days. It's the effects of my blood in you." I tell her as a whine escapes her mouth when I hold her still.

"No! It's you, I'm insatiable for you. Please, please come with me again? I can feel your need just as much as mine." She arches her back to give herself the tiniest bit of friction against my cock buried so deep inside of her and makes a pained noise when it's not enough. I can't resist her for another moment. My hand comes around from the back of her head to tighten around her throat with my thumb brushing over the thrumming of her pulse before I drag it down between her heavy, heaving breasts, over her flat stomach and slip one of my fingers between her slit to find the swollen bundle of nerves that aches for my touch. I flick it lightly and she thrashes against the hold I have on her hips desperate for more. I'm helpless to deny her anything so I release my hold on her and lower my back to the ground not even feeling the cold seep into me as her searing heat clamps around me when she rolls her hips to a steady rhythm, riding my cock with her head thrown back. Little whimpers stutter out of her as she tries to move harder against me and as much as I'm drunk on the slower, sweeter thrill her ride gives me I can't stop myself from thrusting up hard into her. The long, drawn-out "ahhhh" she makes tells me this is exactly what she wants so I do it again and again until I feel her clamp down on me as she explodes in completion for the third time. She drops down onto my chest as she comes down from the high, making it easier for me to lock her hips in place and pinion into her until I feel my own release fill her.

As much as I don't want to let her go I know she'll be begging me to take her again in minutes so I force myself to ignore the pitiful, sexy whine she makes when I slip out of her and take us to our feet. I quickly find her blood-stained blouse from where I tossed it and her lace undergarments. I slip the bloody garment over her head and clench my teeth as the scent of her drying blood on the sleeve wafts up to me and I stuff her undergarments in my breaches so as not to lose them. The temptress is rubbing herself against me like a cat wanting to be petted as I scoop her up into my arms and carry her to my waiting horse. Once I'm settled on the saddle behind her I gather her back onto my lap sideways and guide the mount through the trees and back to the track, turning its head in the direction of home.

Eden squirms on my lap and nuzzles against my neck dragging her teeth against my skin and I'm rock hard again before we've even made it halfway back to the manor. Her mouth trails against my jaw as she takes one of my hands from the reins and presses it between her thighs.

"Luca, I need you so bad. It feels like a piece of me is missing when you aren't touching me. I've never wanted anyone as much as I want you." That devious mouth of hers slides back along my jaw and licks the sensitive skin behind my ear before nipping at my earlobe. It takes all my control not to take her for a third time right here on the back of the horse.

"I hated how you would flinch from me before. The sadness I saw in your eyes every time you looked at me broke my heart. The rare smile you would give me filled me with so much happiness." She tells me with sincerity as she presses my hand harder against her slick folds and I choose to believe she truly means her words and it's not just the intoxication speaking because I need her. I need her to love me and I don't think I can ever let her go. I pull her face to mine and kiss her with all the love that's awakened inside of me, feeling the connection and bond through our blood. When she pushes my hand even harder against her wet heat, I slip my fingers inside of her and stroke her slow and gently curving them slightly to rub against her slick walls with each slow slide. When I add my thumb to press against her clit I have to capture her mouth with mine to swallow down her cries of pleasure. Thank goodness for my well-trained mount who continues home without my guidance because I'm lost to her once again.

My horse is so steady in battle and so accustomed to my brothers in their other forms that it doesn't react when the first huge wolf steps onto the track to walk beside it down the lane that leads to the manor. I'm so lost to the scents of her sweet blood and pleasure that I don't sense them until the second wolf on the other side of my horse nips at my boot. Tearing my lips from Eden's I glance down and meet the glowing gold eyes of Cade in his shifted form. A low growl rumbles from his throat and I give him a curt nod in reply before I remove my hand from between her thighs to grasp the reins once again and nudge my horse up to a trot for the last few hundred feet to the house. Eden spots one of the wolves and grins a silly smile as she reaches out towards it.

"Pretty puppy! I want to pet it!"

The wolves peel off on both sides and race ahead disappearing into the darkness but I know they will be back to deal with me shortly.

When we come to a stop in front of the doors, Sebastian is waiting for us on the steps. His eyes narrow as he takes in the bloody state of us both and when he sniffs at the air his eyes flare red at catching the scent of her blood causing me to drop my own in shame.

Sebastian

None of the villagers will speak to us about the missing or the bodies that have been discovered. We waste a frustrating hour getting nowhere when they all claim to not know anything of what we speak of. The underlying scent of fear that hovers over the squalid village tells me that they've been warned to silence or that someone or thing has compelled them all to silence on the matter. The sheer amount of poverty and despair I see tells me that the Marquis du Corbeil is either incompetent as an overseer or a selfish uncaring one. I make a note to speak to Pierre about the state of things in this area so he may pass on the information to those who will right it. The King is well aware that taxes cannot be collected from those who have nothing to give. For all of Louis's faults, he is at least somewhat in tune with the commoners.

Giving up on learning anything from these pitiful peasants, we enter the forest and once we are far enough from prying eyes, Finn and Cade shift into their wolf forms and disappear in different directions in search of a scent trail to follow. I pack away their clothing and lead our horses to a sun-lit opening between the trees and tether them in the center far enough from the shadows that they will be safe from any newly turned vampires that can't control their bloodlust. I leave them there and begin searching the woods in a grid pattern using my supernatural speed looking for a hovel, cave, or any place a nest might be. While the sun has no danger for me and Luca due to the strength of our bloodline being so close to an Original, newly turned vampires with diluted blood will burn easily under its rays. Prolonged exposure will kill them but the pain of short exposure keeps most in the shadows during daylight hours.

Three hours later my ears pick up the excited yips of a wolf on the hunt and I turn to the west to streak in between trees until I find them. Both wolves are standing still but quivering with teeth bared towards a badly constructed hut that is made more from mud than wood. Tall trees arch over it leaving it in deep shadows that the sun can't penetrate. It's the ideal spot for a nest of newly turned vampires.

Finn shifts and gets to his feet beside me. "We picked up at least eight different scents leading here and also found four more headless bodies drained of blood. They didn't even bother trying to hide them." His eyes flare gold and a snarl comes from Cade still in his wolf form. "Two of the bodies were children. A little boy and girl, siblings based on their head's resemblance." Cade's wolf whimpers as Finn tells me, "They...played with them first before they killed them. There will be no quick death for these fiends today, Bas. We will make them beg for death by the time we're done."

As he shifts back into his wolf, I bring forth my own demon. "So be it."

We find seven in the nest all tangled up together and by the time we step out all three of us are coated in the blood we spilled, making each death more painful than the last. None of the newly turned vampires were able to answer our questions no matter how badly we hurt them, telling me they all had been compelled to silence by whoever sired them. The wolves leave me to find a stream to clean the blood from their fur. I have a change of clothing in the saddlebag on my horse that I will change into once I get back to it. Turning back to the hovel full of the dead I consider burning it to the ground but with no idea who the last vampire is or where to find them, I decide to leave a calling card instead. I pull the silver dagger that caused so many screams from the dead inside from its sheath and stab it into the wood that the door used to be connected to. My du

Gaul crest is stamped into the hilt and will let anyone who finds it know that my house is responsible for the carnage they will discover inside.

I blur at my top speed back to the horses not wanting the sour blood to dry on my skin and quickly strip my clothing and use the water from the skin attached to the saddle to wash away as much as I can before redressing in the fresh clothing I brought with me. By the time I'm done the wolves pad into the clearing and shift back into their human forms and quickly dress as well. None of us speak of what we just did with knife, fang, and teeth. We are all in agreement that our actions were justified and no more needs to be said on the matter. It's a two-hour ride back to the manor so we will arrive home after dark. We have only been riding for twenty minutes when Cade and Finn start exchanging troubled looks and nudge their mounts into a faster trot. I chalk it up to them wanting to get back to their witch faster as we continue.

The longer we ride the more bothered they seem and the faster they ride. I shake my head over the obsession they have with the woman and am about to order them to ease off the pace we are riding at when they both let out strangled cries full of pain and flog their horses into a flat-out gallop. I don't know what has happened and they've pulled too far ahead of me to ask but I trust my life with their senses so if they have a fear that something is wrong then something is wrong. I whip my horse to match their speed and hope whatever has caused their panic is not something that will irreparably damage my family.

Our mounts are lathered and heaving by the time we reach the well-lit manor and the wolves waste no time jumping from their saddles to rush in. I hear them calling out Eden's name with desperation but they race back out the door wild-eyed.

"She's not here and neither is Luca!" Cade barks out, running both his hands through his hair in worry.

"Where would Luca take her? He knows of the threat so why would he have her out after dark?" Finn snarls as his eyes search in every direction.

A hit of unease slithers down my spine as I consider the missive from Pierre might have been a way to lure us away but quickly dismiss it. The witch hasn't left the grounds since we brought her here. No one even knows of her existence. A groom comes running over to lead our horses away so I call out to him in French asking if he knows where Monsieur Soriano and the mademoiselle have gone.

He tells us that he saddled mounts for them in the late afternoon but they have not returned yet. He does not know where they have gone.

I turn and pin the two wolves with a commanding glare. "What is going on? What made you race back here with such urgency?"

They stare back at me with defiant looks but before they can answer, first Cade's and then Finn's head shoots up and they both sniff at the air. They shift so fast it's a blur and as their clothes drop they launch themselves off the steps and into the night. I stand there with my fists clenched and jaw locked at being left with no answers. I'm just about to stomp into the house and pour a large glass of brandy when my hearing picks up the sound of hoofbeats coming from down the lane so I stay put and wait. The unease I felt comes roaring back when I realize that there is only one horse coming this way instead of two. Suspicion fills my mind and I swear if the witch has done anything to harm Luca I will not hold back the demon from getting answers from her this time.

Relief fills me when Luca rides into the torch-lit courtyard and comes to a stop in front of the stairs. I can see that he's holding the witch in his lap but her back is to me. I open my mouth to demand answers when the sweetest smell of her blood hits my senses and my eyes flare red. I track the shame that crosses his features as he drops his head but I'm already striding down the steps and pulling her from his arms. I turn her to face me and with no hesitation at all she wraps her legs around my waist and her arms go around my neck. I stand as stiff as one of Luca's statues in surprised shock but when she kisses my neck my arm tightens across her back to hold her closer and the other moves down to cup her bottom. I almost swallow my tongue when my hand finds bare skin and she licks at my neck. I have no idea what is going on but a few more minutes with this sexy woman in my arms and my cock may explode so I carry her up the stairs and into the house straight to the library where I know a fire will already be lit. Her skin is like ice against my fingers no matter how hot her mouth is on my neck.

Once I have us in front of the fireplace I peel her arms and legs from my body and force her to stand on her own feet. She sways towards me with a pout on her lips that makes me want to devour her mouth with my own and stare into her lust-filled eyes as I brace her shoulders to keep the distance between us and look her over from top to bottom taking in her silky, smooth shapely legs. The hem of the bloody blouse she's wearing barely covers the junction between her legs and my fingers inch with the need to lift it that last inch so she's completely exposed to my eyes. I rip my gaze away from the tantalizing image and move them up taking in the dried blood that had saturated the fabric and see the outline of her hard little nipples against the fabric of the blouse. She moans in desire and tries to move towards me but I hold her in place. One of the sleeves droops down her arm where it's been sliced away and here is where I can smell the sweet blood that I know is hers. My thumb traces an angry red line on her arm where the sleeve has been cut away. It looks like a freshly healed injury. The pieces click into place. The healed wound, the strange sexual behavior she's exhibiting, and the blown pupils. The bloody woman is blood drunk! I push her father away from me, now knowing that it's not me she wants but any cock to satisfy the itch crawling through her mixed blood.

"Luca!"

"I had no choice." He says quietly, in a tone filled with shame.

My head swivels in his direction and I see him, Cade, and Finn standing just inside the door staring at me and the witch. I grind my teeth to try and form a reasonable reply to that as I take in his appearance.

He's bare-chested but covered in blood-soaked squares of fabric that have been bound to his body with long strips of fabric that I can only assume was once the witch's skirt. Cade reaches out and roughly turns Luca so his back faces me and my eyebrows go up at the sheer number of fabric bandages that cover his back as well as the large one sticking to his side.

"Leave him alone!"

A petulant voice whines from beside me as she…stomps her foot? All of our eyes turn to her and we find her erotically sucking on her finger. She begins trailing it down between her breasts as she pouts in my direction.

"Why do you always have to be so mean? Luca was hurt so badly and I saved him. I would do the same thing for you." She tells me, stepping toward me and looking up at me through her long lashes. "Why don't you kiss me instead? I'd like to feel your…" My hand quickly comes up to cover that sweet, tempting mouth and stop her from saying just what she'd like to feel from me. A man can only take so much.

"You will stop speaking." I compel her before sweeping her up into my arms and heading for the door. All three of my brothers block the way with frowns on their faces so I growl out, "I'm taking her to her room and compelling her to bed so we can have a proper discussion on what the hell happened today. After that you can all go and tend to the many needs she will have over the coming days. Now, move!"

The three men I call family all look away with contrition on their faces for thinking the worst of me and move aside so I can exit through the door. As I carry her down the hall her icy cold hand slips inside my shirt and she starts tracing circles around my nipple. I do my best to ignore it and bark orders to the footmen stationed at the foyer that leads to the stairs to the second level. I order a tub and hot water to be brought up and left outside her room as well as food and drink. It should be ready by the time I'm done dragging the answers I want from the three of them and they can bathe and feed her themselves. I block out what else they will be doing to her again and again until the blood she drank from Luca cools enough to mix and dilute with her own.

I drop her back on her feet once we enter her room and the door is closed behind my back. She makes to move up against me so I gently push her back a few feet.

"You will stay there and answer my questions truthfully."

A small whine sounds from her throat at being forced to do what I say.

"Summarize what happened today after you left the house with Luca."

"We went to the village to order more clay and the people there separated us, dragged me towards a post to tie me up and burn me for being a witch. They stabbed Luca so many times in the back and once with an ax in his side. I fought off the men who had me, threw a knife at Bridgette but only hit her in the leg because it was too heavy and went to help Luca. A guy sliced my arm with his sword and then Luca went all vamp and ripped heads off but he had already lost so much blood by then that he could barely stand. The torch and pitchfork mob was coming after us so he managed to get up on the horse so we could get away but he was too heavy for me to hold up on the saddle so I hid us in the trees and he fell off. I ripped my skirt apart and bandaged him up but he was so pale from all the blood loss. He begged me to leave, to run and he was so scared he would hurt me but I made him drink from my wrist and it was fucking amazing. I think I must have passed out cuz' the next thing I know I was sucking his blood from his wrist and then his tongue was in my pussy licking me and when he thrust his fingers inside me I came so hard I saw stars. Then I dropped down on his cock and…"

"Enough! Hell's bells, woman! Enough."

I drag my eyes from her and throw both hands up through my hair to try and keep my head from popping off at the visual she just painted. I swallow hard and reach down to adjust the beast in my pants that is straining to be free. Movement has me looking back to her just as she whips the bloody shirt over her head and tosses it to the side. I take in her full breasts with pink rosebud nipples begging to be sucked on, the matching bite marks on her shoulders, and the four moons branded under one breast in a glance. Her eyes have locked on to the bulge between my legs and she bites her lower lip as she starts to pant in need while one of her fingers slips inside her bare mound and most of my control cracks straight through.

"It's so hot in here. You should take off your pants." She moans. "I'd lick your cock like a lollipop and swallow your cream straight down."

I have her pulled against me, crushed against my chest in less than a breath. My mouth hovers over hers as one hand slides down and roughly drags her soft rounded ass closer so she's pressed hard against my throbbing cock. I manage to stop myself from going any further as my brother's faces flash before my eyes. I growl down at her.

"You will answer my questions truthfully." I see her brow furrow at the command she can't refuse.

"Where are you from?"

"Seattle."

"What year?"

"2028."

"Why did you come here, to this time?"

"I didn't have a choice."

"How do you go back?"

"I don't know."

"Are you a witch?"

"No!"

"Do you have plans to harm or hurt me, Luca, Finn, or Cade?"

I see the hurt flash through her eyes and know she will remember this after the intoxication fades but I need to be sure.

"Never."

I slide my thumb over her bottom lip and her tongue darts out to give it a little lick and I just can't help myself from asking one more question.

"Would you really let me drink from you willingly?"

"In a heartbeat, and so much more."

A shudder rolls through me at her whispered words and the lust that has filled her gaze again. The strain of stopping myself from taking everything she's offering is staggering. My voice shakes as I order her, "Go to the bed and stay in it until your men come in. They will fulfill your every desire."

She turns and walks to the bed giving me the perfect view of her rounded hips and biteable bottom. When she reaches it she lays her chest on it and lifts that ass in the air on her tiptoes so that her wet sex peeks out at me, wiggles it in my direction and then sends me a smoldering look over her shoulder.

"And you? Will you fulfill my every desire too?"

Words refuse to form so I turn and quickly leave the room like hell hounds are on my tail.

Finn

The three of us wait for Bas to return without speaking. Cade is prowling the room with a dark scowl on his face, Luca sits on the edge of his chair with his head down in his hands, defeat and shame clear in every line of his body. I pour myself a glass of Bas's brandy and down it in one go with a shudder. I keep telling myself that Eden is fine to keep my wolf calm but it only keeps the rage barely contained.

The bond we have with her through the claim mark isn't as strong as it will be eventually with more care and tending but it was strong enough to feel a trickle of her fear and panic and when that trickle began to fade and disappear completely it left a spike of pain as emptiness filled the space. It doesn't matter that it came back. The few moments it was severed will haunt me and Cade forever.

It didn't matter to us that we had only known her for a short time when we marked her as ours. We've been with many, many women and shared the majority of them but Eden is different. She blew into our lives like a breath of sweet air we didn't know we needed and at first captured our interest and lust but it quickly changed to love as we learned how strong, kind, and open she would be with us. She had suffered the same loss of family that we did and understood the depths of that sadness we carry.

Eden felt like a long-missing piece of our souls and we both knew immediately when we had her pressed between us, skin on skin, that she was what we needed to be complete.

Sebastian will rant and rave over our marking her as our mate so quickly but I know she's affected him as well even though he would try to hide and deny it.

I look over at my suffering brother and wish I could hear what happened so we can find a way to reassure him but I know he won't speak to us until Bas is back in the room. He's been broken since we met him and I know without a doubt Eden will be the one to mend him and give him back the love and happiness he's lived so long without.

Cade growls low in his throat and kicks a stool out of his way, causing Luca to flinch but he never lifts his head, locked in the misery he's feeling. I catch Cade's eye as he passes by on his next pace and one look and a tilt of my head towards our brother has his expression softening. We both move as one to stand behind the vampire and we each place a hand on one of his shoulders. As much as our brother does not like to be touched, he needs this connection with us right now. We still don't speak, we just stand with our hands on him, showing him that he has our support and love. He is pack and his pain is our pain.

When Sebastian slams into the room his normally perfectly groomed hair is standing in every direction as if he's plowed his fingers through it repeatedly and his eyes are a little wild. I work very hard to conceal the grin that wants to form. If anyone needs a little shaking up it's Bas.

Where Luca desperately needs to be mended, cared for, and loved, Bas needs the rigid control and ice he's formed around himself shattered. I know right down to my toes that with time, Eden will tear all of that away and rebuild him into the man that I catch glimpses of now and again when he lets his guard down.

I hear Cade smother a laugh and know he's thinking about how hard that control must have been for Bas to hang onto with our sexy mate blood-drunk and begging to be pleasured. The next few days will be an orgy of sin as we soothe the sexual intoxication the heated blood running through her veins is causing her to feel. Cade and I have both been through it ourselves three times as Bas shared his blood with us to solidify our pack bond and elongate our lives. The bloody vampire was smart enough to plan each time so that we were in a brothel full of willing women that we fucked our way through for the days it took to mix our blood fully.

With my hand on his shoulder, I feel Luca tense as a shudder ripples through him. With one hard squeeze to let him know I'm here for him, both Cade and I step back so he can get to his feet and face Sebastian who is now pinning him with his signature cold glare. His voice comes at Luca like a whip.

"What were you thinking? You know very well what could have happened. Is that what you want for her? To spend years under the curse of bloodlust? The woman she is today would be erased completely by the acts she would commit under that curse. You yourself should know that better than anyone!"

Luca's face pales even further at the thought of that happening to our woman and he shakes his head.

"No! Of course I don't want that for her. I didn't know she had lost so much blood from her wound before I drank from her! I am lost as to why she wouldn't have bound it before she tended to me. I never would have taken from her if I had known. I was weakened…I was weak. I am sorry."

His head drops again but Bas is not having it.

"Yes, weakened! Why is that? We've battled side by side against seasoned soldiers and you've come away with hardly a scratch so tell me, Luca, how is it that a puny gathering of peasants managed to overcome you and cause such damage?" He waves his hand toward the multitude of fabric patches Eden used to bandage his many wounds. "You look like the seamstress's pincushion! How is that even possible when you are capable of slaughtering a mob in minutes?" He spits out, practically snarling.

Luca's head drops again and his shoulders sag without answering. He stands there in front of his sire unable to answer for himself so I do it for him.

"Aye then, he dinnae want her to see. He dinnae want Eden to see the demon at work," I say quietly.

Bas's gaze tracks between me and Luca before his mouth tightens and he sighs deeply.

"So her opinion of you was worth more than her life? They were going to burn her as a witch! I don't even know how they would get that idea in the first place. Someone tell me who this Bridgette is?"

My whole body tenses when I remember Eden saying something about that a few days ago. I curse under my breath at not following up but the blame is not only mine so I bite back at him.

"Och aye now, how would anyone get the idea in their heids that the woman is a witch when Your Grace only ever refers to her as such in front of all who can easily hear? Tell me, your Grace, have you ever used her proper name? It's a bloody wonder that there hasn't been a fecking mob at our doors sooner!"

I see the guilt flash in his eyes and the twitch of his jaw as my point hits home.

"Bridgette is our fault, aye. She was one of the maids who we had a...dalliance with, ye ken. She turned jealous and spiteful when Eden became ours. Eden told us of the woman's accusation but we didn't put much stock in it being an issue. Aye, we should have known a woman scorned is a dangerous, devious foe."

Sebastian scrubs at his face and then rolls his head to crack his neck.

"Don't think I didn't notice the mate marks you left on her body." He tells Cade and me with a frustrated sigh. "Why would you do that to her? What happens if someday you find your fated mates? You know how that will destroy her!"

Cade shakes his head. "It won't matter. We will reject it. Eden is and always will be the only mate for us. We love her and we will chase her through time if that's what we need to do to keep her."

Bas shakes his head. "You are fools."

"Better to be fools in love than a cold bastard alone." Cade shoots back, causing me to cringe slightly. He always has been the hotter head of the two of us.

I wait for Sebastian to go at him but he just sighs again and turns his gaze to settle on Luca once more, looking him up and down before pulling the dagger he wears at his hip.

Cade and I tense as he walks the few feet between them but we don't interfere. We trust our Alpha to always do what's best for our pack.

Luca tenses as well but keeps his head down, waiting for whatever punishment his sire is about to enact.

I swallow my relief when Bas only slices through the bindings covering Luca's chest and back and peels off the dried on pads. All of his wounds are closed except for the largest gash that looks raw and angry against his ribs. Our brother was truly depleted for the wound to have not closed completely by now. Bas braces a hand on Luca's shoulder and raises his wrist to the man's mouth.

"Replenish yourself. Based on the state of the wi…Eden, when I left her, you will need it to survive the next few days."

Luca's head shoots up and he immediately starts shaking his head. "I couldn't, I don't deserve to be…"

Cade cuts him off. "Aye, you bloody well do and will! Stop being so fucking daft! The lass saw all that you are and still almost died to save you. She needs you, so drink up. I'm afeared even Finn and my prowess won't be enough to satisfy the beast raging between her legs right now but we will endeavor to do our very best by her." He ends with a cheeky grin and eyebrow wag.

Bas just keeps a steady gaze with him. "Go to her. She wants you, blood-drunk or not."

I pour myself another drink to fortify myself for what's to come and watch as the gaping injury in Luca's side stitches itself back together as he drinks from Bas's wrist. When he steps back and his eyes return from red to grey he shoots both Cade and me a grateful look.

"Thank you, brothers. I feared you would not forgive me so easily for putting her in danger."

"Yeah, yeah, wash that dried blood off quickly and join us. Your punishment awaits. By the time Eden's finished with you, your cock will be begging for reprieve." I tell him with a grin.

He nods softly with the smallest of bemused smiles on his face and with one more heartfelt look in Sebastian's direction leaves the room. As Cade and I make to go as well, I look to Bas over my shoulder.

"You know you could join us, right? She would welcome you in her bed just as much as she welcomes us."

A sardonic smile crosses his face as he shakes his head. "No. If I ever end up in her bed it will be when she is clearheaded and of sound mind. Besides, I believe I have a village to raze this night."

I pause and consider that for a moment and then finally nod. "Be sure to send our regards to Bridgette when you find her."

The cold smile that lifts his lips has me shivering slightly as I leave but I'm in full agreement with his plans. I know he will compel the truth from the villagers first, in order to spare the innocents, before he metes out the retribution those that would kill and harm ours based on rumor and superstitions deserve.

As he said earlier, so be it. I'm a firm believer in the "You reap what you sow" mindset.

Cade is waiting for me outside her door when I arrive. I step around the tub and buckets of steaming water filling the hall. We will bring it all in after we see her first. At my nod, he pushes open the door and her sweet moans and gasps reach our ears.

She's splayed out on the bed completely naked with her back arched as her fingers work between her legs in a frantic motion. I can't help the choked groan I let out at the tempting site and my cock surges painfully against my breeches. Her upper body snaps up into a seated position as her eyes zero in on us.

"Thank fuck! I've got a WAP in need of all the hard cocks. Get the fuck over here and fill me up, boys!" She calls to us in desperation.

I don't know what a WAP is but we definitely have the hard cocks handled so we both dive towards her.

Eden

I wake with a wince and groan at the various pains all over my body but the largest ache by far is in between my legs. If a pussy could cry, mine would be bawling. I shift slightly, causing me to gasp at the pain and then choke on the tainted sex aroma that fills the room. What the hell did I do? The question prompts a slide show of one obscenely indecent image after another to flash through my mind. Cade and Finn both inside me at the same time with Luca's cock deep in my throat. Luca buried in me from behind as I rode Cade's face and sucked Finn off. On and on it goes in every possible position and combination. I whimper at the memory of the sounds I made, the grunting like an animal and begging always for more. I have no idea how long it went on but I think it must have been days. Jesus, I think I put every porn star on earth in my time to shame with my performances. And those men! Those fucking sex-god men just kept on at it with hard cocks on demand.

I turn my head slowly to the right and my eyebrows shoot up when I see Cade and Finn tangled up together with Finn as the big spoon. I bite my lip to keep in the laugh but quickly stop when a flash of throbbing tenderness tells me my lips are also swollen and sore from the amount of action they got. I shift my head to the left to see Luca splayed out on his back with one arm tossed over his eyes as if even in sleep he can't face one more orgasm and I'm like, same bae, same. I turn back to stare up at the ceiling and try and swallow some of the embarrassment down as my cheeks flame but I'm so fucking dry I feel my throat close up. I have vague memories of the wolves feeding me nibbles of food in between rounds of sex but I can't remember the last time I drank anything. As much as I know it's going to hurt, I need to get out of this bed and find some water.

I press my swollen lips together to stifle the groans as I shimmy straight down to the end of the bed and climb over the footrest to the floor. I stand perfectly still in a hunched crouch as I wait for the pain in my pussy to subside enough to stand fully. I look around the room and see the tub in one corner so move across to it. The water is cool to the touch but that only helps as I hold a saturated cloth gently against my lady bits and try to clean up without moaning in pain.

I drop the cloth back into the tub and go in search of water I can drink but all I find is a carafe of red wine with only an inch left in it. I need water or I might not make it. I can't stand the thought of getting fully dressed as my overly sensitive skin is screaming at me to not do it but I can't just walk around naked in my search for water either. As gently as I can I slide my bathrobe on and tie it tight to keep everything covered and slip out of the room.

I think it's morning but I can't be sure with all the time I've lost during the orgy marathon party I just hosted so I head to the morning room in hopes of finding water, water, water, and then coffee and some food. As I descend the stairs I offer up my soul to Satan for an ice pack and a bottle of Advil. Sorry, Jesus, I don't think you taking the wheel will cut it on this one.

My nose picks up the smell of food and coffee the closer I get to the morning room so I try and pick up the pace but the Notorious V.A.G. screams "Fuck no, bitch!" so I just whine a little with each step.

My eyes land on the table full of everything I need right now so I'm halfway across the room before I realize Sebastian is sitting at the head of the table in his usual place. I come screeching to a stop and imagine I look like a deer in the headlights of an oncoming car. My eyes go big and wide when they meet his and I remember…and then they slam closed and squeeze tight as waves of well-deserved embarrassment and shame wash over me. I can't believe I said, did…fuck, kill me now!

"I imagine you are in great need of sustenance…Eden. Please, join me and eat and drink your fill."

I crack one eye open with an eyebrow raised at not only his kind tone but also him using my name. I don't think he's ever said it before. My desperation for water outweighs my shame right now so I move to my seat and gingerly lower my abused body down to it, trying to suppress the ah-ah-ah-ah that is stuttering through my head. I finally settle on the hard surface and slide a fake tight smile on my face for him before snatching the filled water glass in front of my plate and guzzling it until every drop is gone. I set it down and search the table for a jug to refill it but instead swipe the one Sebastian holds out to me and chug it as well. A huge sigh of relief gushes out of me as I feel the water doing its magic all through my body. I still hurt like a motherfucker but at least I'm less foggy. When I motion to hand the empty glass back to him, I have to avert my eyes from his when I see just how amused he is by my state. I know words will need to be spoken about what happened between us but I just can't right yet so I reach for food instead to delay it.

"You know, a few drops of Luca's blood would heal your…pains." He tells me in such a casual way that he could have been telling me the weather forecast. I have just shoveled a forkful of eggs into my mouth so I almost choke on them as I frantically shake my head. There's no way in hell I would survive another marathon of whatever Luca's blood did to me the first time. The asshole covers his mouth to hide what I know is a smirk and shakes his head.

"No, no, not to drink. Applied directly to the…area…will result in rapid healing. It won't intoxicate you the way drinking it does."

I groan out a laugh of disbelief at how awkward as fuck this is.

"Is that what we're calling it? Intoxication? Because I'm pretty sure it was more like being possessed by a sexual deviant demon and a priest should have been called to exorcise it!" I tell him with an eye roll.

I clear my throat to get on with the killing the elephant in the room bit but Finn, Cade, and Luca all walk in, causing my face to turn bright red and my mouth to clamp shut. I keep my eyes down on my plate as each one of them comes to me and kisses me on the top of my head before taking their seats.

Silence fills the room as I keep staring down not quite brave enough to look at their faces until Luca clears his throat and speaks.

"Eden, I hope you will be able to forgive me someday, both for what happened in the village and after with our blood exchange. I…"

I cut him off completely when I throw a hand up in a stop motion. I breathe in and out a few times and then take a gulp of my coffee as everyone at the table waits to see how I'm going to react to him.

Once I've drunk half of the coffee in my cup I slowly lower my hand and turn to look down the table at him. His expression is filled with misery and his eyes are pleading. I'm barely dealing with my own issues right now and I don't have the bandwidth to navigate all his dark, self-torture-filled baggage so I lay it out as clear as I can.

"Luca, you will never apologize to me again unless I tell you that you need to. If you can't believe my words, if you don't believe my actions and if what we did together over the last..." I turn to Cade with an eyebrow raised and the cheeky arsehole holds up three fingers with a cocky grin. I close my eyes briefly at the sheer madness of fucking for three days straight and then look back to Luca and continue. "Three days meant nothing to you then you are a fool that can't be helped. Build a goddamn bridge and get...the...fuck...over...it! Once I recover, you are welcome in my bed as much as you are already in my heart."

I lift my eyebrows, daring him to dismiss my words but thankfully I seem to have gotten through to him because he only nods slowly with the faintest smile tugging on his lips.

I go back to ignoring them all and lift my cup to finish the coffee in it.

"Well now, that couldn't be clearer, however, if you could, Eden, clarify what exactly is a WAP?" Cade asks with that same cocky smile plastered across his face.

I have to clamp my lips together to stop from spraying the table with my coffee at the unexpected question. I close my eyes again as the memories assault me of me standing on the bed chanting out WAP to an impromptu cheerleading routine with the three of them waving their dicks at me as they cheered me on. Fuck…my…life so hard right now.

I don't even bother opening my eyes as I grind out, "Worship and prayer, boys. Worship and prayer."

"Hmmm, well we certainly worshipped you but I'm not sure about the prayer part."

"Just fucking go with it, ok?" I groan out - hoping we can let it go for now. Finn rubs my back from beside me and takes pity on me by changing the subject.

"Did you manage to sort out the village?"

My head pops back up and my eyes move between him and Sebastian with a frown and see the grim look cross the Alpha vamp's face as he nods.

"I did. The estate manager has already put out the word that we are accepting new tenants."

A shiver of unease slithers into my belly as I ask, "You did what now?"

His gaze lands on mine and I swallow at the amped-up ice in his eyes. "Let's just say I evicted most of the village to make room for more loyal vassals."

I gape at him and then jerk my head. "Ha! Do you think I'm stupid? I know evicted is code for slaughtered. There were women and children in that village!"

His eyes narrow at my unsaid accusation.

"Do you think me a monster? To be clear, I am, but not that kind of one. I compelled all of them and separated the innocent from the guilty. I don't know how things work in your time but here there are consequences to trying to murder people without trial. It's bad enough what they planned to do to you but Luca is well known to all there. He's known to be my family and under my protection. That they dared to lay hands on him, stab him seventeen times, no, that could not be left unpunished. They did all of that based on the word of a spiteful little wench and never once brought their concerns to me. No, that could not stand."

I glare at him, wanting to dispute that those men didn't deserve to die but I can't. I saw the damage they did to Luca. They stabbed him in the back over and over again and never once tried to justify their reasoning.

"What did you do to Bridgette?"

"I fired her, in an eternal sort of way. Save your sympathies, she was compelled to answer for stirring that pot and confessed it was for jealousy and envy not from any true belief that you were a witch."

The memory of him compelling me to answer his questions in my room flashes through my mind causing me to hit him with my own icy tone.

"Neat trick, that compelling thing. You sure like to use it an awful lot. Tell me, Sebastian, did you get all the answers you were hoping for with me or would you like to ask a few more?"

His eyes shift away from mine and I swear I see a hint of guilt in them. His tone softens with his reply. "No, no need. I know all I need to in regards to you. I'm...I'm sorry I doubted you."

I stare at him for a few more beats and then turn away and push back my chair. I can't hide the wince from the pain as I push to my feet and turn toward the other three.

"I need to go decontaminate my room from the funky sex smell. Then I need a bath and to sleep. You should all know that the pleasure palace is closed for business, the gates are pulled and the door is barred for at least a week. Keep your man parts to yourselves until I say otherwise and the first one of you that brings up anything that happened over the last three days will be cock blocked for double that amount of time."

I'm sure my little speech would have more punch if I could look any of them in the eye but I'm clinging to the last scrap of my dignity here so it will have to do. I grab my empty water cup and scan the footmen standing against the walls until I spot one holding a jug and wave him over. He starts in surprise but scurries toward me. When he's close enough that I can see there's water in the jug I try and take it from him which results in a slight tug-a-war until I growl at him and he releases it. I square my shoulders and try to sail out of the room with a straight back and head held high but it hurts too fucking much and I end up limping toward the door instead with pathetic little whimpers escaping my mouth with each step. I've almost made it out when the Alpha-hole calls out to me.

"Eden, I meant to ask, can you tell me what a lollipop is?"

I freeze to the spot with my back to him as that memory hits me. I wedge the cup under my arm that's holding the jug of water and toss up the middle finger over my head back to him. He won't know what it means but it makes me feel the tiniest bit better. As I start walking again, I mutter under my breath, "Should have just let me burn at the stake. It would have been less painful than this."

By the time I make it up to my room with the cup and water jug clutched against my chest, tears are falling down my face as the pain between my legs kicks up to the next level. I almost sob in gratitude when I shoulder open my door and see someone has opened all the windows to clear the air, changed the sheets on the bed, and replaced the cold water in the tub with fresh steamy water. There is seriously something to be said about having enough money to pay for servants. I plan on kissing each and every one of them once I stop being a sex maimed cripple. I pour another glass of water and down it, refill it again and set it on a small table beside the tub, strip off my robe, and carefully lower myself into the water. I almost scream when the hot water hits my mangled crotch but manage to taper it off to a keening noise. Once I'm fully submerged up to my neck I decide I probably won't be able to get back out without help so hopefully someone comes around to check on me in the next few days before I resemble a raisin.

I'm only in the tub for about ten minutes when I hear the door open. I crack one eye and stay relaxed as Luca comes over and lowers himself to his knees behind my head.

"Let me tend to you." He says softly so I barely nod and lose myself to his talented artist fingers as he washes my hair and massages my scalp. He then runs a sponge with the crumbly rose-scented soap over my arms and legs. I'm a boneless heap in the water by the time he's done and without saying a word he lifts me from the tub bridal style and gently lays me down on the bath sheets he's spread over the bed. He rubs the water from my long hair and pats my skin dry before lifting me again, tossing the damp sheets away and sliding me under the blankets. I feel the bed dip when he joins me and the heat of his body is comforting as I slide into sleep but when I feel his fingers slip between the folds of my pussy I cry out for him to stop.

"No, baby. Please, it hurts too much for more." I say as I reach for his hand to stop him.

"Shh, mi alma, I will make the pain go away."

I want to tell him that an orgasm is NOT the cure-all with women but I catch the coppery scent of blood in the air and realize he's doing what Sebastian had awkwardly suggested earlier so I let him continue, ready to try any home remedy, even blood magic to ease the pain in my cootch. At first, the heat of his touch sizzles painfully and I cry out and try to wiggle away but he bands an arm around me and holds me tight against him as he whispers soothing words in Spanish to me. The burn turns into a warm glow causing the pain to leave me completely and when he slides those fingers up inside of me and gives them a swirl I arch my back as that glow turns into an explosion of need. His mouth drops down onto mine and he hungrily swallows all my cries. When he pulls out of me I clench so hard I'll do anything to have him back inside of me. Who knew Luca had the keys to the gates of the pleasure palace all along? I feel his long hard shaft pressing against my leg and I decide I'm open for business after all. My hand sneaks down under his waistband to wrap around him and slide over his silky smooth length, causing a rough exhale to rush out of him.

I nip his bottom lip between my teeth and when I release it, breathe out the words, "I need you inside of me."

His pants are off and he's nudging down between my thighs in a blink. I stare deep into his gorgeous grey eyes that seem to have fewer shadows than before as he slowly slides into me inch by torturous inch. My knee comes up to give him a deeper angle that sends sparks through my body but as much as I try and rock up towards him he holds me still and continues the slow, sweetly torturous pace of sliding in and out of me. He's not fucking me this time, he's making love to me. His whispered words confirm it.

"Mi alma, you are my soul, my heart. I love you and will for all the days of my existence."

My eyes roll back at the pleasure that fills me from both his movements and words. The small prick of pain on my neck is fleeting as the slowly building wave of ecstasy crests and crashes over me. As my body goes limp under him I barely hear the compelled words he whispers as my eyes flutter shut.

"Sleep my heart, sleep."

Sebastian

I keep myself away from the manor more and more over the next few weeks. I find excuses to visit court and oversee the management of the vassals that inhabit my lands. I'm finding it harder and harder to be around the four of them as the love they all share burns as bright as a flame. I lie to myself often that I'm not jealous but too many times I find myself wishing for her smile to come my way or the little touches and kisses she frequently shares with them to be with me as well. Sleep eludes me most nights and the sounds of her moans, cries, and screams of pleasure echo in my head. I don't know why she haunts me so when it's been a millennium since I made the choice to lock such wants and needs away. I watched too many loved ones wither and die of old age and I won't go through the pain of that again. The brief decades she will be ours is not worth the cost of centuries of grief, loss, and pain that we will all have to live with when she dies.

Luca and I can extend her life somewhat with our blood but it doesn't work the same way for humans as it does for the wolves They already had supernatural blood and extended lives. At best, we could only extend her lifespan by forty years or so, a blink of an eye for immortals. That's not even taking into account the real possibility that she could disappear right before our eyes and return home to her own time. I'm terrified of giving myself over and allowing myself to love her for I'm certain the loss of her will break me for good. My hesitation and absences are causing distance between my brothers and me and that I can't allow so when the invitation is delivered, I call them into the library to discuss it.

"It appears the Marquis du Corbeil has found my calling card," I tell them as I hand the invitation to Finn to look at and pass on to the others. "A small intimate affair means it will be at least fifty of the more adventurous members of the nobility. I'm inclined to accept. It will be the perfect opportunity to sniff out if he does have a pet vampire or if he's the one on a leash." I wait until they are looking expectantly at me to continue before I broach my idea. "I would like Eden to go on my arm."

"That is not bloody happening!" Cade snarls.

"Bas, be serious. The moment the plates are cleared the orgy will begin!"

"I think you should ask her and let her decide," Luca says in a calm voice.

"Ask me what?" Eden says as she steps into the room with a book in her hand. When none of us answer her she frowns. "Ask me what?" She asks again with impatience.

I come around the table and take the invitation from Luca's hand and pass it to her. She looks it over and hands it back.

"Pretty but I don't read French any better than I speak it so…"

I hesitate again wondering if I'm making a mistake but one glance at my brothers reminds me of what they all have with her and how I'm now on the outside.

"It's an invitation to a dinner soirée. The man hosting it is the Marquis du Corbeil. We think he may be dealing with vampires and if so we need to put a stop to it."

Her eyebrows shoot up as a grin tugs at her lips. "Oooh, it's like spy versus spy. Cool! What's it have to do with me and what do you need to ask me?"

"I would like you to attend with me, as my guest," I tell her.

Cade jumps in before she can answer.

"It's not a good idea, lass. The Marquis is a known deviant. His soirées often end in orgies if rumors are to be believed. It's not something you want to be exposed to."

She blinks at him a few times and then throws her head back with a laugh. "Yeah, my delicate sensibilities probably can't handle seeing such scandalous behavior. I mean, it might give me ideas on how to navigate a three-day orgy of my own. Oh, wait! Been there, done that." She rolls her eyes at him and turns back to me. "Sure, it would be fun to get out and do something different as long as no one is coming at me with pitchforks and torches. I'll pass on joining the orgy but otherwise, what do you need me to do?"

"Look beautiful on my arm, dance with me, and smile. There shouldn't be any danger or much intrigue. It's merely a chance to get a feel for the host and possibly sense any other vampires that might be around. I would keep you perfectly safe and we would depart before things degenerated to any group activities that are planned."

"Ahh, so you want me to be your arm candy to distract from your snooping. Got it, I'm in!"

"Eden, I don't know if this is a good idea." Finn steps in and takes her hand bringing it to his mouth to drag his lips over her knuckles. Her eyes narrow at him and she pulls away.

"Why? Don't you trust your Alpha to keep me safe? And let's not forget that I can hold my own against most threats. What's your problem with this?"

He holds up his hands. "Of course we trust Bas with your safety and also your fighting skills but you don't even speak the language. We're just afraid it will make you uncomfortable in that setting, not knowing French or the customs of this era."
She shrugs one shoulder. "Well, not speaking French works to my advantage then. I won't be engaged in idle chit-chat that could give away my lack of knowledge and it will also help sell me as the vapid side piece on his arm that will be dismissed as not a threat. Seriously, I think I'll be fine but I'll need some help from you guys before we go. Um, one of you will need to teach me the proper dance styles of this time." She looks back at me with an excited gleam in her eyes. "You should take a look at the gowns Luca had made for me and pick the one that will best suit this type of party because I have no clue."

I glance over to my brothers to check their reaction and see that they seem to be resigned to her going before I answer.

"I will speak with the seamstress and have a new gown created. This type of soirée hosted by this type of man will require a more…revealing type of gown - If you are comfortable with that?"

A big grin spreads across her face and she wiggles her eyebrows while doing a little hip wiggle.

"Yes! Dress up time!"

She turns away from us to return her book to one of the shelves and I can't stop watching the swaying motion of her hips as she does a walking dance while singing, *"I'm bringing sexy back. Them other boys don't know how to act."*

Luca, Finn, and Cade watch her with bemusement but the love they have for her shines clear in their gazes. I force myself to turn away and ignore the pang of exclusion I feel. I have a seamstress I need to see to discuss a dress that will have all eyes on Eden so I can move freely and discover what I need to know. The only issue will be if I can tear my eyes from her as well.

Eden

I spend the next few days walking around in a cloud of love filled with unicorn sparkles. Sometimes it is hard to believe that only a month ago I was on my knees in my shower sobbing over how sad and empty my life was. I feel like a completely different woman than that hot mess. It's amazing how the love of three men can change everything. I don't even care about the lack of indoor plumbing anymore. Modern conveniences are great and so is being a modern woman with all the rights that go with that but the way these men care for me, tend to me, love me, and want to protect me mends the damage to my soul like no therapist ever could. I feel…free and complete like I never have before. I never want to go back to the time, place, or woman I was.

The only bump in my new life is Sebastian. I see how he's distanced himself from the wolves and Luca and I hate that I feel a little like Yoko Ono breaking up the band. I was thrilled at Sebastian's invitation to go with him to this dinner party or soirée as they call it. It's a chance to build a stronger bridge between us. It's not that I expect him to jump into my harem dick first or anything, even though there's always been an underlying sexual tension between us. It's more that I hate that he's excluding himself from the new dynamic. He rarely stays long with us in the library after supper when we play cards or other games and I always catch a hint of sadness when he leaves us to our fun. The coldness he treated me to from the start has eased and he hasn't referred to me as a witch since the whole village incident. I know his suspicions of me were cleared up when he compelled the answers he wanted from me that night but I'd like more than to just exist in the same house with him. If possible, I'd like to be friends at the very least. The hot picture of him crushing my naked body against his and the rock-hard bulge pressed against my pussy flashes through my mind as I try unconvincingly to tell myself I want to be friends with him.

I step through the training room doors and find Luca, Finn, and Cade waiting for me for my final dance lesson before the party tonight. I wish Sebastian would give me a hint on what the dress will look like but all he's been willing to say so far when pressed is that it will be daring. For all I know that could mean a hem above the ankle. The bugger won't even tell me what color it will be. I smile as I step into Luca's arms, Finn hits play on my phone and Lindsey Stirling's haunting violin strains fill the room.

Most of the dances they've taught me are based on the traditional waltz so they haven't been too hard for me to pick up. It's the one that has constant shifting partners that I'm struggling with but Luca assures me that I can choose to sit that one out without anyone noticing. The song finishes with Luca dipping me back over his arm and he takes the opening to run his mouth up the stretched column of my neck causing me to giggle. When he tips me back onto my feet he flourishes an elegant bow towards me.

"You are ready. Every man present will want to claim a dance with you." He tells me.

"Which you won't accept!" Cade snaps out.

I tilt my head in his direction and send him an amused smile. "No worries, wolf boy, my dance card is completely filled with all of you."

I shake out my arms and hands trying to shake off the creeping anxiety of messing up somehow and embarrassing Sebastian in some way. I'm excited to go but filled with nerves all the same. I bounce on my feet in place feeling the need to move and burn some of it off so I stride over and swipe my phone from Finn and scroll through my playlists looking for the right song. When I land on the one that will work, I hit the guys with a devious smile.

"My turn! You taught me how to dance your way now it's my turn to teach you boys some moves."

I hit play and Bang Bang by Jessie J and friends begins playing. Flashing an "I dare you" smile I pull Finn to his feet and start dancing, my hips rolling to the beat. My hands on his hips help him get into the motions and I soon have Cade grinding up behind me like a pro club player. I spin away from them with a few thrusts so my arms can lift above my head and sway as I lose myself to the fun beat but seconds later Luca is there pulling me so close that our hips roll as one in a sexy Spanish dance style. The man has mooooooves! By the time Britney is banging out Toxic my nerves are gone, the four of us are shaking our asses and howling with laughter as Cade pretends to hump Finn's leg to the beat and Luca thrashes an air violin to match the songs iconic sound.

I spin with my arms in the air and my hips rolling and jutting and catch sight of Sebastian standing in the door watching us. I dance my way over to him mouthing the words teasingly to him, point a finger, and curl it back in a come hither motion. I feel a thrill when his eyes drop to my rolling hips and a small sexy smile pulls on his lips. I just know if I can break through his iron control and get him to join us for some fun everything will shift back into balance between all of us but he just shakes his head.

"I find myself disappointed this style of dance won't be in vogue for quite some time I'm sure." He tells me. "Nonetheless, I look forward to dancing with you tonight in the more sedate style of this time." He lifts heated eyes back up to mine and tips his head slightly. "Madam Claudette awaits you to begin the ministrations to prepare you for our outing."

I wrinkle my nose. "Ah, I mustn't keep my favorite beauty sadist waiting then." His brow furrows in confusion making me laugh. "You see how it feels to be squeezed into a corset and then having your hair yanked and pulled repeatedly for the perfect style. That woman is a master at what she does," I tell him with a wink and then reach out to clasp his hand and make him launch me into a twirl back towards the others as I call out, "Be right there!"

Cade shuts the music off and gives me a disgruntled look. "It's going to be maddening waiting all night for you to come back. I don't see why we couldn't have accompanied you as well," he pouts.

I balance against his chest with one hand so I can go up on my tiptoes to kiss that sexy mouth and swipe my tongue over that pouty bottom lip of his. When I pull back the pout's gone and amused love fills his eyes.

"Because you weren't invited," I say, running a gentle touch along his square jaw and then plucking my phone from his hand. A few quick swipes locate the app I've been saving for a moment that I need to distract them. I open it up and wave the other two closer. "Here, it's a game you can play while you're waiting for me to come back. It's very simple, all you have to do is swipe to match three or more candies in any direction. If you get bored with that, there's a few movies downloaded you could watch that I think you might like." I show them where to find the movies and how to turn them on before going back to the addictive Candy Crush game and handing Cade the phone back. "Ok, have fun. I'm off to hair and makeup!"

I try not to laugh as all three of them crowd together with heads pressed close over the screen as I walk towards the doors. I do end up laughing when I hear them start bickering over what combination to match first.

I head up to my room and pass a maid dusting art that lines the walls and I'm a few steps past her when I choke out a laugh when I realize she's singing Icona Pop's, I Love It under her breath. I'm in such a good mood that I turn back to her and sing the next line back at her.

"*I threw my shit into a bag and pushed it down the stairs. I crashed my car into a bridge…*" I pause there and point to her with a challenging look. It takes her a beat but the smile forms and she leans towards me.

"I don't care, I love it. I don't care!"

We end up laughing with each other and it's a really nice moment, even if she probably doesn't understand the English words. I don't even care how badly I'm probably messing up music history especially since I caught the Spanish chef singing Despacito the other day in the kitchen as he kneaded dough, accompanied by some pretty lewd groin thrusts for a man of his girth. Another shared smile and a wave to my new favorite maid and I turn back to head to my room only to find Sebastian once again watching me. I can't read the expression on his face so I just cock my head to the side and walk towards him.

"What's up?" I ask.

He stares at me for a few more moments before he seems to shake himself out of whatever's on his mind.

"I was just dropping off the jewelry I think will complement the gown you will be wearing tonight."

I clap my hands together in glee. "Oooh, sparklies! Seriously though, thank you for inviting me and for the gown and jewelry to wear with it. I'm really looking forward to going with you tonight. I promise I will try very hard not to embarrass you." I tell him with a sincere smile.

He does that weird lost stare thing again and then slowly nods and turns and walks away in the opposite direction down the hall. I frown at his back at how hard the guy is to crack and hope I have a little better success tonight with bridge-building. I step into my room and spot the sheet-covered mound on my bed that I just know is my new gown and head straight to it with my hands held out and my fingers making grabby motions but freeze mid-step when a stern French "NON!" snaps out at me. I set my expression in the most petulant child look I can muster and turn slowly towards Claudette.

"YOU are SO mean!" I whine at her. I can see the tremble as her lips fight off a smile but she finally caves and throws her hands up with an indulgent smile but still drops one hand to wag a finger at me and then points to the stool in front of her.

"Ici!"

I roll my eyes at her but do as I'm told and walk away from the dress I'm dying to see and take a seat on her stool. I look up at her with a wink and wave my hands in front of my face dramatically.

"You may begin…the transformation of me," I tell her with a laugh and she shakes her head at my antics and smooths my hair back before turning me on the stool. It's the last nice moment between us for a while before she yanks the first fistful of hair in her quest to tame it.

For the next half hour, my head gets pulled in every direction as I let my mind wander to tonight and try not to let the nerves come back. Partway through the scalp torturing Claudette shows me a pair of gorgeous stiletto-type daggers that have ruby-encrusted hilts before anchoring them in the updo she's creating on top of my head. It gives me a thrill and makes me feel like a badass assassin. I let a montage of scenes play through my mind of me pulling them out during the party and letting them fly across the room to take out the bad guys as Claudette goes to work on my makeup. It's just a little silly amusement to pass the time as I know

Sebastian will handle any possible danger that might present itself. He's not like Luca and doesn't worry about how I will react to his monster being on full display. I sigh wistfully. I doubt Sebastian worries or cares about anything I do or think. I've been pretty ruthlessly suppressing my feelings and attraction for him and trying to keep them at bay is sometimes exhausting. It's especially hard when I catch him looking at me with longing or heat in his eyes. In a lot of ways I think the Alpha vamp is just as broken as Luca was, he just holds it all locked in with an iron control made of ice. If I can just find a crack or a way to melt some of that ice we might be able to start being friends at the very least. It doesn't matter that I want more. That I want his hands on my body and love in his eyes is just plain old greed. I have three amazing men who give me that already. I will happily settle for friendship with Sebastian if it's all I can have.

Claudette taps me on my shoulder, bringing me out of my thoughts to let me know she's done with the hair and makeup portion and is ready to strap me into the rib-cracking corset. I stand and move to the bed so I can use one of its posts to brace myself but she surprises me by whipping the sheet off of the gown and lifting it up for me to see. My eyes flare wide and my mouth opens in a surprised gasp as I take in the work of sexual art that no seventeenth-century seamstress should be able to create.

Here I was thinking it would be scandalously indecent, showing a lot of cleavage and a high hemline but what I see before me would be daring even in my timeline.

The satin is blood red that edges into cherry and has black lace overlaid around the edges. The front and back have deep Vs that will go all the way to my waist with built-in boning to perch my breasts in. It's essentially a dress made of two panels, front and back that are tied together on either side by crisscrossing black ribbon lacing. It's a dress that can only be worn over a naked body with no supports as any undergarments would show through the front, back and sides. It's fucking epic.

I strip naked in front of Claudette with no shame at all as I can't wait to see this glorious creation on my body. I have to hold the front and back against me in place while she tightens the ribbons on both sides and I wonder if this time frame has the equivalent of double-sided body tape because I can just see me breathing a little too hard and my tits popping out for all to see. By the time she's done tugging, adjusting, and tying things off I'm confident that everything will stay where it's supposed to as long as I stay upright and make no sudden movements. She leads me over to stand in front of the mirror and I have to swallow hard at what I see.

My breasts are pulled apart and pushed up as high as they'll go by the built-in boning leaving almost all of my center chest and waist exposed to just above my belly button. It's A LOT of fucking skin. I turn slightly to the side and see black ribbon crisscrossing from under my arm to the floor-length hem. The ribbons grip my skin from the top to just under my hip and then the skirt widens from there. Turning further I look over my shoulder and see the wide deep V that drops down to stop just above my ass and my eyes almost bug out at the heart shape the dress has turned my ass into. It won't matter what direction I turn, a lot of skin will be exposed for all to see. This dress, this fucking dress was made to capture men's gazes and hold them as prisoners with its blatant sexuality. Its sole purpose is for eye fucking and I can't wait for my men to see me in it. It also makes me wonder if Sebastian either knew what it would be or had a hand in the design.

Claudette answers that question when she brings over the jewelry and swings the necklace in front of me so she can secure the clasp and that clasp better fucking be a padlock because where the dress made my pussy damp with how sexy it is, the necklace fucking terrifies me.

A long double strand of pea-sized diamonds with a ruby every few inches drops down my chest and ends in a teardrop-shaped ruby the size of a robin's egg. The huge stone sits at the bottom of my breastbone and this dress was clearly built to showcase it. Sebastian definitely had a hand in the design so he's either serving me up as the ultimate distraction or he wanted to see me looking like this.

Either way, I'm now wracked with nerves over wearing something so completely priceless and terrified I will somehow end up losing it. Claudette clips on the dangling matching earrings that have slightly smaller versions of the teardrop ruby, making my nerves even tighter. My hair is piled high in curls on top of my head with only a few loose tendrils drifting down, meaning there's no hiding the jewelry or all the skin on display. My eyes lift to my face in the mirror and I admire the dark smoky eye with winged eyeliner she's created and the blood-red lips perfectly match the color of the dress. I'm feeling a little shaky at the overall effect and my hand clutches Claudette's as my panicky eyes meet hers in the mirror.

"I ca-can't. It's too much!" I tell her with a tremble in my voice.

She turns me away from the mirror to face her and takes both my hands in hers pinning me with a determined, fierce look.

"*Non*, it is not too much. This *ici*, er, here. This here is *pow-er*. Ladies have so little *pow-er* in this world. This is your *wea-pon*. You will use it, wield it for control to master them, n'est-ce pas?"

I slowly nod as I blow out a deep fortifying breath. She's right, so fucking right! This dress, this look, it will stop men in their tracks. I need to own it and use it to my advantage. I pull our joined hands up and kiss the backs of hers before letting go and squaring my shoulders.

"Thank you, Claudette. Thank you."

She beams a smile at me and shoots me a wink before dropping down to her knees and helping me slide my feet into the matching red shoes with small inch and a half heels. I pat at my hair, run a slightly shaking hand over the necklace, and walk out the door she holds open for me. As I walk down the hall to the stairs all I can think of is one of those fuckers better have my phone on them because I need a damn picture of me in this dress!

Eden

When I hit the top of the stairs I pause dramatically and wait until all four of them turn and look up at me. As much as I want to see my guys' reaction, I can't tear my gaze from Sebastian. He's the one who put me in this dress and I want to see if it has the effect on him I think it will. I feel the heat and lust in his stare as I slowly and carefully descend the staircase but when my shoes hit the floor a wall of ice blocks it out and all I get from him is a slight nod as he holds out a red matching cape with black lace overlaid along the edges. Talk about a fucking underwhelming reaction. The bitch inside of me is raging to grab my tits and shove them his way in a taunt while asking if the look was all he wanted. Something about being draped in diamonds and rubies forces me to keep it classy so I turn away from him ignoring the outstretched cape and finally get the reaction my self-confidence needs from Cade, Finn, and Luca. Based on the flames dancing in their eyes and the way Cade and Finn's hands are fisted at their sides, I would be nailed against a wall as they stripped me bare if I didn't have a party to attend. My lips curve in a sensual smile and I turn slightly so they can see the ribbons holding the dress on me and murmur, "I'll let you untie me when I get home."

They move in unison towards me like they aren't going to wait that long but Luca steps in front of them with his own smoldering look. He lifts one of my hands and runs his hot mouth over my knuckles, tugging me closer and taking my breath away with the intensity in his eyes.

"Are you ready for this?"

I think he's talking about the party at first but his next words make his meaning clear.

"You were meant to complete us, Eden. Tonight, I think you will."

I just stare back into his eyes, having no idea how to respond to that and just nod in a dazed way as he brushes his lips lightly over mine and steps back. I'm about to turn back to accept my cape when the Alpha-hole growls at me.

"Enough, we must be on our way."

I shoot him a bitchy look over my shoulder before asking, "Who has my phone? I want pictures!"

I can practically hear his teeth grind from here but too fucking bad, he should have at least told me I looked nice. I make him wait while Finn runs to get it and then a little bit longer as they all take turns snapping pictures of me and them together. Luca finally takes the phone from Cade and waves towards Sebastian.

"Let's have one last one with you and your escort."

I make a face but move his way, admiring the all-black outfit he wears with a red cravat that matches my dress at his throat. He's so tall and broad that I feel dainty standing beside him. I pose with a tight smile on my face but Luca frowns and waves me closer causing Sebastian to growl and slip an arm around my waist and yank me towards him.

The unexpected move has me unbalanced so I'm forced to turn into him and brace a hand on his chest while looking up at him in surprise. His head is tilted down at me and the heated desire is back in his eyes as his fingers slide over my bare skin between the ribbons on my side. My breath catches in my throat being this close to him but the spell is broken when Luca calls out.

"Done! You should get going as it will take you a few hours to get there."

His arm drops away from me and he bends to snatch the cape from Finn who had picked it up from the floor where Sebastian dropped it. He holds it out for me and drapes it over my shoulders and then grasps me by my elbow to pull me from the house. I get one last look over my shoulder at my three men before he lifts me into the enclosed carriage and calls for the driver to be on our way.

I sit on the cushioned bench across from Sebastian and pull my cape closed, no longer wanting his eyes on my skin. The fucker runs so hot and cold it gives me whiplash trying to keep up. We spend the first hour avoiding even looking at each other and I'm at the point where I'm ready to tell the driver to turn this carriage around when I force myself to take a deep breath and stop being so immature.

It's not like this is something new. He's been like this from the start and I don't know why I thought an over-the-top sexy dress would change it now. I need to find a way to break through his walls and build some kind of relationship or my men will be the ones to suffer. I square my shoulders and paste a pleasant smile on my lips.

"Is there anything I should be on the lookout for while we're there?" I ask to try and break the ice.

He raises an eyebrow in the most condescending look and the small smirk of amusement has me digging my nails into my palms.

"There is nothing for you to worry about except being charming and decorative. This night is only a chance for me to see if I can sense others of my kind nearby. It would be best if you spoke as little as possible to any of the other guests," He tells me in a dismissive tone.

My smile tightens, my eyes narrow and I give him a jerky nod. "Right, just a brainless piece of ass on your arm. Got it."

He sighs out a breath that's seeped in annoyance. "Eden, the other guests there will be the worst representation of the nobility. They are cruel, selfish, and self-serving with only one thing on their minds tonight, their own pleasure. A piece of ass, as you say, will be all they see when they look at you. It's imperative that you school your reactions to anything you see tonight no matter how lewd it is. If they see any weakness from you it will only make them want you more. Next to perverse pleasure, they love nothing more than to corrupt the innocent."

I grit my teeth to stop from snapping at him. He can be so insufferable. Instead, I force a measured tone out.

"One, I'm far from innocent and can handle anything I see tonight. And two, if you have so little faith in me then why did you even invite me to come?"

He leans back on his bench and scans me but I'm completely covered by my cape so he blows out a breath.

"I invited you because having you on my arm will be distracting, allowing me a greater latitude to observe the other guests and also because I do have faith that you can handle the setting. I am just cautioning you to show no shock at what you may see. From what you have told us about your era, sex seems to be more open in society compared to this time. Your...relationship...with Cade, Finn, and Luca and the ease you seem to navigate it tells me that your sensibilities won't be offended."

I brush a wispy curl away from my face and decide he's given me the perfect opening to discuss the dynamic that has shifted between us all.

"Does it bother you? Does all three of them being with me bother you?"

He scoffs. "Why would it bother me? I haven't seen my brothers this happy, well, ever. You fill a need that they have been missing. As for you being with three men at once, that's your business."

"Yes, it is. I can tell you they've filled a hole in my heart that I didn't think could ever be fixed. I've never been with more than one man before and it's certainly not common in my time, no matter how open and accepting sex is for my generation." I look down breaking the eye contact. "Before I came here, my life…my life wasn't very happy." I huff out a sad laugh. "That's an understatement. There was no happiness in my life at all, for many years. All the people I loved are dead and for a long time…I wished I was too." I tell him, ending in a whisper. I close my eyes and shake those memories off before looking back up at him. "What I've found here, experienced here, with the others has changed everything for me. I finally feel like the woman I'm supposed to be. Their love has given me everything I ever dreamed of and so much more. But, I can't help but feel like my relationship with the others has…intruded on the bond you have with them. Sebastian, you all have been a family for so long and I'm terrified that I might be causing a wedge between you and them and that's not something I would ever want to be responsible for." I tell him as sincerely as I can hoping he can see the truth of that in my eyes.

I wait, hoping for something from him I can't even name and see the shift of emotions in his eyes and expression that has my heart speeding up in hope but it is quickly dashed when the familiar ice frosts over once again and cold amusement sets his lips in a smirk.

"My dearest, Eden, how charming of you to think you ever could come between us. We have been together for hundreds of years and will be a family long after your bones have turned to dust in your grave."

A small gasp slips out at the cold words he hits me with. There's no getting through his ice walls and I'm done with trying and this conversation so I just tilt my head slightly to acknowledge his point.

"Yes, well I'm glad you will always be there for them after I won't be."

Just as I go to turn my eyes away from his, I think I see a flash of regret in them but I'm no longer interested in trying to understand this man so I sit quietly staring down into my lap for the last of the trip wishing the night was already over.

The carriage coming to a stop has me finally lifting my head to meet his gaze. I lift my lips into an empty smile and nod to him.

"Distraction ready to launch."

He stares back at me with a slight frown and opens his mouth to say something but just then the driver opens the carriage door so instead, he climbs down and turns holding his hand out for me to take. I step down and my first look at the home we've arrived at has my eyebrows shooting up.

I thought the manor house was huge but this place is three times as large and has major castle vibes going on. Sebastian takes my elbow and guides me up the large front stairs that lead to an impressive set of double doors that are standing open with footmen flanking it. We step into a foyer that goes up three stories and I try not to gawk like a country hick as he takes my cape off and hands it to a waiting servant. I can hear music coming from ahead and spot another pair of footmen standing on either side of a set of heavy red curtains. He leads me to them and we pause as the curtains are drawn apart. Two steps into the room and he brings me to another stop as someone calls out,

"Sa Grâce, le Duc du Gaul et invité!"

We are standing at the top of a short staircase leading down into a ballroom giving me a perfect view of the entire room. At first, all I see is the large crowd of people dancing in their finery with the many jewel colored gowns swishing as they move. I try and ignore the large number of eyes that have just turned our way and are studying every inch of me as my gaze moves to take in the rest of the room. I'm proud of myself when my only reaction to what I see is a slight indrawn breath and a tightening of my fingers on Sebastian's arm.

Lining the sides of the room on both sides are what look like fancy gilded cages and in each one are various groups of naked people having sex, a lot of sex, on raised platforms. They range from all men together to women with women and a mix of both. Not one grouping is just plain old vanilla man and woman going at it alone. Based on the ecstasy on all their faces it's all consensual and having eyes on them just makes the experience even better. This isn't a dinner party, this is a fucking sex club and this, this I can handle.

I turn my head back to look up at Sebastian before tilting it slightly down the stairs with the same empty smile that hasn't slipped once since we left the carriage to let him know I'm good to carry on. He takes an extra moment to study my face as his eyes narrow slightly and his mouth tightens before he guides me down the stairs to the main level and straight to the dance floor. He drops my elbow to clasp my hand and gives me a leg and bow before moving into me so his hand can rest on my bare back. I keep my back and neck ruler straight with my chin lifted as we step into the rotating dancers in time to the music. I feel utterly ridiculous and like royalty at the same damn time. I keep my eyes firmly on his chin and my vapid smile in place as he moves me around the floor in a waltz trying my best to channel a Stepford wife but when his thumb begins to rub circles on the exposed skin closest to my ass an involuntary shiver runs through me. I lift my eyes to meet his and tilt my head, hoping he can read the "What the fuck are you doing?" look in them. His eyes flash with amusement and his head dips towards mine.

"You look like an exquisitely beautiful but empty doll."

My smile slips slightly and I huff out an annoyed breath.

"Do you know what mixed signals are? Because you are a master of them. I thought this was what you wanted me to be."

His hot fingers slide up my bare spine as he gives a little shake of his head and his voice is low and husky when he says, "No, never this. I want you…"

He trails off without finishing as the song comes to an end.

Eden

Someone nearby calls out to him in French but all I understand is his title as he moves us to the side of the dancing area as the next song begins. He turns me to face a man at least a foot shorter than me. He's decked out with a high pile of curls that have been powdered and way too much lace for any man to carry off. The wispy thin mustache and chin beard go with his slim frame and painted lips for the overall slimy Frenchman look. The guy's eyes are practically licking all my exposed skin as he takes me in with a sleazy smirk. Sebastian says something to him in French and all I pick out of it is the French word for English so I'm assuming he's telling the guy I don't speak the language. His eyebrows shoot up in interest and he reaches for my hand as Sebastian does the introductions.

"Mademoiselle Eden Kelly, may I present the Marquis du Corbeil, our gracious host for the evening."

I dip down into a half curtsey thankful that Luca ran me through the dumbass customs of etiquette as he brings my hand to his mouth for an open kiss that has his tongue swiping over my knuckles. I lock my muscles down to suppress the shudder that wants to wrack me at his creepiness.

"Enchanté, you honor us with your beauty." He tells me with a heavy accent. His eyes are frozen on my tits like they're about to do tricks but his next words are for my escort.

"I was surprised to see you accepted my invitation. I do not believe you have ever joined us for one of my more intimate soirées."

Sebastian's fingers are back to trailing up and down my bare arm as if he's making clear to the Marquis his ownership of me when he replies,

"It was an invitation I felt would be beneficial to accept and of course I thought my companion would find pleasurable. I believe we have mutual interests to discuss."

The Marquis shoots him a pointed look before his eyes slide back to my breasts. "Ah, oui on both counts. She will receive much pleasure this night I am sure but let us enjoy the festivities first before we discuss such interests more privately, oui?"

I'm bored with this guy's fixation on my breasts so I look over his shoulder to scan the crowd just as it parts and I see one of the hottest, sexiest women I've ever seen in my life walking towards us. Her black hair falls to her waist in a pin-straight glossy curtain. She's too far away for me to see what color her eyes are but they're a light color, either grey or blue. Her face is sculptured perfection with her lips set in a sexy amused pout. I thought I was daring with the dress I'm wearing but this woman has almost bared it all. A flowing column of black lace is all that covers her heavy breasts, continuing down over her stomach and the center of her legs. It has to be glued on somehow because there's no straps or ribbons holding it in place. Her sides are bare with her dipped in waist and rounded hips, thighs, and the rest of her legs on full display. Because I'm studying her so closely I see the moment her confident steps falter and she comes to a quick stop. My eyes look up to her face and I see a brief flash of fear before she whirls away and heads back the way she came, disappearing into the crowd. I frown slightly, wondering what made her flee but when I feel clammy fingers trailing down the skin between my breasts all thoughts of her vanish. My eyes turn to the douche bag touching me and I cast a side-eye glance at Sebastian, digging my nails into his arm. I can see he's distracted though as his head moves in every direction searching the room for something.

I'm fine being the distraction for him and I don't want to fuck this up but I won't be groped by this asshat either, so my hand flashes out and latches onto his wrist in a tight grip. I give him a smile that's all teeth and purr, "No touchy, bad boy!"

I know I've hit the right tone when his eyelids drop to half-mast and he shivers as he licks his lips. I want a shower with buckets of soap knowing I just gave him a sexual thrill by being dominant. This guy is a total sub if that's all it took to get his engine revving. He twists his wrist in my hand so he can rub his fingers over my own and then slides them against my palm before breaking contact.

"I look forward to spending more time with you after the supper is completed and the real festivities begin." He tells me with smoldering eyes.

I try hard not to snort and murmur, "Can't wait."

The minute he turns to walk away I'm rolling my eyes so hard I almost make myself dizzy. Sebastian's still looking over the crowd and apparently missed the whole exchange so I swipe a tiny glass with a long stem from a passing waiter's tray and after sniffing the pink foamy liquid that smells like strawberries, shoot the whole thing in one go. It's not bad, whatever it is, and hopefully the shot-sized liquor will ease some of the tension I'm feeling in my shoulders and neck at standing with perfect posture for so long. It's not as easy as it looks without a corset holding you up.

I reach out and exchange my empty for another drink when a different waiter passes, this one with lime green liquid in it. I've already decided to just sip at it, not wanting to get loaded, but before it even reaches my lips, Sebastian is snatching it from my hand.

"Hey! I was drinking that!" I whine but he ignores me and takes a sip of the drink himself.

His eyebrows raise in surprise at whatever he tastes and the glass is handed off to another server passing by. He takes my elbow and leads me back onto the dance floor for another dance.

"Don't drink anything else offered to you," he tells me as he twirls me around the floor.

I wince and give him an "Oops, too late" look.

"Um, kinda already drank one. What's in the drinks?"

He hits me with an exasperated look like I should have known better because apparently roofies are a thing in every century.

"You should be fine. It will only lower your inhibitions, just don't drink anymore."

Fuck, that's just great. Just what a girl needs when attending a middle ages sex club where everyone wants to fuck me. And they all do. Everywhere I turn I find hot, lust-filled eyes roaming over my body from both men and quite a few women. I'd like to say it makes me uncomfortable but my sex drive has leveled up since taking on three men because all I feel is sexy and confident under the attention. It sucks great big donkey balls that the only man in the room that I secretly want looking at me that way seems indifferent to me. I try and just focus on the loads of sex I'll be having when I make it home tonight and remind myself that three cocks is more than enough.

We dance three songs in a row and it's a lot of work to ignore his hot fingers siding up and down my bare spine and the hard muscles I can feel under my hand. I'm almost grateful when he walks us off the floor because I'm ready to rub myself against him like a cat in the hopes he'll pet me some more. He moves me from group to group, exchanging pleasantries but it's all in French so I let my eyes wander and they land on the nearest group of sex performers.

There's one man and three women in the enclosure and I find myself moving away from Sebastian and closer to the cage for a better look.

The single man is slamming into the main woman from behind and his eyes are clenched closed with his head thrown back. I can see how tightly his fingers dig into her hips as he anchors her for the hard, fast pace of his thrusts. There's another woman on her knees in front of the main woman that has her tongue sliding in and out of her pussy so she's getting fucked and licked at the same time. Hanging from the bars on the top of the cage is a swing that hangs at head height with the last woman sitting on the edge of it and she has her legs draped over both the standing couple with the woman that's getting pleasured from both sides' mouth and tongue working her pussy over with moans of pleasure. This is like watching real live porn and my body feels flushed, hot, and heavy as my own core begins to ache to be touched. For half a second I don't even care who presses up against me from behind and wraps an arm around my waist, sliding a hot hand over to rest on my lower belly. My core clenches with the need to be filled as his thumb traces circles against the skin bared by the V of the dress and my breathing is heavy, almost panting.

"Look at their eyes," Sebastian whispers against my ear. Their eyes are not what's turning me on so I have to force my gaze from all the licking and fucking happening in front of me and try and concentrate on what he's noticed. I see two of the women's eyes have completely blown pupils. I swallow hard and tilt my head back to rest against his chest.

"Are they drugged?" I whisper back.

"Either that or blood-drunk like you were." He tells me.

More memories flash through my mind of that three-day sexathon, making my pussy throb even harder. I tip my head back even further to meet his eyes and I know he can tell just how turned on I am because he pulls me even closer against his chest and I swear I can feel the rigid length of him pressing against my ass through the dress. His eyes drop to my lips and stay there for a few beats before he pulls back completely, leaving me desperate for the contact to return.

"Supper has been announced. We need to find our seats."

Motherfucker, I can't wait to get back to my men who I know will take this ache away in the best possible ways. I let him lead me away from the sex show with only a quick glance over my shoulder and ignore the throb between my legs when my thighs rub together as we walk into another room with the longest table I have ever seen.

There has to be seating for at least a hundred and I roll my eyes remembering the Marquis saying this is an intimate gathering. We find our seats roughly in the middle of the table and I'm happy to be off my feet when Sebastian helps me into my chair. I reach for one of the goblets in front of me but stop with it halfway to my lips before handing it to Sebastian.

"Please check this for me? I'm parched and desperate for a drink."

He takes it from my hand and has a small sip before handing it back to me with a slight nod so I take a few healthy gulps, happy that it's plain water and not wine. My inhibitions don't need any more lowering as I'm pretty sure that last drink is the reason I'm so turned on right now.

Sebastian makes small talk in French to the couple on the other side of him but the two on my side are wrapped up in each other and other than a leering look at my cleavage the guy beside me focuses all his attention on his companion. It's actually a good thing as I need a few moments to myself. I just focus on taking a few bites from each course that is served, skipping the fish dish altogether, and just people watch. I scan down the table and notice that the seating is alternating male, female so that no two women are beside each other. I take in the elaborate hairdos and the sheer amount of cleavage showing. The table is higher than most so it almost looks like every woman's breasts are sitting on it, displayed like on a shelf.

After a few goblets of water and some food I'm feeling better about the night and I've got my pussy wrangled back into a dormant state. The last thing I want is to be stuck in the carriage for a two-hour drive while I'm wiggling in need on the bench across from him. I know we will be leaving shortly after the meal is done so we won't be present for the orgy that everyone seems to know about. As soon as Sebastian has his private conversation with the Marquis, we're out of here. When the cheese and grapes are set in front of me I know the meal is almost done. After it's cleared away a hush falls over the long table and I turn my head along with everyone else to see our host, the Marquis standing at the end of the table on a small platform.

His eyes look to each person, taking way longer than it should as a pleased smirk sits on his lips.

When he finally speaks it's in French so I have no idea what he says but giggles and gasps erupt.

"Le cours final ne sera servi qu'aux dames. Profiter des desserts, la petite mort!"

I turn to Sebastian to ask him what the guy said but he's already cursing under his breath as his eyes lock onto mine.

"Eden…" Is all he manages to get out before I'm flinching in my seat as my skirt is pushed up my legs and a face slides between my thighs. My body freezes as my eyes frantically look down the table and see every woman's expression change. Their heads fall back and their eyes glaze over at what's being done to them and I'm almost helpless when a hot tongue slips between my folds and goes straight to my clit and begins circling it in expert motions. My hand comes down hard on Sebastian's arm and my nails dig into his sleeve as a jolt of pleasure rocks through me. My eyes dart to his and my voice is a stuttered whisper.

"Th-there's…ah…ah…oh fuck. Oh my G-God it's…" Is all I can stutter before a moan escapes me and I'm no longer capable of stringing more words together as waves of pleasure pass through me.

The master between my legs soothes the ache I've been living with for the last hour with hot flicks and licks over my sensitive clit. No one else at the table has bolted and based on the sounds I'm hearing, everyone is fully on board this pleasure train. I could shove the head between my legs away and just pretend it's still happening but the truth is…I like it and it just feels so damn good.

I've fully embraced my whoredom since coming here and taking on three cocks so I'm just going to own this too and love every fucking minute of whoever is licking my pussy in such an erotic, delicious way.

Sebastian

Her eyes roll back under half-closed lids as another sexy moan slips between her lips. I want to rip whoever's under the table away from her and fill the spot with my own mouth. I'm desperate to taste her sweet arousal but instead I torture myself by watching the pleasure overtake her.

This whole night has been a mistake. It's been a true test of my will and control to have this woman looking like she does in my arms with my hands on her silky skin. She's so open and responsive to carnal pleasures. It might be the drugged drink she had but based on her times with my three brothers it's not just that. She's a naturally sensual woman and it took everything I had not to find the nearest hard surface to throw her on so that I can strip this maddening dress off of her and devour her beautiful body with my hands, mouth, and cock for most of the night. The only thing stopping me is the knowledge that once I have her, I will never be able to stop and the pain and agony of living on centuries without her after she dies her mortal death will be excruciating. My brothers will already be facing that pain to come and someone will have to hold us together after she's gone. And now this is happening to her. I knew exactly what was coming when the Marquis announced that the dessert course would only be served to the ladies, especially when he said for them to enjoy la petite mort. It is a common term in French to describe an orgasm.

I lean closer to her and murmur in her ear, "I can have us out of here in a flash if you want me to stop this. You don't have to do this for me, Eden."

Her hazy eyes meet mine and her back arches against her seat as her mouth drops open with a stuttered gasp before she manages to give the tiniest shake of her head as she clutches my arm harder. Her cheeks and chest flush with a pretty pink blush and she bites down on her bottom lip but when she licks her lips and whines with need, my hand comes up and cups her face so she's forced to stare into my eyes. I use my thumb to caress her lips and barely suppress a moan of my own when they open and she sucks and licks at it. My cock is as hard as it's ever been and straining painfully against the confines of my pants as I watch the orgasm build just by the way her expression changes. When her head falls back and her body arches against the table I lower my hand and cup her throat, squeezing gently. Her eyes have never left mine so I see the moment she finds release and almost spill my seed in my pants when her pupils blow out and I feel the tremors rock her body against my hand. Except for the quietest gasps she manages to keep her release between us. I would barter my soul to hear her scream my name in pleasure.

We sit staring into each other's eyes with so much to say but neither of us speaks. The minute people start rising from the table I pull her up and lead her quickly out of the room, through the ballroom, and up the stairs. I pause only long enough to snatch her cape from the pile that a servant holds and usher her straight out the doors. I keep a firm grip on her elbow as her legs are still unsteady and give a loud wolf whistle that my driver will recognize and bring the carriage around. As we wait I watch her out of the corner of my eye. Her head is tilted back and her eyes are locked onto the stars that fill the night sky, no doubt trying to process what just happened. When the carriage comes to a stop in front of us I don't wait for the driver to get down to open the door just do it myself, ushering her up into it.

I search for the words that should, no - need to be said, and come up blank. She still won't look at me so I stay silent, giving her the space and time she probably needs right now as images of her face while being pleasured continue to flash through my mind.

My fingers begin to ache after clenching my hands in fists for the twenty minutes we've been traveling in silence and the air is thick with tension as she stays locked in place, unmoving and staring at her lap. When she does finally move it's simply because a shiver wracks her body and I curse myself for a fool as I swipe her cape from the seat beside me and move to drape it over her exposed skin to protect her from the evening chill.

As I bring it around her shoulders to clasp it closed the back of my fingers slide along the soft skin of her neck and a different type of shiver travels through her. Her eyes finally move to mine and when I see the desire and need in them the ice-cold control I've mastered shatters. I snatch her from her seat with a snarl and yank her against me, my mouth dropping to hers in a savage kiss. There's nothing sweet about the kiss as I ravage her mouth with my tongue prying her lips apart for access to her sweet depths. Her hands slide into my hair and make a fist to pull me even closer and even that isn't enough. I need my hands on all of her. I need to explore every part of her, learn her body's secrets, and consume it all.

My hands drop to the skirt of her dress to gather the material so I can have her straddled on my lap, pressing against my throbbing cock, but the damn thing is so tight over her hips I growl with frustration at being denied the access I need. Ripping my lips from hers I reach up and pull one of the small ruby daggers from her hair and slide it between her skin and the black ribbons holding the garment to her. The ribbons part with next to no effort and the entire dress drops away from her body, leaving her entirely bare for my eyes to feast upon. With one hand I grip her rounded hip to hold her steady against the swaying of the carriage as she stands between my thighs and I look my fill.

Utter perfection is what I see and I'm unable to stop my other hand from caressing her heavy breasts with my fingers circling one of her taut, pebbled nipples. The contact has her moaning and arching against my hand to beg for more. I can't deny her so I pull her closer so that my lips can replace my fingers. I roll the bud between my lips and use my tongue to flick it before sucking hard on it. Her gasps of pleasure go straight to my cock as it demands contact but her clever little hands are already there and she works to free the beast from its fabric prison.

When her hot, supple fingers wrap around my shaft and begin to stroke I almost spill my seed. It's been centuries since I've been touched in this way and the need I've been bottling up behind ice feels explosive. I release her nipple with the intention of traveling lower to finally get a taste of her sweet cream that I can smell in the air but she takes control by pushing me back against the seat and straddling my lap. Her grip on my cock never falters as she slides the tip of it back and forth between her folds drenching it with her wetness. The sounds she's making as she uses my cock's head to pleasure herself is the most sinful music to my ears but they are drowned out by my roar when she aligns me with her opening and sinks straight down onto my shaft taking every large inch of me as deep as I can go.

My fingers dig into the soft flesh of her hips in a bruising grip when she arches her back at being filled so deeply. It takes her a moment to recover from the stretch I cause her channel with her eyes wide with the shock of it but then she's rolling her hips in a fast rhythm over my shaft sending fireworks of pleasure pulsing through me. I want to thrust up into her but I hold myself back as I watch her milk every ounce of pleasure for herself from riding my cock. Her velvet heat grips me tightly inside and I feel the first gentle clutching flutters around me as her release begins to build. I want to feel her come apart around me more than I've ever wanted anything in my long life so I release one of her hips and slide a finger between her wet folds in search of her most sensitive spot. I work it with just enough pressure in my flicking and rubbing to feel her start clamping down on me as her release takes hold. Her slick heat squeezes my cock like a vise again and again as she milks me through her orgasm and it rips my name from her sweet lips. Hearing her say it in such a way has the last shred of my control crumbling away and I clamp back down on her hips so that I can thrust hard up into her. I'm ruthless and relentless in my thrusts, prolonging the orgasm that is shattering her until my own explodes so hard that my vision dims and greys.

Eden collapses against my chest and her hot little breaths against my neck as she pants only make the moment that much sweeter. My arms come around her to hold her even tighter against my chest and I know I will never be able to let her go. We stay like that until her breathing slows and when my softening cock slips from her heat I feel her shiver against me. I use a linen handkerchief to gently clean my seed from between her legs, causing a small smile to form on my lips when she moans softly and then rearranges herself on my lap sideways. I swipe her fallen cape from the floor and wrap it around us both to warm her. We still haven't spoken once but our actions screamed louder than any words could.

I hear her breathing even out when she slips into sleep and with her precious body cradled gently against me my thoughts are consumed by her. The attraction I've had for her has been there since day one but the other feelings that I've been denying have built and sneaked through the cracks of my walls. This would be so much easier if it was just sexual relations but I won't lie to myself any longer. Every joyful laugh, teasing look, and considerate act from her has chipped away at my will to resist her. The woman came to us so damaged and desperate for love and I've watched her true personality flourish under our care and attention. I don't think she even realizes that she no longer flinches from touch or that the mindless rage she would lose herself to has been mastered.

The kindness she shows everyone, even the servants and her concern for me at being excluded from the foursome her and my brothers have made even after I've treated her so coldly tells me just how big her heart is and I can't help but love her no matter how hard I tried not to. But it's a dangerous, distracting kind of love that will have to be managed properly. First Luca almost got them both killed by trying to hide his true nature from her and now tonight, I was so consumed by her that I ignored the main objective for going to that deviant's soirée in the first place. Eden sighs softly and burrows closer to me in her sleep and my heart aches from the love I feel. If we are not careful we will lose ourselves in our love for her and miss the many threats this world has over mortals. We all must stay on guard to protect her so that we may have as much time with her as possible before her natural cycle ends. The thought of the time she will leave us in death has me baring my teeth and considering the possibility of changing her into one of my kind for the first time since I sired Luca. I close my eyes against the crushing weight of knowing that isn't an option. Eden would stop being the woman we now all love the moment the bloodlust hits her. The curse of those years and all the things she would do to satisfy the fire in her veins would break someone as sweet and kind as her. No, I'd rather see her die a natural death than have her hate me for what I've turned her into. Instead, we will treasure every moment we have with her and carry her in our hearts and memories until the day our own cycles eventually come to an end.

The slowing of the carriage brings me from my musings and a quick glimpse out of the window surprises me that we have made it home already. Eden stirs in my arms and I tighten my hold on her not ready to end our time together. Selfishness washes over me and I decide that my brothers will have to cede their time with her for at least the rest of this night. I've only sampled a fraction of Eden's charms and it is not nearly enough. I wake her with soft kisses and when her long lashes flutter open and her green eyes meet mine filled with contented satisfaction a wave of warmth fills my chest. This woman owns me now without saying a word.

I sit her up and drape the cape around her properly so that her nakedness is covered completely. When the driver opens the door for us her cheeks fill with heat as she blushes and clutches the edges of the cape tightly to keep all of her skin covered. I step down first and turn to grasp her by the waist and lift her from the carriage. She tries to walk up the steps but I'm not ready to not have her in my arms so after I lean in and grab her ruined dress I scoop her up into my arms and carry her up the stairs and through the doors the footman has opened. Luca, Cade, and Finn are just coming into the foyer, alerted that we have returned.

"How did it go, then?" Cade asks but rather than reply I just flick my wrist, sending the ruined dress his way.

He catches it easily and holds it up with a grin and a laugh.

"Aye, I'd say it went very well." Finn chokes out while trying not to burst out laughing.

Luca says nothing as he takes in Eden's expression and the way she rests her cheek on my shoulder. He merely nods knowingly with a slight smile.

I ignore them all and stride straight to the grand staircase to carry her to my chambers. She shifts slightly in my arms so she can look over my shoulder and lifts a hand to send them a lazy little finger wave. When we reach the door to my chambers I kick it open and place her on her feet so I can close and lock it behind us. I turn to face her with burning eyes and try to find the words I need to speak to her but again, come up blank. Instead, I flick the clasp on her cape so that it drops and pools at her feet and burn the skin of her body with my heated gaze. It's a body I'm about to ravish in so many ways.

Eden

I stand naked except for the rubies and diamonds draped around my neck and feel hot wet heat pool between my legs at his hungry stare. He hasn't spoken a single word to me since the...event...happened under the table but my brief concern that he would think badly of me for allowing it to continue was washed aside by what we did in the carriage. I chew on my bottom lip as the concern comes back. He probably thinks I'm a wanton whore that will take all comers into my body and that's why he took his shot. If that's his true feelings then I'll take whatever he offers tonight and deal with the aftermath as best I can. When he finally moves it's to reach for my hair and I stand stock still as he carefully begins removing the many pins anchoring it in place. His voice is low and thick with his promise as he finally speaks.

"What happened tonight, under the table, will never happen again. No man other than myself and my brothers will ever touch or pleasure you again until the day you die, Eden. You are mine...ours...and only we will bring you to such heights in pleasure. I'm sorry I put you in such a position." He pulls the last pin and gently rubs the ache from my scalp before spreading my hair out to fall over my shoulders.

I feel a hint of tears burning in my eyes as I nod in agreement.

"It was my choice to allow it to continue but no, no one else will ever touch me except all of you. I am yours and always will be. Nothing will ever change that."

I reach up to unclasp the heavy necklace from around my neck but he stops me.

"Leave it." He tells me taking my hand and walking me over to a tall mirror against one wall. He stands behind me in front of it and runs a hand down from my neck between my breasts over the heavy jewels and down to rest over my lower belly with his fingers splayed out and his thumb caressing my heated skin. He uses his other hand to pull my hair away and back behind me so that his mouth has access to my neck. His lips land on the sensitive skin just behind and below my ear and when his tongue tastes me a tremor ripples through me. Our eyes are locked in the mirror as his mouth slides down the column of my throat and his other hand pulls me back against his hardness to press against my ass.

"Look at yourself, do see how exquisite you are? I would see you like this at all times, naked and draped in the finest jewels. Your beauty drives a man to madness." He whispers against my skin as his hot mouth travels to the dip between my neck and shoulder. "Watch, watch how I drag you down into that madness with me." He tells me as his long thick fingers spread my wet sex apart and slide deep into my folds. My head drops back against his chest as I arch into his touch searching for the delicious friction my pussy craves and I see the small smile that lifts his lips in the mirror and the wanton pleasure staining my face. His thumb circles my clit as two of those fingers thrust up into me. I'm so wet with need his hand is coated with my arousal as he slowly slides them in and out of me with just enough curl to hit the perfect spot inside me to have me bucking against him. His other arm is quick to wrap around my hips like a band of steel holding me still and causing a whine of want to escape my lips.

"Please…I need you!" I beg, needing so much more from him. The arm holding my hips sweeps up my body to grip my throat and his fingers jerk my chin towards him so his mouth can capture mine with a brutal, bruising kiss that I feel all the way to my soul. I've never felt such need and want from a man before and my head swims in dizziness as his fingers and thumb stroke me to the edge of orgasm. His lips and fingers leave me so abruptly at the same time that I sway and would have fallen to my knees if he wasn't holding me up. I meet his eyes in the mirror with a pleading look but he just chuckles and scoops me back up into his arms and carries me to his bed.

"No my little witch. The next time you find release will be on my tongue. I will erase any memory of another's on your body." He threatens while laying me out on the bed.

My hands reach for him, desperate to help remove his clothes but he catches them in one big hand and holds them together. He removes his cravat and uses it to tie my wrists together to a dowel on his headboard.

I groan, "Bas, Bastian, please, I want to touch you!"

The Alpha-hole laughs softly. "You'll just have to wait. I've been dreaming of all the things I'm going to do to your sweet, curvy body since you got here. I'm not letting you go until I've tasted, touched..." he grins, "And fucked every inch of you."

I have to press my thighs together hearing that word that I'm sure the wolves taught him come from his usually formal, proper aristocratic mouth. It's so fucking hot. I'm forced to watch him slowly undress and my eyes lick at the broad chest filled with a Roman Centurion's muscles. My pussy clenches hard at the drool-worthy V cut of muscle that leads down into his pants. Who knew Bas was hiding the body of a God under all that formal clothing he always wears. When his pants slide over his hips and his cock springs forth my eyes go round and my mouth waters. I want him inside me again so badly. He's long and thick and I already know just how much he'll stretch me, so damn sweetly, that I'll feel every inch of him.

Once he's naked he climbs onto the bed at my feet and lifts one to his mouth. He works his way up the inside of my leg with a trail of hot wet kisses and licks. The closer he gets to my core the more I strain to lift my hips to meet his mouth but he detours around and continues upward, leaving me panting and moaning. My whole body is thrumming in need as his tongue circles my naval. His chest slides over my mound as he moves further up to my breasts and I shamelessly grind against it causing him to drop his weight down to hold me in place. I strain against the bonds holding my arms over my head and buck as hard as I can to try and loosen them so I can touch him but he's not having it. Sebastian lifts his mouth from my skin and pins me with a look.

"Little witch, the more you fight this the longer I'll make you wait."

I glare a pout at him and turn my head away on the pillow stilling my body but when his mouth captures one of my aching nipples I arch against him involuntarily and moan his name. His tongue lashes the sensitive peak causing a deep ache in my core before he moves to bestow the same treatment on the other one. By the time he makes it to my lips, I'm a quivering, panting ball of need. I plead with him as he nibbles and sucks on my lips.

"Bas, please...I n-need you. I ache..."

He smiles against my mouth. "You beg so prettily, how can I resist?"

He slides off of my body and with strong hands flips me over so my hands twist and my front hits the mattress. I moan as my sensitized nipples press against the blanket and his hot mouth trails down my spine. His hands grip my hips and lifts them up until my knees rest on the bed with my elbows supporting me. His fingers cup and squeeze my ass cheeks and when his teeth nip at them my whole body bucks. He spreads my thighs apart and lays down with his face under me so that his mouth can finally capture my aching center. Bas licks, sucks, and flicks every part of my soft, sensitive core and when his tongue spears into my opening again and again I give up all restraint and grind down to ride and fuck his face. After so much teasing it only takes seconds for the orgasm I've been on the edge of to take hold and blow through me. His tongue never stops spearing into me as he prolongs it as long as my body will allow.

When my muscles give out and I crash down to the bed he licks me from top to bottom one last time and slides out from between my legs. I'm fucking dead and gone from the heights of that one and don't think I can take anymore. He soothes me with long soft sweeps of his hands up and down my back and ass and I just lay there in the afterglow of the best orgasm of my life, ready for a long nap. The sharp crack of his hand coming down on my ass has my traitorous pussy clenching for more, especially when he licks away the burn, causing me to moan in pleasure. Hard fingers pull my hips back up into the air and his knees knock mine further apart so I'm spread wide for him when I feel the big round head of his cock nudge against my opening. When he slides an inch into me, the burn of the stretch feels so damn good that I push back against him wanting more, wanting to feel him fill me completely. His fingers flex on my hips and dig in deeper before he slams his length balls deep inside of me and I'm howling.

"FUCK, YES!"

I'm a mindless animal as I buck and rock back at him to take him deeper, reveling in the slick burn of how tight I am around him and wishing I could see his face to see if he's feeling the same sweet agony I am. His chest drops against my back with a growl in my ear as he reaches out and tugs on the fabric holding my wrists captive, releasing me. Holding me against him as he continues to thrust hard into me he sits us up onto our knees and his mouth latches on my neck.

"I need to taste you," he growls. "Say yes. Say you want me to."

There's nothing I'll say no to for this man.

"I'm yours, Sebastian. Yes, take what you want. Anything!"

The pain of his fangs sinking into my neck is only a brief flicker of pain before the spike of ecstasy consumes me and I scream for God, Satan, and the whole fucking continent to hear me as I shatter around his throbbing, jerking cock and we come together.

I either doze off or pass out because the next thing I'm aware of is being cradled against his chest with our legs tangled together and his lips pressed against my forehead. He's somehow gotten us under the blankets and I feel warm, safe, and thoroughly fulfilled in all ways possible. I tilt my head back to meet his eyes and see so many emotions in them I can't even begin to sort or understand them all. I have the same extreme range washing through me so I look away not ready to deal with them and put a pin in it for later.

I snuggle up closer to the deliciously hard warm body next to me and feel his cock hard and ready for another round pressing against my hip. Damn, I take stock to see if I'm even capable of hitting that again and after a moment decide, hell yeah, I am. Besides, turnabout is fair play and if anyone needs to have control taken away, it's Sebastian. I grin evilly to myself and push him onto his back so I can straddle him. His brows shoot up and a small, smug smile tugs at his lips as he reaches for my breasts.

"Uh-uh, nope," I tell him as I grab his wrists and push them over his head. "You had your turn. Now it's mine and the more you fight this, the longer I'll make you wait." I sing-song his words back to him making him narrow his eyes at me and causing me to grin. "Make use of that iron control you're famous for and keep those hands up there. Trust me, it'll be worth it." I tell him as I lower to his neck and kiss my way down to his chest and abs licking an outline of each ridged muscle and feel the thrill of his tremors. I settle between his legs and roll my eyes up to meet his as my tongue darts out to swipe the bead of pre-cum from the slit in his head. He jerks at the contact and his hands move to reach for me so I pull back with a cagey smile. "Uh-uh-uh, control yourself, Sebastian."

He growls at me but does as I say so I reward him by taking his head into my mouth and gently swirl my tongue around it while sucking gently. His body shakes under me, making heat pool between my thighs and I can't resist going deeper and taking as much of him as I can into my mouth. He roars and snatches me up from between his legs causing me to giggle but when he slams home deep into my cunt my laughter turns to moans.

Eden

When I wake in the morning, Sebastian is gone and my two wolves are pressed on either side of me. I stretch between them to ease some of the delicious aches that fill my body after a long night with Sebastian. Cade nuzzles at my shoulder and licks the faint bite mark he left on me causing a sweet glow to fill me. Finn sweeps hair back from my face and meets my eyes with love and tenderness.

"Morning, love. How are you feeling?"

I breathe the scent of them in and sigh wistfully. "Honestly? A little overwhelmed and a lot terrified."

He frowns at that. "Why? We felt your pleasure last night many times. Did Bas do or say something to hurt you?"

"No, I...wait...you *felt* my pleasure? What does that mean?" I ask with narrowed eyes.

When he looks away with a hint of guilt I push away from him and Cade and sit up against the headboard with the blankets pulled up to cover my chest. Both of them scramble into seated positions in front of me.

"Finn, Cade? One of you had better start talking. How could you feel my pleasure?"

The wolves exchange a silent look causing me to growl at them so Cade jumps in with a cautious tone.

"Aye, well now, it's the wee bite marks we left on your body, ya ken?"

I pin him with a look. "No, I don't *ken* and don't think for a minute I don't *ken* what you're doing by thickening your accent. Just because you know it makes me hot doesn't mean you can use it to manipulate me. Now, what about the bite marks?"

He shoots me a devilish grin. "It's a shifter custom to mark our mate. When Finn and I bit you during our lovemaking it bonded us to you."

Finn reaches for my hand and brings it to his lips. "The bond lets us feel any strong emotions you have and it will only get stronger as time goes on."

My eyes dart back and forth between them as I process that. I'm a little bit in awe that they feel so strongly for me to do such a thing and also a little bit annoyed that there wasn't any conversation around such an intimate action.

"So when you like a woman, you bite her during sex and you get to feel her pleasure as well as your own? How does that work out if you stop being with her, like if you break up?" I ask in confusion. "I mean, can you imagine feeling your ex get her rocks off with her new guy?"

Cade's expression turns more serious than I've ever seen it and he grabs my free hand.

"No, lass. Not women we have sex with, just our mate, just you and there is no break up as you say. The bond...the bond is for life."

My eyes dart to Finn and he's just as serious as he nods. Jesus! I need a freaking beat on this. They made me their life mate with no conversation and after only...?

"Three days! I was only here for three days before we...before you...oh my God! Are you two insane? I've taken longer to pick out a Netflix movie to watch and you two decided after three days that I was your mate...for life?"

A defiant look fills Cade's eyes. "Three minutes or three days, it dinnae matter! We felt that you were our missing piece. Neither one of us ever hoped we would find our mate so when we felt the tug we locked it down. You can be angry all you want, Eden, but we willna let you go!"

I lunge toward him and grab a handful of his shirt, balling it in my fist. "Don't yell at me you asshole! I never said I wanted you to let me go!" I let go of his shirt and lean back with a huff. "All I'm saying is it was fast and maybe a conversation with your supposed mate might have been in order before you locked it down." I look to Finn. "What will happen if whatever brought me here sucks me back to my own time? Is that something you ever even thought of?" I ask sadly.

He cups my cheek and brushes his thumb over my lips before whispering, "Then we'll wait three hundred and sixty-one years to get you back. We'd wait ten lifetimes for you, lass. We'd fight time herself to keep you."

This time when I lunge forward it's to capture his sweet lips in a soul-searing kiss. My other hand flashes out and pulls Cade towards us so I can turn and show him the same love. When I break the kiss I hold onto them so all three of our foreheads are touching and breathe out the words swelling inside of me.

"I love you. I love you so much it hurts and that's what terrifies me. I'm so scared of losing any of you.

How does one woman hold so much love for four men and how do I live without it if something goes wrong?"

Cade rubs a hand up and down my back. "You trust us. Trust that all four of us will do whatever it takes to keep you no matter what year we find ourselves in. The fates brought you here to complete our pack and nothing will ever change that. You own our hearts and souls and nothing can take that away. Time be damned."

Finn is the first to pull back and gently wipe the tears from my cheeks. "We brought your cloak for you, love, and a bath is waiting for you in your room. Go and tend to yourself and join us in the breakfast room. Luca is anxious to see you as well."

I lay back on Sebastian's bed for a few moments once they leave, trying to process all the emotions swirling inside of me and imagine spending the rest of my life with the four men who have captured my mind, body, and heart. So much has changed in the last month since coming here. I can't even imagine going back to the life I had or the woman that I was.

I know deep in my soul that this is exactly where I'm supposed to be so with a sigh of happiness and acceptance I bounce out of the bed and slide my bathrobe on, gather the cape from the floor and the jewels tossed carelessly aside and take them all back to my room to put away properly.

I bathe and dress quickly, eager to see all four of my men…and coffee. I'm feeling beautiful and loved so I slide a pretty gown of cream brocade with red ribbons on and pop my head out the door to ask Claudette to lace me up but find a new girl I haven't met before waiting in the hall. She quickly gets the gown laced up for me and I breathe deeply, happy I skipped the corset. I braid the top half of my hair into a crown and just because they are so damn pretty slide the ruby mini daggers into the braids so the jeweled handles look like hair combs. I thank the new girl but she doesn't speak any English so I just give her a happy wave and head out to find my guys and coffee.

I only make it halfway down the hallway before a hand reaches out and drags me into an alcove and I land against a broad, hard chest. I'm turned and pushed against the wall with Sebastian's muscular arms caging me in and his hot mouth pressed against mine. My knees give out from the brutal assault he wages with his lips and tongue and when he finally pulls back I'm gasping for breath and wishing he'd take me right here against the wall. A laugh spills out of me at how quickly my body responds to these men and I can't help but tease him.

"Your Grace! How scandalous. What will the servants think?"

He tips my head to the side to nuzzle at my neck, sending shivers down my body straight to my core and growls, "Toss the servants, how do you think they will react if I spread you out on the breakfast table and sample your sweet cunt for my meal?"

An instant image of him doing just that has wet heat filling my panties. I tip my head back further as he runs his mouth over the tops of my breasts that are pushed up from the gown and marvel at how this man plays my body like an instrument. My fingers thread into his hair and I tug so he's looking up at me intending to tell him how badly I want him even after spending the entire night in his arms but what I see in his eyes chokes the words to a stop.

It isn't just desire I see but also a fierce, possessive love shining through. My heart surges in response. How is this even possible? Yes, the sex was insanely amazing but this man has run hot and cold with me from the moment I got here. Attraction is one thing but love? Can I really be in love with him too? My heart is screaming at my rational brain that it wants what it wants so fuck right off and I just give in and let myself fall. My hands slide from his hair to cup his strong jaw and the words just slip out. "Sebastian, I love you."

He rocks back like I just set off a bomb and says something in Greek that sounds like a curse before his mouth lands on mine again but this time it's an achingly sweet kiss that makes my knees weak for a different reason besides passion. His forehead rests against mine so I see every gold fleck in his gorgeous cinnamon-colored eyes and all the truth as well.

"If I had a soul, it would belong to you. I will love you for the rest of your days and all the hellish days I'll have to live without you."

My heart swells and aches at the same time from his words. To have not just one but four men love me this way is a gift beyond belief but he's referenced me not living as long as they will before and I can't help but feel like this love will someday be turned into a curse for them. He must read something in my expression though because he pulls back and goes to say something but changes his mind and just kisses me again. A small squeak of surprise by a maid passing through the hall has me jerking and then bursting out into a fit of giggles. With a last kiss, Bas pulls me out of the alcove and escorts me down to the breakfast room.

Cade, Finn, and Luca are already at the table and rise when we enter the room. My wolves have their customary grins in place when they see Sebastian and my fingers twined together but my eyes go straight to Luca and I bite my lip worrying how he will respond to this latest development. Any worries I have wash away at the love I see in his eyes as he nods briefly towards us with the softest smile lighting up his face.

I take my seat and look at each one of them and wonder how someone like me who a month ago had very little reason to want to keep living could now have four men who love me and a future I can't wait to live. So I sit and sip my coffee with a glow of happiness surrounding me and think about my men. Luca, my quiet tortured love who was so full of despair and self-loathing that he couldn't bear to be touched. Only two days ago he allowed me to undress him and kiss, suck and nibble every inch of his body on a canvas sheet that was spread out on the floor of his studio. It was a wild raw love I saw in his eyes as he clenched my hair in his fist while I took him in my mouth and refused to stop until his hot seed poured down my throat.

Cade and Finn, their matching grins that are so similar, hide how different they are the more I come to know them. Cade has a quicker temper that flares hot where Finn is the peacemaker. Cade loves to catch me alone and get me wet with dirty filthy words whispered in my ear before fucking me hard and fast against the nearest hard surface. Finn prefers to take his time and toy with my body until I beg for his cock and only then will let me find my release. Alone they make me pant with desire but when they come together to love my body it's an explosion of lustful desire that leaves me shattered in pleasure. But it's the constant touches, smiles, and looks that show me their constant love.

My eyes swing to Sebastian as I finish my coffee. He's so rigid in his control over his emotions and even before last night, I caught glimpses of the feelings he tried to hide from me. He tries to mask how he feels with ice but I know our love will be filled with heat and passion as I push back against his iron control and melt all the ice walls he's constructed. This love is still new but I can imagine it being the most volatile of the four with the battles we will have.

"What about you, Eden?" He asks me, breaking me out of my internal musings.

"I'm sorry, what was that?"

A small smug smile tugs at his lips as if he knows what I was thinking about.

"We are discussing the Marquis soirée. I was not able to speak with him due to our abrupt departure. I was just saying that I thought I sensed another of my kind there for a brief moment but it was gone too fast to be sure. Did you happen to see anything untoward while we were there?"

His eyes have a gleam of amusement as my cheeks redden with a deep blush at the memories of all that I saw and experienced at that party. I shoot him a pointed look before shaking my head.

"You mentioned that the…entertainers may have been under a sexual intoxication similar to how I was after drinking Luca's blood but other than that I didn't see anyone walking around with fangs and red eyes."

He rubs his chin in thought but then shakes his head. "It's possible but they could just as easily have been drugged in some way. No, I will have to pay the Marquis another visit to get the answers we seek." When my eyes widen at that, he laughs and reaches out to cup my cheek. "No, no. I will not be letting you anywhere near that man again. I believe you have been corrupted enough by your time in his home."

I roll my eyes at him thinking that the four of them aren't a corrupting influence on me and turn my head in his hand so that I can nip at his fingers with my teeth before soothing the bite with my tongue. The action has him snatching me out of my seat and onto his lap in one smooth move that has me giggling and then gasping as his hand finds its way under my skirt and up my inner thigh. His voice is a growl against my ear that sends shivers down my spine.

"Recall the warning I gave you earlier about spreading you out on this table and feasting on your body."

My eyes flash around the room filled with at least six servants as well as the others. I feel the heat spread between my legs at the thought of all four of them at once but the servants watching is a great big hell no. I clamp down on his wrist through the fabric of my skirt to stop his hand from going higher while frantically shaking my head before his touch makes me throw the last shreds of my modesty right out the window. His lips kiss at the delicate skin behind my ear and his voice is thick when he asks me,

"Do you see your men and what you do to them? The way you blush so prettily. The quickening of your breath as you imagine my hand sliding in between your thighs. The soft, sweet desperate moans that escape you as my fingers explore your slick, hot wetness. Look at them. Their cocks are hard and straining from what they want to do to you. For what we all want to do to you…together."

My breathing picks up even more when my eyes take in how rigidly Luca sits in his seat. His heated eyes are locked onto my chest and when his tongue slips out and licks his lips a tremor of need rocks through me. My glance moves to Cade and I see the naked desire on his face as the fork in his hand is clenched so hard it begins to bend. Finn's eyes meet mine with a promise of all he will do to me as he drops a hand into his lap and begins stroking himself.

My grip on Sebastian's wrist relaxes, letting him move higher between my legs, and his thumb rubs slowly up and down against my slit. When I try and lift my hips for more friction his other arm tightens to stop me from moving and holds me closer so that I feel the entire length of his hardness pressing against my ass through my dress. I feel the smile form on his lips against my neck and want to bite his lips for the tease he's forcing on me.

"Say you want it. Say you want all of us on you at once. Luca and I buried deep inside of you at the same time with Cade's cock between your sweet lips and your fingers wrapped around Finn's shaft stroking him. Eight hands exploring you. Four tongues licking you in all your most sensitive, secret places. Four cocks fucking you until you scream your pleasure to the heavens. Say you want that and it's yours."

And just like that, with his hot, dirty words filling my ear and the lightest touch of his thumb against my pussy an orgasm rocks through me while sitting at the breakfast table surrounded by servants. I bite my lip hard to stop the cries that want to escape but it doesn't block the grunts and moans that my men make at seeing me come. When my eyes clear and I can think again, I feel my cheeks flush red and I shove Bas's hand from my body and scramble to my feet, straightening my dress. I can't fucking believe I just did that in front of six servants. When I see the cocky grins on Luca, Cade, and Finn's faces and hear the low satisfied chuckle coming from Sebastian my face gets even redder.

"Assholes! You're all assholes!"

I keep my eyes straight ahead so I won't accidentally meet any of the servants' looks and try to keep my head up as I walk toward the doors. I almost make it before the Alpha-hole calls out.

"Eden, we all look forward to…enjoying…your company this evening."

With a shaky deep breath to fortify myself, I give a sharp nod without turning because who the fuck wouldn't want every single thing he described done to them? I slowly walk the rest of the way out of the room, bitching under my breath about him always getting the last word when I try for a dramatic exit.

Luca

The clay feels like warm silk between my fingers as I mold it to my current work in progress. For the first time in centuries, I'm not pouring agony and pain into my work. Since the blood lust left me a few years after being changed, I've only been able to create pieces that reflect the damage and misery I wrought upon my victims. My mind has been filled with their screams and the horror etched on their faces as they died. Eden has changed that. I will live with what I have done for eternity but for the first time since I came out of that savage haze, I now feel something other than self-hatred and loathing for the fiend that I am. I am filled with the love she has blessed me with and even though I know I'm not worthy of it, I will clutch it close to my soul and take every bit of it I can for as long as she gives it.

Everything about her consumes me. Her laugh, so freely given makes me smile where before I found nothing to ever smile about. Her compassion and understanding tempers the guilt I live with to a manageable level so that I am able to feel other emotions for the first time in what feels like forever.

The way she is so generous with her affections and body is truly a gift I will never grow tired of. Every touch and kiss she bestows upon me reassures me of her love. The passion she shows at my touch is intoxicating and I want her every moment of the day and night. Now that Sebastian has finally allowed himself to love her the way the rest of us do, I know that our family is complete. For the first time since I was reborn into this form, I feel like I am truly alive once again.

As my hands mold the clay that will form her image a smile fills my face as I think of the cries of pleasure the four of us will wrench from her sweet lips when we join together tonight in loving her and her body. I'm so lost in my creation and the images in my mind of all our hands upon her tantalizing curves that I don't hear the door of my studio opening. It takes her soft arms circling my waist from behind and her small warm fingers slipping under my shirt to trail over my stomach to bring me back. My body stills briefly but I know it's just muscle memory of how I used to react to being touched so I relax into her before spinning around and shifting to block her view of my half-completed project. I keep my clay encrusted hands away from her so as to not soil her gown and use my body to shuffle her back towards the door with a small smile.

"Mi alma, you mustn't come in here. You will ruin the surprise I'm working on for you!" I tell her enjoying the intrigued look that widens her eyes. With a cagey grin, she tilts slowly to the side to try and see around me but I move to block her again, causing her to laugh.

"Fine!" She tells me with a sparkle of happiness in her eyes and rises up on her toes to brush my lips with hers. "But you need to take a break and get cleaned up. We're having a picnic, all of us! Meet us out at the back of the gardens where the woods begin. The wolves have promised they'll shift for me and I need you and Bas to come and protect me from the hairy beasts." She says teasingly. "Who knows what they'll do to me in their animal forms?"

I can't help but laugh when she wiggles her eyebrows up and down suggestively at that.

"Of course. I would be delighted to join you all but I fear you may need protection from me as well as I'm having a hard time keeping my hands off you as it is."

I reach for her with my filthy clay-covered fingers with a playful leer on my face causing her to dance back away from me while laughing.

"Promises, promises! Round up Sebastian for me, please? I want to check on the food for our picnic." She slips through the door at my nod but pauses and looks at me over her shoulder. Desire fills her eyes as she looks at my dripping hands and she licks her lips before meeting my gaze again and nods towards my hands. "Maybe another time you could lay me out on one of your canvases and paint my body with your clay-covered hands." She swallows and her voice gets breathy. "We could make some living art with our bodies."

Her words paint a vivid image in my mind of our two naked bodies, covered in clay and pressed together, causing my cock to harden painfully as I look down at my dripping hands. When I look back up, the doorway is empty and I move quickly to the basin of water to clean up so that I can join her and the others.

Sebastian

I toss down the last report of the Marquis' movements, holdings, and close companions that Pierre sent to me by runner. There's nothing in the reports that tell me if he's consorting with vampires. Other than his frequent soirées and rumors of his many dalliances, the most interesting thing about the man is that he returned not long ago from a voyage to the Orient. The last thing I wish to do is have further dealings with the deviant but I will have to pay him yet another visit. When Luca steps into the room, it's a welcome distraction to my frustration.

"There you are. What say you to joining me tomorrow on a visit to the Marquis du Corbeil's?" I ask him. He nods with a frown.

"Of course. I feel the need to settle this matter once and for all." He looks down at his hands as his frown deepens. "I find myself overly concerned that Eden may be at risk now that he is aware of her."

I study him for a moment before slowly nodding my head. "Agreed. Having her accompany me was perhaps a miscalculation on my part. The thought of her possibly being in danger has me regretting that I exposed her to such a man." I look away when I see a flash of reproach in his eyes and straighten the missives on my desk into a neater pile. "I…I have come to care deeply for Eden and regret how I sometimes treated her carelessly." I tell him in a stilted tone.

"And yet she forgave you and accepted all that you are into her heart, didn't she?"

My eyes dart back to his and I nod sharply. He steps closer to my desk with an intent look on his face.

"She is a treasure that we do not deserve. We must stay on guard to always protect and care for her for we both know our time with Eden will be but a blink of an eye to our long existence. I plan on dedicating the short time we will have with her to making her deliriously happy and soaking up all of her love to savor once she is gone. I suggest you do the same. I do not believe we will ever find another that will so capture our hearts and complete our family, our pack, as the wolves say."

I run a rough hand through my hair, already dreading the moment she will slip from our lives and what it will do to all of us after she's gone.

"You can start right now. Eden has requested our presence for a picnic. Cade and Finn have promised to shift for her so that she may see their wolf forms. They are waiting for us near the woods."

I nod in agreement. Yes, I will treasure every moment we are blessed to have her in our lives, starting right now. Luca turns and reaches for the door but I have to ask,

"Luca? Do you think it will be worth it?" When he looks back at me in question, I swallow the knot lodged in my throat. "The pain. The pain we will have to live with after she's gone? Will it be worth it?"

A soft smile crosses his face. "It already was." And then he leaves me to my uncertainties.

I close my eyes and remember the way her body reacted to my touch with such passion. The sound of her laughter and the way she rolls her eyes when I'm being a bastard to her and finally the truth that shone from her eyes when she told me she loved me. I let out the breath I'm holding and feel my shoulders relax as I rush towards the door to join them because he's right. Her love is already worth whatever pain will come.

I catch up to Luca as we make our way through the maze of gardens and we hear her laughter and the wolves' playful shouting before we come around the last hedge obstructing our view. Eden is sitting on a blanket, spread out on the grass with a basket of food nearby and is leaning back on her hands as Finn and Cade stand a few feet away, acting out something that makes her laugh. The sun shines down on her, turning her hair to a rippling fire of reds and golds and her green eyes dance with happiness as she laughs at the wolves' antics. I want to freeze the image of this moment of perfection and hold it close. It has been so long since I felt happiness that it feels like a pressure in my chest that wants to burst free and I can't stop the smile that spreads across my face.

As Luca and I walk the last few feet that separate us Cade and Finn freeze in place and lift their heads as one to sniff at the air. Cade's expression morphs to one of fury and it swings my way as his eyes begin to glow and he begins to shift with his canines lengthening and fur sprouting. He manages to snarl, "Vampire!" before his wolf overtakes him and he drops to all fours beside Finn who is also shifting just as the first arrows fly through the air towards us. Luca roars in rage and dives towards Eden, taking her down to the blanket and covering her with his body as arrows sprout into his back. I let my demon come forth as I'm struck again and again in my chest and I feel the instant burn of the silver tips embedded in my flesh. It will weaken me but it won't be enough to stop me from slaughtering whoever has dared to attack us on our own land.

I strain with all my will to move towards the threat but something is spreading through my veins and locking my muscles in place. As I crash down to one knee, fighting the poison that is keeping me paralyzed, my eyes flash between Eden who is screaming underneath a still Luca, and the woods where the first line of men step from the shadows and run towards us. My eyes search each face looking for the vampire Cade had scented and finally come to rest on my worst nightmare. She's just as beautiful as the first time I saw her over a millennia ago and mistook her for an angel sent by God to save me.

Her long black hair streams to her waist in a waterfall of shine and when her cornflower blue eyes meet mine across the distance, her plump red lips lift in a smug smile that shows the demon she truly is. As I topple sideways, I manage to whisper a curse before my lips freeze. I had hoped to never see this demon again. Keket, goddess of the darkness and my maker.

Eden

I can't stop screaming their names. It happened so fast. One second we are laughing and the next my loves are being shot full of arrows. Luca is a heavy dead weight on top of me pinning me in place but my head is turned enough that I can see Bas on the ground. He's so still and with his eyes wide open I'm terrified that he's dead. My screams turn to whispers as I say his name over and over again like a prayer. I manage to free one arm from under Luca and I stretch it out toward Sebastian but there isn't even a flicker of life as I reach for him causing my whispers to turn to sobs. I don't even turn my head away from him when Luca's body is dragged off of me I'm so frozen with grief at losing them all so abruptly. Whoever has attacked us and killed my loves can do whatever they want to me because without them I am nothing and I won't go back to that dark place again.

"Oh, how poignant and pathetic." A female voice mocks me causing me to finally turn my head away from Sebastian's blank stare. I look up to see who is responsible for my heartbreak but the sun has backlit her and I'm forced to squint to try and make out her features. The woman crouches down beside me and her hair, eyes, and features come into focus and I recognize the beauty I had seen at the Marquis' party. I shake my head in confusion.

"Why? Why did you kill them?" I cry.

Her expression fills with mocking compassion. "Oh, no, no, dear girl. I didn't kill them! They are merely disabled for the moment. Gelsemium, a darling little plant I picked up in the Orient. It causes paralysis. That combined with the silver-tipped arrows will weaken them long enough for my men to shackle them properly. I'm sorry darling but I have need of your pets. Sebastian especially. But don't worry, I will bring you along as well. All the better to control them with the threat of your life in the balance." She leans forward with her sickly sweet smile and pats my cheek before the smile slides into a snarl and she barks, "Now go to sleep!" I try and fight it but my eyes drop closed and darkness takes me.

"Wake up!"

I jerk awake like a bucket of water has been thrown at me and blink my eyes to try and clear the haze from them. My head turns from side to side but it's dark and damp wherever I am. The only light is from a sputtering torch against a far wall so I push myself to my feet and stagger in that direction until I come up against a wall of iron bars and that's when I realize I'm in some kind of cage or prison. My fingers whiten as I squeeze the bars holding me in and memories of what happened rush through my mind. Not dead! My loves, my men, she said they weren't dead! I need to get out of here and find them! I rattle the bars as hard as I can but the iron is set snugly and I know I'll have to find another way.

A door slams closed further down the dark passageway to my right and the sharp click of heels heads my way. I know it's the bitch who did this to us before she even steps into the dim light of the torch.

"Well, hello! I'm so glad you could join us. You look refreshed from your little nap. Let me introduce myself. I already know you are Eden, my name is Keket." She scans me from head to toe while tilling her head from side to side before meeting my gaze again. "You are a pretty little thing. I can see why my Bastian would enjoy playing with you but alas that time is over. I'm afraid I don't enjoy sharing. At least, not with other women anyway."

She pauses for my reaction and the only thing I can do is laugh. Seriously? A psycho, jealous ex? Why the fuck not, I've lived through everything else so why not this too. At first, my laughter takes her by surprise and her eyes go wide in shock but they quickly narrow in fury as she steps towards the bars.

"You won't be laughing once I've had my fun with you!" She spits at me. "I won't kill you as you are an easy means to controlling Bastian and the others but you will wish I would before I'm done."

I shrug one shoulder and shoot her a wink. "Take your best shot."

I know antagonizing her isn't the best strategy but as Sebastian taught me, rage makes people lose focus and control. It makes them make mistakes and all I need is one little opening and I can take this chick down.

Her hands wrap around the bars above mine and I bite down hard on my tongue not to react when her eyes flare red and she grins so that her fangs show. Instead, I lean closer to her and fake shudder.

"Eeeeewwww, scary!" I say mockingly with an over-exaggerated scared voice before stepping back and waving my hand in dismissal. "Yeah, sorry to disappoint you but been there, done that. You're just a basic bitch at this point."

The red eyes and fangs disappear and I swear I can see a hint of respect in her eyes before she throws her head back and roars with laughter. When she finally gets it under control she has a wide smile on her face and she leans even closer to the bars and speaks in a friendly tone.

"I *like* you! I think we are going to be friends. After I pull all the pain that I can from your body, of course."

I give her a tight smile right back. "Of course," I say sarcastically, wanting to punch her right in her chick dick.

"KK, where are you my dove?" Rings out from somewhere deeper in the dark and I snort a laugh, causing her to raise an eyebrow at me in question.

"I'm sorry but KK? Really? Doesn't exactly fit the whole villainous thing you've got going on, does it?"

She rolls her eyes like a champ and shrugs one shoulder before talking to me like we are girlfriends gossiping about a boy.

"Yes, well - he's not the brightest sunbeam, if you take my meaning, but he does have his uses."

The Marquis in question steps into the light and claps his hands in delight when he sees me behind bars.

"Oh, goodie! I'm so glad you haven't broken her yet! Now don't forget, you promised me you would compel her to play all my favorite games with me," he gushes.

I feel the bile rise in my throat as his eyes lock on to my breasts. My eyes flash to hers as I feel the first real stirrings of fear at being compelled to act out this sick fuck's sexual fantasies but she merely shrugs again with a "what are you going to do" look and turns to him.

"Of course I haven't forgotten, my sweet but I also said that you get yours after I get mine." She ends with a snap in her tone.

The Marquis grasps her hand and dots her knuckles with kisses.

"That's why I was looking for you! His Majesty has just sent word that he will grant you a royal audience. We must make haste to the palace. One does not leave the King waiting!"

Her expression beams approval at him before she turns back to me.

"Excellent! Can you imagine how disappointed I was to learn that Bastian has had the King's ear all this time and has done nothing of substance with that power? Then again, Bastian has never lived up to his full potential. He's a complete disappointment to me. So ungrateful! I went to all that trouble to turn him and then train him through his savage years only to have him run away and desert me the first chance he got. You can be sure we will be discussing that once I've made him pay for his disloyalty." She harrumphs in annoyance before shaking her head.

"Very well, I will leave you for now to enjoy your last hours of peace while I claim my place beside the Sun King. Do try and get some more rest, darling. You will desperately need your strength when I return."

I back further away from the bars until I'm standing in the shadows as the happy couple leaves arm in arm. This is bad. This is so fucking bad. Luca told me Bas was turned by an Original. I can't even wrap my head around how powerful that bitch must be. More powerful than my Alpha, that's for sure. I need to get out of here and find my guys. I can't even think about how fucked up things will be if she gets control of the King. History as I know it will be completely altered with her in control. I need to do something to stop it and that starts with freeing my men.

Once I hear a door slam closed in the distance, I move back into the light and listen closely for any sounds of guards nearby. When I guess five minutes have passed in silence, I dig my phone out of the side band of my bra and tap on the flashlight feature.

Only days ago I was complaining about these gowns not having any pockets and now I'm eternally grateful they don't or I wouldn't have my phone secreted away to use now. I drop to my knees in front of the bars and use the flashlight to search for the lock that has to be on it. When I find it closer to the wall I crawl over and tuck my phone into my cleavage so that the light shines on the lock plate and my hands will be free. I reach up and yank the two ruby-encrusted stiletto daggers from my hair and take a deep breath sending the light bouncing for a second. I lean closer to the lock plate and hold one of the daggers in one hand and use my fingers on the other to explore the lock hole on the other side of the plate by touch. This can go super, stupid fast, or take forever.

Since inheriting Adera's house, I've been forced to become something of a master at antique lock picking. The woman had at least twenty locked chests and cupboards that I had to find a way to open as I cleared each room of junk. All thanks to the YouTube Gods for conveniently posting hundreds of lock picking videos for armatures like me to learn from. I was getting so into the whole thing for a while there that I even learned how to open modern padlocks and door locks. When I started watching videos on how to hotwire cars, I shook myself out of it and gave myself a thirty-day ban from YouTube. I close my eyes and shake my head at how shitty my life was before I came here but...silver lining, I guess.

I wedge myself as close to the bars as I can and tap off the flashlight. I can't see shit on this side of the door so I don't need it anyway. This will all be done by feel. I place my ear against the plate and slide one of the daggers into the hole slowly until I feel resistance. Turning the blade carefully I hear the slight scrape of the tumbler bar moving and a small smile tugs at my lips until the blade screeches sideways and I have to start again. By my fourth attempt, sweat is starting to trickle down my back and my lip throbs from biting on it so hard. I'm just about to try and see if I can get the second dagger into the hole with the first when I go flying forward and smack into the cold stone floor of the passageway outside of my cell. I push myself back up to my knees and hold a hand to my ear where one of the lock plates bolts has scratched it as I flew forwards. I wince when my fingers come away wet with blood but it's not a mortal wound so I use the bars to pull myself up onto my feet. I close the cell door as quietly as possible hoping it will buy me a few extra seconds if I'm discovered missing and make my way down to the right hoping I'm going in the right direction.

I pause at each cell door as I go and find them all empty. I'm desperate to find the guys as every minute ticks past and I end up getting sloppy when I rush around a corner and almost plow into a guard's back. A scream is locked in my throat as I backpedal as silently as I can and duck down into dark shadows between torches. My heart is roaring in my ears as I wait to be discovered but time passes with no one yelling out an alarm. Once my breathing is under control and I can no longer hear my pounding heart, I tiptoe back to the corner and strain to hear any movement from the guard. The minutes pass and I've almost worked myself up to take a peek around the wall when I finally hear a harsh laugh that is quickly followed by an animal's vicious snarl.

My body goes still as a statue while I pray to God that was from one of my wolves and not some rabid beast they have down here guarding prisoners. An ugly curse rings out followed by a thud and then heavy steps stomp my way causing me to scurry back into the shadows. I see the guard pass across the opening of the passageway I'm in and disappear, followed quickly by a slamming door. I wait for three beats and then dash back to the opening and peek around to find an empty intersection that has four passageways leading into it and no guard.

I race across the open space and dart down the way I think the noises came from, quickly tapping the flashlight back on and holding the phone out at each cell. The fifth one down has my men in it. The cocky guard is so sure of the silver shackles holding my guys in place that he left the cell door wide open. I grab the two nearest torches and bring them in with me so I can have as much light as possible to work with as I pick the locks that hold them in place.

Sebastian is front and center. He's been crucified to a cross-shaped post with a wide silver band around his throat and two bands holding his arms suspended to either side. Luca is in a similar state against one of the walls and both Cade and Finn are still in their wolf forms with thick silver collars that connect to silver chains attached to rings in the stone wall.

All of their eyes are on me as my face crumples in relief at seeing them alive. I hold a shaking finger to my lips to tell them to be quiet as I send each one a trembling smile full of love. I move to Bas first and get to work on his arm shackles with the hope he will be able to use the second stiletto to free one of the others while I work on the other two. The hole in the silver clasp is much smaller and I end up mangling the lock more so than picking it to the point that I can pull it open when I hang my weight from it. When his arm comes free I see an angry red blistered welt that encircles his wrist from where the silver burned his flesh on contact. His hand wraps around the back of my head and pulls me to his chest for a brief moment and then tips my head back so he can look into my tear-streaked face.

The love and relief I see shining from his eyes are all I need to wipe away the horror of his lifeless eyes staring back at me when the arrows took him down. My head bobs a few times as I try and silently convey all that I feel but time isn't on our side and the guard could come back at any moment so I dash the tears from my face and get to work on freeing his other arm. I whisper Keket's plan to compel the King and seize power as I work. I tell him we have to go and stop her before it's too late and she changes history. Once it's done, I work carefully on the lock of his collar, terrified that the blade will slip and I'll stab him in the throat. His eyes never leave my face and it helps steady my hand so when the lock clicks open, I step back a few feet with a huge smile on my face to give him room to step out of the collar.

I did it. I fucking rescued my own ass and rescued my men too. A silent laugh bubbles in my chest at all the ways I'm going to tease Bas about being rescued by a girl in the future.

He steps out from the collar and a smile begins to form when his eyes widen at something behind me. I frown at a sharp pinch in my back and my head rocks forward as I cough involuntarily, spraying wetness over my lips and chin. My eyes focus on the blade of a sword protruding from in between my breasts and I lift my gaze and arms up to reach for Sebastian as sadness fills my slowing heart. My wolves begin to howl mournfully and Luca is raging and thrashing against his shackles but my eyes are locked onto Bas's. I see the despair fill his eyes and his lips are moving but I can't hear his words as a roar begins to fill my ears. A flickering has my eyes dropping down to look at my hands that are still held out, reaching for him and I frown in confusion as my fingers start to turn transparent and then disappear. My arms are next and I realize in an instant that I'm going back. Back to my own time.

I try and tell him that I love him one last time but whiteness blanks out my vision and then I'm tumbling end over end until my back hits something solid. I gasp in a deep breath to fill my empty lungs and my hands go straight to my chest to try and pull the blade free but it's gone and so is the wound it caused. I frantically pat at my chest and then my lips but there is no blood on me at all. My stomach heaves and I roll quickly to my hands and knees to empty the contents onto the floor. When the last bit of it has been expelled from my body, I crawl away from the puddle and grab the nearest piece of furniture to help pull me to my feet. A keening noise is escaping my mouth with every exhale as my eyes scan the room where this all started. When they land on the mirror, I stagger toward it and clutch the jeweled frame.

"Send me back!" I scream. "Please, let me go back!"

I beg and plead but the mirror is dead and dark with not even my reflection showing in it. My knees give out and I crumple into a heap in front of it sobbing my loss. Sometime later when the tears have stopped and my mind has cleared I breathe out and close my eyes as I make a vow. Someway, somehow, I will find a way to fix the mirror and I will go back.

Back to my men, my loves - and I will never leave them again.

Afterword

Hey, so that happened…sorry! Cliffies are my jam so not sorry? lol. Really, it was kind of insta-love for our harem and that just doesn't seem right so I'm going to make them work for it and then work some more to finally get their HEA…it's going to be a rollercoaster of a ride. I mean, what coud possibly go wrong when you start fucking with time, right?

I have to give a HUGE thank you to all you readers that took a chance on my debut standalone, Dying to Love, and then raved about it to anyone who would listen. You posted screenshots of the funny bits, blogged about it, TikTok'd it and those reviews! OMG they just made me melt with all the love you threw my way. Thank you SO much for loving Kelsey and her guys as much as I did!

I hope you will stick with Eden through the next 3 books in this series as she makes her way through different eras, chasing her happy ever after.

Xoxo - Reese

DYING TO LOVE

662 – Days since the dead rose up
413 – Days since I've spoken to another living human
4 – Men who have climbed my fence looking for safety
1 – Last chance for Love

Kelsey survived the start of the apocalypse and thrived in the new world with help from her friends but now they're gone. Alone for over a year and mentally broken with high anxiety, she pushes through every day trying to find the will to keep going. Until three sweet, sexy men and one hot a**hole climbs her fence looking for sanctuary.

With her best friend, Tara, haunting her with outrageous antics, she needs to decide if she wants to keep dying a little bit day by day or if she can grab on to what these sexy men offer her and maybe find love.

Also, zombies make a few cameos.

This isn't a blood and gore zombie novel. It's full of comedy, over protective men that just want to take care of her and a ton of sexy steam that happens behind a set of double fences.

YA Post Apocalyptic Titles Written as Theresa Shaver

<u>The Stranded Series</u>

Land – A Stranded Novel, Book One

Sea – A Stranded Novel, Book Two

Home - A Stranded Novel, Book Three

City Escape – A Stranded Novel, Book Four

Frozen – A Stranded Novel Book Five

<u>The Endless Winter Series</u>

Snow & Ash – An Endless Winter Novel, Book One

Rain & Ruin – An Endless Winter Novel, Book Two

Sun & Smoke – An Endless Winter Novel, Book Three

Fire & Fury – An Endless Winter Novel, Book Four

Scorched – A Dry Earth Novel (Standalone)

<u>The Flare Series</u>

The Journey – A Flare Novel, Book One

The Line – A Flare Novel, Book Two

The Bridge – A Flare Novel, Book Three